CORRIGAN

THE PENGUIN BOOK OF EIGHTEENTH-CENTURY ENGLISH VERSE

Dennis Davison was born in Sheffield and graduated from Sheffield University with Dual Honours in English and French. His M.A. thesis on Marvell and his Ph.D. thesis on Augustan literature were supervised by L. C. Knights. At New England University he took a Litt.B. in German, with a thesis on Max Frisch.

He has published five books – editions of Marvell and Restoration comedies, and critical studies of Marvell, Dryden and Auden. Three of his plays have been produced, and his poems have been reprinted in anthologies, including *Best Poems of 1970*.

After four years as an actor at Sheffield Little Theatre he became Lecturer in English at Rhodes University, Cape Province, under the South African poet and playwright, Guy Butler. He is now Senior Lecturer at Monash University in Melbourne.

He helped to found a Yorkshire mobile theatre and also staff drama groups at Rhodes University, New England and Monash. He is a play reader for Melbourne Theatre Company, and is collecting Australian plays and translating Mexican plays for projected anthologies.

He is married and has three children.

D0180023

THE PENGUIN BOOK OF

EIGHTEENTH-CENTURY ENGLISH VERSE

*

EDITED AND INTRODUCED BY
DENNIS DAVISON

PENGUIN BOOKS

Penguin Books Ltd, Harmondsworth, Middlesex, England
Penguin Books Inc., 7110 Ambassador Road, Baltimore, Maryland 21207, U.S.A.
Penguin Books Australia Ltd, Ringwood, Victoria, Australia
Penguin Books Canada Ltd, 41 Steelcase Road West, Markham, Ontario, Canada
Penguin Books (N.Z.) Ltd, 182–190 Wairau Road, Auckland 10, New Zealand

—

Published in Penguin Books 1973
Reprinted 1975

—

Copyright © Dennis Davison, 1973

—

Made and printed in Great Britain by
Hazell Watson & Viney Ltd,
Aylesbury, Bucks
Set in Monotype Fournier

This book is sold subject to the condition
that it shall not, by way of trade or otherwise,
be lent, re-sold, hired out, or otherwise circulated
without the publisher's prior consent in any form of
binding or cover other than that in which it is
published and without a similar condition
including this condition being imposed
on the subsequent purchaser

à ma femme, Geneviève
à nos enfants, Marc, Pascale, et Rémy

CONTENTS

2. 'The proper study of mankind is man.'

3. 'Dear, damned, distracting town, Farewell!'

CONTENTS

4. 'And yet my numbers please the rural throng.'

CONTENTS

5. 'Blest with each talent, and each art to please.'

CONTENTS

CONTENTS

8. 'Go wondrous creature! mount where Science guides.'

9. 'Go, work, hunt, exercise!'

CONTENTS

ACKNOWLEDGEMENTS

THE copy-texts for poems selected for this anthology are either first, or early, editions, or standard collections such as Anderson's *Poets of Great Britain* (1792–5), Dodsley's *Collection of Poems* (1748), and, in particular, Chalmers's *The English Poets* (1810) in the ten-volume reprint edited by David P. French, retitled *Minor English Poets 1660–1780* (Blom, New York, 1967). Few of the minor poets have appeared in modern critical editions, but I have, of course, been able to consult the excellent modern editions of the major poets and check doubtful readings. I have also consulted such useful collections as K. W. Campbell: *Poems Written in the Eighteenth Century* (Blackwell, 1926), R. H. Case: *English Epithalamies* (John Lane, 1896), C. Peake: *Poetry of the Landscape and the Night* (Arnold, 1967), R. Quintana and A. Whitley: *English Poetry of the Mid and Late Eighteenth Century* (Random House, 1963), D. Nichol Smith: *The Oxford Book of Eighteenth Century Verse* (Clarendon Press, Oxford, 1926), J. Sutherland: *Early Eighteenth Century Poetry* (Arnold, 1965), and H. T. Swedenberg, *English Poetry of the Restoration and Early Eighteenth Century* (Knopf, New York, 1968).

For early editions I am mainly indebted to the Baillieu Library, Melbourne University, and Monash University Library (in particular to its Rare Books section and its librarian, Susan Radvansky). I wish also to thank Maureen Mann, who helped me considerably with the biographical notes, and Sadie Stephens, Heather Phillips, and Denise Hill for assisting with the production of my typescript.

INTRODUCTION

TODAY many historians regard the political and religious turmoil of the middle years of the seventeenth century not simply as a 'Puritan' or 'Cromwellian' rebellion but as an early type of bourgeois revolution by which society was radically transformed. The two civil wars, the execution of the king and the Archbishop of Canterbury, the sequestration of royalist estates, and the purging of 'disaffected' elements in the universities, were harsh aspects of a profound historical movement which eventually led to parliamentary democracy and the astounding achievements of the capitalist economy. Whether the violence of the civil wars, or the persecutions and plots (real and fabricated) of the Restoration period, could have been avoided is a matter for speculation, but as time passed more and more voices welcomed the prospect of an age of serenity and prosperity. Dryden, in 1681, had set the tone with his lines in *Absalom and Achitophel*:

> The sober part of Israel, free from stain,
> Well knew the value of a peaceful reign;
> And, looking backward with a wise afright,
> Saw seams of wounds, dishonest to the sight:
> In contemplation of whose ugly scars,
> They cursed the memory of civil wars.

In 1713 Pope's *Windsor Forest* recalled the violent past in a more grandiose idiom, and acclaimed a new era of peace, justice and prosperity:

> Oh fact accursed! what tears has Albion shed,
> Heavens, what new wounds! and how her old have bled!
> She saw her sons with purple deaths expire,
> Her sacred domes involved in rolling fire,
> A dreadful series of intestine wars,
> Inglorious triumphs and dishonest scars.
> At length great ANNA said – 'Let discord cease!'
> She said! the world obeyed, and all was peace!

Characteristically, the verse of this new era was deliberately social in content, urbane and conventional in style. The cultivation of neo-classical balance and correctness, of decorum in the choice of vocabulary or genres, and the adoption of the values of a polite, urban society, are significant features of a culture which had, of course, its own contradictions, but which did manifest an overt uniformity.

Two important components of this new culture were the decisive shift from a religious to a rational world-view (which included Christian rationalism), and marked improvements in living conditions in London, now the largest city in the world. The English architects of this Age of Reason were Hobbes, Locke and Newton. Hobbes, whose *Leviathan* was published as early as 1651, conceived all life as matter in motion. He envisaged the mind as a kind of machine, and asserted that all knowledge is gained through the senses. When perceived objects are removed, all we have left are fading impressions of them: these are memories, and from these residues of sense we build our imaginative pictures. To quote Hobbes's own words: 'Imagination is therefore nothing but decaying sense'. Thus the mind does not create, or even re-create: it merely remembers. All that a poet can do is reshuffle the fading images his memory has retained, and to do this he uses Reason, or Judgement. Hobbes wanted metaphors to be either abolished or kept under severe control: his follower, Bishop Parker, even suggested that they should be excluded from sermons by Act of Parliament. Hobbesian materialism thus undermined the creative, imaginative role of poetry. The poet Cowley compared the 'desserts of poetry' unfavourably with the 'solid meats' of science, and Sir William Temple described poetry and music as 'amusements' which 'serve to revive and animate the dead calm of poor or idle lives'. Admittedly no Augustan poet actually published his imaginative works as *Poems of Decaying Sense*: indeed they were more prone to exclaim, with the excessive confidence of a Walter Harte, 'Once more inspired, I touch the trembling string.' But beneath this artificial pose there is the widespread suspicion that 'divine poesie' had been revealed as a mere system of verbal devices.

Similarly John Locke, in his *Essay Concerning Human Understanding* (1690), denied that there were innate principles in the mind and likened mental processes to the acts of storage and nomenclature: 'The senses at first let in particular ideas, and furnish the yet empty cabinet, and the mind by degrees growing familiar with some of them, they are lodged in the memory, and names got to them.' No doubt Locke was being provocatively drab, but he consistently described the mind as a mere recipient of experience – an 'empty cabinet', or a 'white paper void of all characters', or a '*tabula rasa*' – able only to receive sensations and reflect upon its own operations. In *Some Thoughts Concerning Education* Locke dismissed poetry, music and painting from his proposed syllabus, adding that if a child showed poetic talent 'the parents should labour to have it stifled, and suppressed, as much as may be . . .'

Newton's immense achievements astounded and impressed his age and caused Pope to write admiringly:

> Nature and Nature's laws lay hid in night:
> God said, Let Newton be! and all was light.

It was as though the entire physical universe had suddenly been explained: it was revealed as a complicated but nevertheless comprehensible machine. To many in the eighteenth century this 'clockwork universe' was reassuringly understandable and predictable, but from at least the Romantic period onwards there have been voiced deep fears that it would logically follow that man too was merely a comprehensible machine. Moreover, as H. T. Pledge remarks, 'Newton reinforced Descartes' critical process of stripping matter of its more sensual attributes, leaving only a bare universe of hard particles to the 18th century.'

However, mechanistic materialism proved tremendously stimulating as a working guide to scientists, and in other areas it played an indirect role – for instance, in the growing scepticism towards witchcraft. But can poetry thrive on a theory which describes the mind and the emotions deterministically as mere reflections of physiological processes? Is there not something mechanistic in the psychological theories of Pope's *Moral Essays*, which assert too neatly that all human behaviour is based on the 'ruling passion'? Indeed, neo-classicism itself, (which Pope presented sympathetically in *An Essay on Criticism*), seems both an imaginative reaction against the dehumanizing tendencies of science and yet also a parallel to mechanistic philosophy, in that it provides a set of fixed rules, dogmatic metrical formulae, or strict genre categories – in short, recipes for concocting poems. No good poet sticks to the recipe any more than does a good cook, but the underlying assumption that poetry can be fabricated by following an instruction manual is really in line with the type of thinking we have noted in Hobbes, Locke, and Newton. It is not surprising that when William Blake wished to liberate himself from everything he found oppressive in the eighteenth-century ethos he made a vigorous attack on Newton:

> May God us keep
> From Single vision & Newton's sleep!

Eighteenth-century culture was also influenced by improved living conditions: indeed, an anthropologist would regard them as part of the 'culture'. The streets (of Gay's *Trivia*, for instance) were still muddy and dangerous, but they were being lit at night with oil-lamps. Lady Mary Wortley Montagu had brought back from Turkey the secret of a vaccine against smallpox. Wigs were obligatory, and shaving the head beneath these weighty symbols of 'conspicuous waste' helped, as W. H. Auden reminds us, to delouse the upper classes. Gentlemen met to talk in the fashionable coffee-houses over their novel drinks – coffee, tea and cocoa. (A price-list of goods for January 1732 quotes Pekoe tea at 14s. a pound, though a pound of opium was only 10s. 6d. and French brandy 6s. a tun.) The publishing trade was launching weekly periodicals, such as the *Tatler* and the *Spectator*, and forming a new reading public, which, significantly for the future novel, included women. Witches were no longer feared or hunted, and scientific wonders now included improved telescopes, microscopes, barometers, airpumps, accurate clocks, adding-machines, automatic looms, magic lantern 'movies', pressure-cookers and a mechanical music-composer: earlier blood-transfusion experiments, with sheep and criminals, had proved fatal, but inoculation and better surgical techniques were signs of striking medical progress.

The growing comfort and security was partly due to the expanding merchant economy: London had become the emporium of the world as Dryden had prophesied in his *Annus Mirabilis*. One must remember, however, that England was still basically agricultural, with the great majority of the population living outside the towns. But the sophisticated poets, the professional men of law, medicine and politics, together with leisured members of fashionable society, formed an urban group conscious of its well-built metropolis, its elegant city life, and its intellectual and artistic achievements. The more optimistic spokesmen of this society (leaving aside for the moment the equally vocal satirists) would no doubt have felt in accord with these lines from James Thomson's *The Seasons*, which list the benefits of English civilization in this period:

> ... the softening arts of peace,
> Whate'er the humanizing muses teach,
> The godlike wisdom of the tempered breast,
> Progressive truth, the patient force of thought,
> Investigation calm whose silent powers
> Command the world, the light that leads to Heaven,
> Kind equal rule, the government of laws,
> The all-protecting freedom which alone
> Sustains the name and dignity of man ...

The 'metaphysical shudder' which wracked, and perhaps redeemed, the seventeenth-century poet is no longer manifest in his eighteenth-century counterpart. Perhaps Newtonian physics combined with national prosperity provided a more comforting environment: perhaps the Augustan poet was less concerned with sin and personal anguish, and more inclined to employ his powers of reason to understand society and the individual's relation to it. Sometimes the poet agreed with both Mandeville and Pope that God and Nature 'bade Self-love and Social be the same', but at other times he agreed with the satirists and critics (among whom Mandeville and Pope are again found) that man and society were corrupt and repugnant.

'Dryden and Pope are not classics of our poetry, they are

classics of our prose' runs Matthew Arnold's well-meaning but backhanded compliment. Few poets can survive being classed as prose-writers: Pope has survived to be hailed by F. R. Leavis as an Augustan Metaphysical, and his *Dunciad* has been imitated by Roy Campbell in remote South Africa and by A. D. Hope in remoter Australia. Gray's *Elegy*, Gay's *The Beggar's Opera*, Goldsmith's *The Deserted Village*, Cowper's *John Gilpin*, Crabbe's *The Village*, and the poems of Burns and Blake are works which still have popular appeal, though Dr Johnson and Dean Swift are now better known as the inspiration of a famous biography and as the author of *Gulliver's Travels* respectively. But what of Thomson's *The Seasons*, Gay's *Trivia*, Akenside's *The Pleasures of the Imagination*, Smart's *A Song to David*, Churchill's satires, Collins's odes, and the lengthier poems of Blackmore, Somerville, Goldsmith, Cowper, Crabbe and Shenstone? Perhaps some modern readers find eighteenth-century works formidably long, and no doubt others would accuse them of being wordily descriptive, earnestly didactic, snobbishly neo-classic and upper-class, artificial in style and unreal in content. How quaintly remote are the upper classes at their country hunts and their watering-place distractions, and the lower classes at their rustic games on the village green. Lords, squires, beaux, belles, milkmaids, link-boys, street-tradesmen, coffee-house wits and ladies of leisure, or pleasure, are part of a vanished world where periwigged gentry chase the stag across a Miltonically-painted landscape, or coquettish nymphs in Vauxhall Gardens display enough of their charms to inspire a waspish epigram, a playful epistle, or a dozen lines of rococo flattery. Admittedly there is a certain period charm about the antique bric-à-brac – sedan chairs, fans, swords, snuff-boxes, fire-screens – but can one take it seriously? And dare one really resurrect such forgotten names as Byrom, Anstey, Toplady, Jago, Lovibond, Jenyns or (Geoffrey Grigson's find) William Diaper?

My answer is twofold. A good deal of Augustan verse is as dull as – well, as a good deal of minor Elizabethan verse. So we have to sort the dusty curios until we find genuine works of art. And secondly, we have to acquire a taste for genres other than the lyrical and the satirical (modes which most people can respond to without difficulty). The truly catholic reader could surely find delight in the short, genial fables of William King or Christopher Pitt; in the ingenious, meticulous, verbally inventive, scientific descriptions of Diaper, Blackmore, or Darwin; in the burlesque pastorals of Gay and Somerville; in the Miltonic-scientific panorama of Thomson; in the musing travelogues of Goldsmith; and in the methodical madness of Christopher Smart. In other words, there is a variety in eighteenth-century poetry which has partly been ignored because of the overshadowing role of satire in the period. I would personally deny that Pope is 'prosaic', except in his philosophical verse essays, but certainly the stylistic variations in the writers mentioned above are typical of widespread attempts to avoid what we, perhaps wrongly, assume was the dominant heroic couplet form. A random sampling affords evidence of quite a range of effects:

> While reading pleases, but no longer, read;
> And read aloud resounding Homer's strain,
> And wield the thunder of Demosthenes.
> The chest so exercised improves its strength;
> And quick vibrations through the bowels drive
> The restless blood, which in unactive days
> Would loiter else through unelastic tubes.
> Deem it not trifling while I recommend
> What posture suits: to stand and sit by turns,
> As nature prompts, is best. But o'er your leaves
> To lean for ever, cramps the vital parts,
> And robs the fine machinery of its play.

These lines of blank verse, from John Armstrong's student-counselling muse, could be contrasted with William Broome's jocular rhythms:

> 'Twas sung of old how one Amphion
> Could by his verses tame a lion,
> And, by his strange enchanting tunes,
> Make bears or wolves dance rigadoons:
> His songs could call the timber down,
> And form it into house or town.

7

This comic tone is found in scores of poets who wrote in the very popular Fable genre. Typical of the more facetious kind is Elijah Fenton's *The Fair Nun*, who challenges the Devil to dekink one of her pubic hairs which 'curled like any bottle-screw'. On the other hand Edward Moore's *The Spider and the Bee* exploits the didactic-erotic note:

> When Celia struts in man's attire,
> She shows too much to raise desire;
> But from the hoop's bewitching round,
> Her very shoe has power to wound.

The mock-epic manner is, of course, a familiar one, but sometimes the comedy gives way to descriptive realism. Somerville's rustic wrestlers, somewhat snootily presented in burlesque classical style, are disturbingly real:

> No rest, nor pause allowed,
> Their watchful eyes instruct their busy feet;
> They pant, they heave; each nerve, each sinew's strained;
> Grasping they close; beneath each painful gripe
> The livid tumours rise, in briny streams
> The sweat distils, and from their battered shins
> The clotted gore distains the beaten ground.

Similarly Gay's mock-pastorals modulate from playful pretence to a detailed, sensitive response which invites sympathy as well as laughter:

> If by the dairy's hatch I chance to hie,
> I shall her goodly countenance espy;
> For there her goodly countenance I've seen,
> Set off with kerchief starched and pinners clean.
> Sometimes, like wax, she rolls the butter round,
> Or with the wooden lily prints the pound.
> Whilom I've seen her skim the clotted cream,
> And press from spongy curds the milky stream;
> But now, alas! these ears shall hear no more
> The whining swine surround the dairy door;
> No more her care shall fill the hollow tray,
> To fat the guzzling hogs with floods of whey.
> Lament, ye swines, in grunting spend your grief,
> For you, like me, have lost your sole relief.

Milton, cunningly described by a critic as one of 'the greatest poets writing in a language other than English', is certainly a pervasive influence throughout the century: even Keats in the next century was almost strangled by the python-grip of his coiling lines, but escaped just in time by leaving *The Fall of Hyperion* unfinished. It is, of course, the more obvious, external features of Milton's verse which are imitated in order to achieve the sublime tones and grandiose dignity which were so much admired. Frequently the imitations are so ludicrous that it is hard to distinguish them from the deliberate parodies and burlesques. But just as the Restoration period had manifested itself both in saucy, satirical comedy and romantic, bombastic, heroic tragedy – Dryden indeed switched from one to the other with professional ease – so did the eighteenth century criticize itself with merciless satire and at the same time laud its heroes, its culture, its patriotism and its enlightenment with a panegyrical whitewash concocted from fragments of *Paradise Lost*. Facile Miltonic pastiche of this kind we no doubt find nauseating, but we can still enter into the good-natured Miltonic parody of John Philip's *Cider*, or *The Splendid Shilling*, from which the following lines are taken:

> So pass my days. But when nocturnal shades
> This world envelop, and th'inclement air
> Persuades men to repel benumbing frosts
> With pleasant wines, and crackling blaze of wood;
> Me lonely sitting, nor the glimmering light
> Of make-weight candle, nor the joyous talk
> Of loving friend delights; distressed, forlorn,
> Amidst the horrors of the tedious night,
> Darkling I sigh, and feed with dismal thoughts
> My anxious mind ...
> But if a slumber haply does invade
> My weary limbs, my Fancy, still awake,
> Thoughtful of drink, and eager, in a dream
> Tipples imaginary pots of ale:
> In vain; awake I find the settled thirst
> Still gnawing, and the pleasant phantom curse.

But James Thomson's lengthy major work, *The Seasons*, is another matter. Here the Miltonic apparatus is matched by a religious and scientific vision of eighteenth-century man and landscape which results in a genuinely new poetic amalgam. The tone of reverent intellectual wonder is heard in the well-known passage on the rainbow (as fascinatingly explained by Sir Isaac Newton's theory of prismatic colours):

> Meantime, refracted from yon eastern cloud,
> Bestriding earth, the grand ethereal bow
> Shoots up immense; and every hue unfolds,
> In fair proportion running from the red
> To where the violet fades into the sky.
> Here, awful Newton, the dissolving clouds
> Form, fronting on the sun, thy showery prism;
> And to the sage-instructed eye unfold
> The various twine of light, by thee disclosed
> From the white mingling maze . . .

From here it is but a step to the grandiose description of a spider catching a fly, or this dignified, epic treatment of – a lad having a dip in a pool:

> Cheered by the milder beam, the sprightly youth
> Speeds to the well-known pool, whose crystal depth
> A sandy bottom shows. Awhile he stands
> Gazing the inverted landscape, half afraid
> To meditate the blue profound below;
> Then plunges headlong down the circling flood.
> His ebon tresses and his rosy cheek
> Instant emerge; and through the obedient wave,
> At each short breathing by his lips repelled,
> With arms and legs according well, he makes,
> As humour leads, an easy-winding path;
> While from his polished sides a dewy light
> Effuses on the pleased spectators round.

Ludicrous, of course – from the point of view of naturalism. But this is the eighteenth century's poetic equivalent of opera and dance. The artifice is accepted because it presents human life as idealized, sublime, histrionic, intensified, meaningful. For Thomson and many writers of his age life was, or could be, magnificent – a fascinating pattern of natural and social phenomena, illuminating the wisdom of God and the ingenuity of man, and inviting the passionate curiosity of the scientist as well as the descriptive talents of the poet. In *The Seasons* Thomson paints the back-breaking task of haymaking as a joyous operatic spectacle, bursts into a hymn of praise to the pineapple, and sings rapturous arias about sheep-dipping and the latest insecticides (when a new one came on the market he had to revise his lines). Perhaps only an eighteenth-century poet or a Soviet collective farmer could voice such agricultural enthusiasm: for Thomson, farming is all 'happy labour, love, and social glee', and another writer, John Dyer, devoted the four books of *The Fleece* entirely to the wool industry. Blistering satire is one well-known aspect of eighteenth-century culture, but equally strong is the note of optimism, often Christian or deistic, of vigorous faith in Society, Work, Patriotism and Prosperity. So, after Pope's or Swift's astringent criticism of society, it is salutary to turn to Thomson's buoyant tones of confidence: one may dismiss them as sentimental or idealistic, but they do represent a vision that was widely shared in a century which was more diversified, and contradictory, than is often supposed. Here is that tone at its most positive:

> Happy Britannia! where the Queen of Arts,
> Inspiring vigour, Liberty, abroad
> Walks unconfined even to thy farthest cots,
> And scatters plenty with unsparing hand.
> ... On every hand
> Thy villas shine. The country teems with wealth;
> And Property assures it to the swain,
> Pleased and unwearied in his guarded toil.
> Full are thy cities with the sons of art;
> And trade and joy, in every busy street,
> Mingling are heard: even Drudgery himself,
> As at the car he sweats, or, dusty, hews
> The palace stone, looks gay. Thy crowded ports,
> Where rising masts an endless prospect yield,
> With labour burn, and echo to the shouts
> Of hurried sailor, as he hearty waves
> His last adieu, and, loosening every sheet,
> Resigns the spreading vessel to the wind.

What an amazing contrast to Dr Johnson's sombre pessimism,

or Hogarth's harsh exposure of vice and stupidity. The poor who were dying of poisonous gin, or the mothers who could expect half their children to perish in infancy, could hardly have been the most sympathetic readers of Thomson's cheerful muse.

Thomson's relish for scientific farming reminds us that one new field of poetic exploration in this century is science. It is true that earlier Donne had responded sensitively to the 'new philosophy', that Milton's archangel had lectured Adam on the Copernican system, and that Davenant had waxed eloquent about stuffed animals in a museum, but the bulk of scientific verse came later. There was a rather specialized genre inspired by Newtonian colour theory, but it is advances in the practical sciences which gave birth to eighteenth-century 'text-book' verse. Characteristic topics are Yalden on coal-mining, Moore on fen-drainage, Thomson and Dyer on agriculture, Diaper on fish, Philips on glass-blowing, Aaron Hill on vaccination, Garth on medicine and the medical profession, Darwin on botany and Blackmore on physiology. The poets showed an admirable social conscience in attempting to absorb and popularize the new knowledge, despite the jibes of Pope in *The Dunciad* or Swift in *Gulliver's Travels* against virtuosos, zoologists and Royal Society experimenters. Frequently the writers on scientific or similarly 'unpoetic' areas of learning were partly responding to neoclassical enthusiasm for the Ancients – Diaper's *Halieutics* was translated from the second-century Oppian, and William King's *The Art of Cookery* was an avowed imitation of Horace's *Art of Poetry*. Whereas Thomson and others offered detailed descriptions of cattle diseases in the Miltonic grand style, Garth employed classical mythological machinery, and Diaper and Darwin wrote of the sex-life of eels or cowslips as though they were beaux and belles. But Blackmore and others tended to reduce the 'fanciful' element and concentrate on imparting information, as in this passage from Blackmore's immense treatise *Creation*:

> The large arterial ducts that thither lead,
> By which the blood is from the heart conveyed,
> Through either lobe ten thousand branches spread.
> Here its bright stream the bounding current parts,

And through the various passes swiftly darts,
Each subtle pipe, each winding channel, fills
With sprightly liquors, and with purple rills;
The pipe, distinguished by its gristly rings,
To cherish life aërial pasture brings,
Which the soft breathing lungs, with gentle force,
Constant embrace by turns, by turns divorce;
The springy air this nitrous food impels
Through all the spongy parts and bladdered cells,
And with dilating breath the vital bellows swells;
Th'admitted nitre agitates the flood,
Revives its fire, and re-ferments the blood.

Blood circulation, geology, gout, gymnastics, sheep-rot, insect life, hunting, fishing, climatology – these and dozens of other topics demanded the muse, and forced poets to expand enormously the range of their interests, thus foreshadowing Shelley's claim that every subject is poetically valid. Whether eighteenth-century scientific verse is poetry is another matter. To contemporary readers it was possibly as novel and exciting as is to us James Kirkup's *A Correct Compassion*, a sensitive account of a modern surgical operation. (Incidentally, in 1717, Marin Marais, Louis XIV's chief bass viol player, wrote a words-and-music piece, for viola da gamba, harpsichord and speaker, which described the removal of a kidney stone without anaesthetic.) At all events, this kind of verse did encourage first-hand observation and concrete detail, as well as realistic content, at a time when heavy generalizations, stale poetic diction, neoclassical pastiche, and frivolous high-society verse threatened to stifle genuine poetry. We may smile to read that James Hurdis wished to celebrate 'carrots, parsnips, onions, cabbages', or that Cowper was stirred by the success of manned balloon flights in 1783 and the American hand-propelled submarine of 1775, but such reactions to the limited verse produced for fashionable urban society did after all lead to the realism of Crabbe's survey of provincial village life, to Burns's and Blake's accounts of peasant and proletariat, and to Wordsworth's portraits of leechgatherers, idiot boys and shepherds.

The satirical verse of the eighteenth century is rightly

esteemed today, and there is no need here to praise once more the exhilarating critical irony of Pope, exhibited with such marvellous verbal ingenuity within the small compass of the heroic couplet, nor the calculated and thoroughly healthy nastiness of Swift, nor the journalistic vivacity of Gay. Lady Mary Wortley Montagu displays an unladylike venom in her attack on Pope or men of fashion; Edward Young and William Whitehead enjoy peeping at young nymphs intent on their intricate boudoir rituals; but to my mind the most inventive of all these minor women-baiters is Soame Jenyns, whose satires *The Art of Dancing* and *The Modern Fine Lady* deserve reprinting in a chic edition with slightly naughty illustrations.

Delightful and formally ingenious though so much eighteenth-century satirical verse is, an inordinate amount of it does seem to be about hoop-petticoats, card games and tea-drinking, together with a few other feminine vices such as vanity and coquetry. When we remember the social targets vigorously attacked in the novels of Fielding or Smollett, or in the drawings of Hogarth and the (later) Rowlandson and Gillray, we are surprised at the limited topics handled by the poets. Even Pope's acute sense of human folly seems directed too much towards the frivolity of a Belinda, raped of a lock of hair, or towards the dullness of third-rate authors and the maddening pretensions of the *nouveaux-riches* in their fake palaces and vulgar gardens. Of course, the new-rich are always with us, and Pope was defending good taste in literature, architecture, and manners, as well as advocating charity towards the poor and urging common-sense as a guide to social behaviour. But the context is usually upper-class life, its follies and its vanities: there is little about political and legal corruption and its effect on the victims, little indeed about middle- and lower-class life – for which one has to go to the novelists and the racier ballads. Where is the verse satire on incompetent country magistrates, on seedy charity schools, the stagnant universities, harsh landlords, aggressive merchant wars, the slave trade, life in the colonies? I have unearthed a little – John Langhorne on the rural J.P. or Cowper on the slave-trader – but there isn't very much. James Miller, in

On Politeness (1738), has a few biting remarks on upper-class education:

> To Eton sent, o'er every form you leaped,
> No studious eves, no toilsome mattins kept,
> Thence Christ's quadrangle took you for its own;
> Had *Alma Mater* e'er so true a son!
> Half seven years spent in billiards, cards and tippling,
> And growing every day a lovelier strippling;
> With half a college education got,
> Half clown, half prig, half pedant and half sot;
> Having done all that ought to be undone,
> Finished those studies which were ne'er begun;
> To foreign climes my Lord must take his flight.

Charles Churchill, it is true, jabbed his vitriolic quill at politicians, actors and homosexuals, but his vehement denunciations are monotonous and verbally unsubtle. The young Chatterton, famed for his medieval 'forgeries', was a promising satirist of Methodism, but for deeper criticism of the social order and its religion one must read the compelling, off-beat ballads and songs of William Blake. But this red-hatted revolutionary, who hid Tom Paine, who was tried for sedition, and who attacked 'priests in black gowns' and praised 'lovely copulation', is not typical of what we usually label the Age of Reason, or the Enlightenment, or the Neo-classical Period. Eighteenth-century Good Taste and Common Sense, which had genuinely sustained the civilization and culture of a minority class, were unable to comprehend, much less solve, the problems symbolized by the French Revolution.

A NOTE ON THE TEXT

SPELLING has been modernized, and capitals, italics, etc., have been brought into conformity with modern practice. It has not been found necessary to alter the original punctuation. Many eighteenth-century poets were fond of using abstractions, with varying degrees of personification, and a case could be made for spelling these with capitals. However, determining the degree of personification present is a difficult task and I usually allow the reader to detect it without the rather crude signal mechanism that capitalization provides.

The headings to each section are all taken from the verse of Alexander Pope.

Subtitles have been provided for passages extracted from longer poems, and are printed in small italic type.

I

*'Woman's at best a contradiction
still.'*

From *The Modern Fine Lady*

But soon th'endearments of a husband cloy,
Her soul, her frame incapable of joy:
She feels no transports in the bridal-bed,
Of which so oft sh'has heard, so much has read;
Then vexed, that she should be condemned alone
To seek in vain this philosophic stone,
To abler tutors she resolves t'apply,
A prostitute from curiosity:
Hence men of every sort and every size,
Impatient for Heaven's cordial drop, she tries;
The fribbling beau, the rough unwieldy clown,
The ruddy templar newly on the town,
The Hibernian captain of gigantic make,
The brimful parson, and th'exhausted rake.

SOAME JENYNS

Song for Ranelagh

Ye belles, and ye flirts, and ye pert little things,
    Who trip in this frolicsome round,
Pray tell me from whence this impertinence springs,
    The sexes at once to confound?
What means the cocked hat, and the masculine air,
    With each motion designed to perplex?
Bright eyes were intended to languish, not stare,
    And softness the test of your sex.

The girl, who on beauty depends for support,
    May call every art to her aid;
The bosom displayed, and the petticoat short,
    Are samples she gives of her trade.
But you, on whom fortune indulgently smiles,

And whom pride has preserved from the snare,
Should slyly attack us with coyness, and wiles,
    Not with open and insolent war.

The Venus, whose statue delights all mankind,
    Shrinks modestly back from the view,
And kindly should seem by the artist designed
    To serve as a model for you.
Then learn, with her beauty, to copy her air,
    Nor venture too much to reveal:
Our fancies will paint what you cover with care,
    And double each charm you conceal.

The blushes of morn, and the mildness of May,
    Are charms which no art can procure:
O be but yourselves, and our homage we pay,
    And your empire is solid and sure.
But if, Amazon-like, you attack your gallants,
    And put us in fear of our lives,
You may do very well for sisters and aunts,
    But, believe me, you'll never be wives.

WILLIAM WHITEHEAD

From *Satire VI*

ON WOMEN

Lavinia is polite, but not profane;
To church as constant as to Drury Lane.
She decently, in form, pays Heaven its due;
And makes a civil visit to her pew.
Her lifted fan, to give a solemn air,
Conceals her face, which passes for a prayer:
Curtsies to curtsies, then, with grace, succeed;
Not one the fair omits, but at the Creed.

Or, if she joins the service, 'tis to speak;
Through dreadful silence the pent heart might break:
Untaught to bear it, women talk away
To God himself, and fondly think they pray.
But sweet their accent, and their air refined;
For they're before their Maker – and mankind:
When ladies once are proud of praying well,
Satan himself will toll the parish bell.

Acquainted with the world, and quite well-bred,
Drusa receives her visitants in bed;
But, chaste as ice, this Vesta, to defy
The very blackest tongue of calumny,
When from the sheets her lovely form she lifts,
She begs you just would turn you, while she shifts.

*

Go breakfast with Alicia, there you'll see,
Simplex munditiis, to the last degree:
Unlaced her stays, her night-gown is untied,
And what she has of head-dress, is aside.
She drawls her words, and waddles in her pace;
Unwashed her hands, and much besnuffed her face.
A nail uncut, and head uncombed, she loves;
And would draw on jack-boots, as soon as gloves.
Gloves by queen Bess's maidens might be missed;
Her blessed eyes ne'er saw a female fist.
Lovers, beware! to wound how can she fail
With scarlet finger, and long jetty nail?
For Harvey, the first wit she cannot be,
Nor, cruel Richmond, the first toast, for thee.
Since full each other station of renown,
Who would not be the greatest trapes in town?
Women were made to give our eyes delight;
A female sloven is an odious sight.

EDWARD YOUNG

The Toilette
A TOWN ECLOGUE

LYDIA

Now twenty springs had clothed the park with green,
Since Lydia knew the blossom of fifteen;
No lovers now her morning hours molest;
And catch her at her toilette half-undressed;
The thundering knocker wakes the street no more,
No chairs, no coaches, crowd her silent door;
Her midnights once at cards and hazard fled,
Which now, alas! she dreams away in bed.
Around her wait Shocks, monkeys, and macaws,
To fill the place of fops and perjured beaux;
In these she views the mimicry of man,
And smiles when grinning Pug gallants her fan;
When Poll repeats, the sounds deceive her ear,
(For sounds like his once told her Damon's care);
With these alone her tedious mornings pass,
Or, at the dumb devotion of her glass,
She smooths her brow, and frizzles forth her hairs,
And fancies youthful dress gives youthful airs;
With crimson wool she fixes every grace,
That not a blush can discompose her face.
Reclined upon her arm, she pensive sate,
And cursed th'inconstancy of youth too late.
   'O youth! O spring of life! for ever lost!
No more my name shall reign the favourite toast;
On glass no more the diamond grave my name,
And rhymes misspelt record a lover's flame:
Nor shall side-boxes watch my restless eyes,
And, as they catch the glance, in rows arise
With humble bows; nor white-gloved beaux encroach
In crowds behind, to guard me to my coach:
Ah, hapless nymph! such conquests are no more;
For Chloe's now what Lydia was before!

"'Tis true, this Chloe boasts the peach's bloom,
But does her nearer whisper breathe perfume?
I own, her taper shape is formed to please;
Yet, if you saw her unconfined by stays!
She doubly to fifteen may make pretence;
Alike we read it in her face and sense.
Her reputation! but that never yet
Could check the freedoms of a young coquette.
Why will ye then, vain fops, her eyes believe?
Her eyes can, like your perjured tongues, deceive.

'What shall I do? how spend the hateful day?
At chapel shall I wear the morn away?
Who there frequents at these unmodish hours,
But ancient matrons with their frizzled towers,
And grey religious maids? My presence there,
Amid that sober train, would own despair;
Nor am I yet so old; nor is my glance
As yet fixed wholly to devotion's trance.

'Straight then I'll dress, and take my wonted range
Through every Indian shop through all the Change;
Where the tall jar erects his costly pride,
With antic shapes in China's azure dyed;
There careless lies the rich brocade unrolled;
Here shines a cabinet with burnished gold:
But then remembrance will my grief renew,
'Twas there the raffling dice false Damon threw;
The raffling dice to him decide the prize;
'Twas there he first conversed with Chloe's eyes.
Hence sprung th'ill-fated cause of all my smart;
To me the toy he gave, to her his heart.
But soon thy perjury in the gift was found,
The shivered china dropped upon the ground;
Sure omen that thy vows would faithless prove;
Frail was thy present, frailer is thy love.

'O happy Poll! in wiry prison pent,
Thou ne'er hast known what love or rivals meant;
And Pug with pleasure can his fetters bear,
Who ne'er believed the vows that lovers swear!

How am I cursed (unhappy and forlorn)
With perjury, with love, and rival's scorn!
False are the loose coquette's inveigling airs,
False is the pompous grief of youthful heirs,
False is the cringeing courtier's plighted word,
False are the dice when gamesters stamp the board,
False is the sprightly widow's public tear;
Yet these to Damon's oaths are all sincere.

'Fly from perfidious man, the sex disdain;
Let servile Chloe wear the nuptial chain.
Damon is practised in the modish life,
Can hate, and yet be civil to a wife.
He games; he swears; he drinks; he fights; he roves;
Yet Chloe can believe he fondly loves.
Mistress and wife can well supply his need;
A miss, for pleasure, and a wife for breed.
But Chloe's air is unconfined and gay,
And can, perhaps, an injured bed repay;
Perhaps her patient temper can behold
The rival of her love adorned with gold.
Powdered with diamonds, free from thought and care,
A husband's sullen humours she can bear.

'Why are these sobs? and why these streaming eyes?
Is love the cause? No, I the sex despise!
I hate, I loath his base perfidious name!
Yet if he should but feign a rival flame?
But Chloe boasts and triumphs in my pains;
To her he's faithful, 'tis to me he feigns.'

Thus love-sick Lydia raved. Her maid appears;
A band-box in her steady hand she bears.
'How well this ribbon's gloss becomes your face!'
She cries, in raptures; 'then, so sweet a lace!
How charmingly you look! so bright! so fair!
'Tis to your eyes the headdress owes its air.'
Straight Lydia smiled; the comb adjusts her locks,
And at the playhouse Harry keeps her box.

JOHN GAY

The Choice

Had I, Pygmalion like, the power
To make the nymph I would adore;
The model should be thus designed,
Like this her form, like this her mind.

Her skin should be as lilies fair,
With rosy cheeks and jetty hair;
Her lips with pure vermilion spread,
And soft and moist, as well as red;
Her eyes should shine with vivid light,
At once both languishing and bright;
Her shape should be exact and small,
Her stature rather low than tall;
Her limbs well turned, her air and mien
At once both sprightly and serene;
Besides all this, a nameless grace
Should be diffused all o'er her face;
To make the lovely piece complete,
Not only beautiful, but sweet.

This for her form: now for her mind;
I'd have it open, generous, kind,
Void of all coquettish arts,
And vain designs of conquering hearts,
Not swayed by any views of gain,
Nor fond of giving others pain;
But soft, though bright, like her own eyes,
Discreetly witty, gaily wise.

I'd have her skilled in every art
That can engage a wandering heart;
Know all the sciences of love,
Yet ever willing to improve;
To press the hand, and roll the eye,
And drop sometimes an amorous sigh;
To lengthen out the balmy kiss,
And heighten every tender bliss;
And yet I'd have the charmer be

By nature only taught, – or me.
 I'd have her to strict honour tied,
And yet without one spark of pride;
In company well-dressed and fine,
Yet not ambitious to outshine;
In private always neat and clean,
And quite a stranger to the spleen;
Well-pleased to grace the park and play,
And dance sometimes the night away,
But oftener fond to spend her hours
In solitude and shady bowers,
And there, beneath some silent grove,
Delight in poetry and love.
 Some sparks of the poetic fire
I fain would have her soul inspire,
Enough, at least, to let her know
What joys from love and virtue flow;
Enough, at least, to make her wise,
And fops and fopperies despise;
Prefer her books, and her own Muse,
To visits, scandal, chat, and news;
Above her sex exalt her mind,
And make her more than womankind.

SOAME JENYNS

The Widow and Virgin Sisters

BEING A LETTER TO THE WIDOW IN LONDON

While Delia shines at hurlothrumbo,
And darts her sprightly eye at some beau;
Then, close behind her fan retiring,
Sees through the sticks whole crowds admiring:
You sip your melancholy coffee,
And at the name of man, cry, 'O fie!'

Or, when the noisy rapper thunders,
Say coldly – 'Sure the fellow blunders!'
Unseen! though peer on peer approaches:
'James, I'm abroad! – but learn the coaches.'
As some young pleader, when his purse is
Unfilled through want of controversies,
Attends, until the chinks are filled all,
Th'assizes, Westminster, and Guildhall:
While graver lawyers keep their house, and
Collect the guineas by the thousand:
Or as some tradesmen, through show-glasses,
Expose their wares to each that passes;
Toys of no use! high-prized commodities
Bought to no end! estates in oddities!
Others, with like advantage, drive at
Their gain, from store-houses in private:
Thus Delia shines in places general,
Is never missing where the men are all;
Goes even to church with godly airs,
To meet good company at prayers;
Where she devoutly plays her fan,
Looks up to Heaven, but thinks on man.
You sit at home; enjoy your cousin,
While hearts are offered by the dozen:
Oh! born above your sex to rise,
With youth, wealth, beauty, titles – wise!
O! lady bright, did ne'er you mark yet,
In country fair, or country market,
A beau, whose eloquence might charm ye,
Enlisting soldiers for the army?
He flatters every well-built youth,
And tells him everything but – truth.
He cries, 'Good friend, I'm glad I hap'd in
Your company, you'll make a captain!'
He 'lists – but finds these gaudy shows
Soon changed to surly looks, and blows:
'Tis now, 'March, rascal! what, d'ye grumble?'
Thwack goes the cane! 'I'll make you humble.'

Such weddings are: and I resemble 'em,
Almost in all points, to this emblem.
While courtship lasts, 'tis, 'Dear,' 'tis, 'Madam!
The sweetest creature sure since Adam!
Had I the years of a Methusalem,
How in my charmer's praise I'd use all 'em!
Oh! take me to thy arms, my beauty!
I dote, adore the very shoe-tie!'
They wed – but, fancy grown less warming,
Next morn, he thinks the bride less charming:
He says, nay swears, 'My wife grows old in
One single month;' then falls to scolding,
'What, madam, gadding every day!
Up to your room! there stitch, or pray!'
    Such proves the marriage-state! but for all
These truths, you'll wed, and scorn the moral.

WILLIAM BROOME

*On Seeing a Tapestry Chair-Bottom Beautifully
Worked by His Daughter for Mrs Holroyd*

WRITTEN IN THE YEAR 1793

While Holroyd may boast of her beautiful bottom,
I think of what numberless ills may bespot 'em;
'Tis true they're intended for clean petticoats;
But beware of th'intrusion of bold Sansculottes;
Who regardless of Charlotte's most elegant stitches,
May rudely sit down without linen or breeches:
Would you know from what quarter the mischief may come,
When the battery's unmasked then beware of the bomb.

RICHARD OWEN CAMBRIDGE

From *The Art of Dancing*

Now haste, my Muse, pursue thy destined way,
What dresses best become the dancer, say;
The rules of dress forget not to impart,
A lesson previous to the dancing art.
 The soldier's scarlet, glowing from afar,
Shows that his bloody occupation's war;
Whilst the lawn band, beneath a double chin,
As plainly speaks divinity within;
The milkmaid safe through driving rains and snows,
Wrapped in her cloak, and propped on pattens goes;
While the soft belle, immured in velvet chair,
Needs but the silken shoe, and trusts her bosom bare:
The woolly drab, and English broadcloth warm,
Guard well the horseman from the beating storm,
But load the dancer with too great a weight,
And call from every pore the dewy sweat;
Rather let him his active limbs display
In camblet thin, or glossy paduasoy,
Let no unwieldy pride his shoulders press,
But airy, light, and easy be his dress;
Thin be his yielding sole, and low his heel,
So shall he nimbly bound, and safely wheel.

*

Dare I in such momentous points advise,
I should condemn the hoop's enormous size:
Of ills I speak by long experience found,
Oft have I trod th'immeasurable round,
And mourned my shins bruised black with many a wound.
Nor should the tightened stays, too straightly laced,
In whalebone bondage gall the slender waist.

*

Let each fair maid, who fears to be disgraced,
Ever be sure to tie her garters fast,

Lest the loosed string, amidst the public ball,
A wished-for prize to some proud fop should fall,
Who the rich treasure shall triumphant show;
And with warm blushes cause her cheeks to glow.

*

But let me now my lovely charge remind,
Lest they forgetful leave their fans behind;
Lay not, ye fair, the pretty toy aside,
A toy at once displayed, for use and pride,
A wondrous engine, that, by magic charms,
Cools your own breasts, and every other's warms.
What daring bard shall e'er attempt to tell
The powers that in this little weapon dwell?
What verse can e'er explain its various parts,
Its numerous uses, motions, charms, and arts?
Its painted folds, that oft extended wide
Th'afflicted fair-one's blubbered beauties hide,
When secret sorrows her sad bosom fill,
If Strephon is unkind, or Shock is ill:
Its sticks, on which her eyes dejected pore,
And pointing fingers number o'er and o'er,
Dies to consent, yet fears to own her flame;
Its shake triumphant, its victorious clap,
Its angry flutter, and its wanton tap?

SOAME JENYNS

From *The Poet and His Patron*

Why, Celia, is your spreading waist
So loose, so negligently laced?
Why must the wrapping bed-gown hide
Your snowy bosom's swelling pride?
How ill that dress adorns your head,
Distained, and rumpled from the bed!

Those clouds, that shade your blooming face,
A little water might displace,
As Nature every morn bestows
The crystal dew, to cleanse the rose.
Those tresses, as the raven black,
That waved in ringlets down your back,
Uncombed, and injured by neglect,
Destroy the face, which once they decked.

Whence this forgetfulness of dress?
Pray, madam, are you married? 'Yes.'
Nay, then indeed the wonder ceases,
No matter now how loose your dress is;
The end is won, your fortune's made,
Your sister now may take the trade.

Alas! what pity 'tis to find
This fault in half the female kind!
From hence proceed aversion, strife,
And all that sours the wedded life.
Beauty can only point the dart,
'Tis neatness guides it to the heart;
Let neatness then, and beauty strive
To keep a wavering flame alive.

'Tis harder far (you'll find it true)
To keep the conquest, than subdue;
Admit us once behind the screen,
What is there further to be seen?
A newer face may raise the flame,
But every woman is the same.

Then study chiefly to improve
The charm, that fixed your husband's love.
Weigh well his humour. Was it dress,
That gave your beauty power to bless?
Pursue it still; be neater seen;
'Tis always frugal to be clean;
So shall you keep alive desire,
And Time's swift wing shall fan the fire.

EDWARD MOORE

From *Satire V*

ON WOMEN

Britannia's daughters, much more fair than nice,
Too fond of admiration, lose their price;
Worn in the public eye, give cheap delight
To throngs, and tarnish to the sated sight:
As unreserved, and beauteous, as the sun,
Through every sign of vanity they run;
Assemblies, parks, coarse feasts in city-halls,
Lectures, and trials, plays, committees, balls,
Wells, bedlams, executions, Smithfield scenes,
And fortune-tellers, caves, and lions' dens,
Taverns, exchanges, bridewells, drawing-rooms,
Instalments, pillories, coronations, tombs,
Tumblers, and funerals, puppet-shows, reviews,
Sales, races, rabbits, (and, still stranger!) pews.

*

O'er the belles-lettres lovely Daphne reigns;
Again the god Apollo wears her chains:
With legs tossed high, on her sophee she sits,
Vouchsafing audience to contending wits:
Of each performance she's the final test;
One act read o'er, she prophesies the rest;
And then, pronouncing with decisive air,
Fully convinces all the town – she's fair.
Had lovely Daphne Hecatessa's face,
How would her elegance of taste decrease!
Some ladies' judgment in their features lies,
And all their genius sparkles from their eyes.

*

Lemira's sick; make haste; the doctor call:
He comes; but where's his patient? At the ball.
The doctor stares; her woman curtsies low,

And cries, 'My lady, sir, is always so:
Diversions put her maladies to flight;
True, she can't stand, but she can dance all night:
I've known my lady (for she loves a tune)
For fevers take an opera in June:
And, though perhaps you'll think the practice bold,
A midnight park is sovereign for a cold:
With colics, breakfasts of green fruit agree;
With indigestions, supper just at three.'
'A strange alternative,' replies sir Hans,
'Must women have a doctor, or a dance?
Though sick to death, abroad they safely roam,
But droop and die, in perfect health, at home:
For want – but not of health, are ladies ill;
And tickets cure beyond the doctor's bill.'

*

The languid lady next appears in state,
Who was not born to carry her own weight;
She lolls, reels, staggers, till some foreign aid
To her own stature lifts the feeble maid.
Then, if ordained to so severe a doom,
She, by just stages, journeys round the room:
But, knowing her own weakness, she despairs
To scale the Alps – that is, ascend the stairs.
My fan! let others say, who laugh at toil;
Fan! hood! glove! scarf! is her laconic style;
And that is spoke with such a dying fall,
That Betty rather sees, than hears the call:
The motion of her lips, and meaning eye,
Piece out th'idea her faint words deny.
O listen with attention most profound!
Her voice is but the shadow of a sound.
And help! oh help! her spirits are so dead,
One hand scarce lifts the other to her head.
If, there, a stubborn pin it triumphs o'er,
She pants! she sinks away! and is no more.
Let the robust and the gigantic carve,

Life is not worth so much, she'd rather starve:
But chew she must herself; ah cruel fate!
That Rosalinda can't by proxy eat.

*

    Few to good-breeding make a just pretence;
Good-breeding is the blossom of good-sense;
The last result of an accomplished mind,
With outward grace, the body's virtue, joined.
A violated decency now reigns;
And nymphs for failings take peculiar pains.
With Chinese painters modern toasts agree,
The point they aim at is deformity:
They throw their persons with a hoyden air
Across the room, and toss into the chair.
So far their commerce with mankind is gone,
They, for our manners, have exchanged their own.
The modest look, the castigated grace,
The gentle movement, and slow-measured pace,
For which her lovers died, her parents paid,
Are indecorums with the modern maid.

EDWARD YOUNG

An Elegy,

TO AN OLD BEAUTY

In vain, poor nymph, to please our youthful sight
You sleep in cream and frontlets all the night,
Your face with patches soil, with paint repair,
Dress with gay gowns, and shade with foreign hair.
If truth, in spite of manners, must be told,
Why really fifty-five is something old.
    Once you were young; or one, whose life's so long
She might have borne my mother, tells me wrong.

And once, since Envy's dead before you die,
The women own, you played a sparkling eye,
Taught the light foot a modish little trip,
And pouted with the prettiest purple lip.

To some new charmer are the roses fled,
Which blew, to damask all thy cheek with red;
Youth calls the Graces there to fix their reign,
And airs by thousands fill their easy train.
So parting summer bids her flowery prime
Attend the sun to dress some foreign clime,
While withering seasons in succession, here,
Strip the gay gardens, and deform the year.

But thou, since Nature bids, the world resign,
'Tis now thy daughter's daughter's time to shine.
With more address, or such as pleases more,
She runs her female exercises o'er,
Unfurls or closes, raps or turns the fan,
And smiles, or blushes at the creature man.
With quicker life, as gilded coaches pass,
In sidling courtesy she drops the glass.
With better strength, on visit-days she bears
To mount her fifty flights of ample stairs.
Her mien, her shape, her temper, eyes, and tongue,
Are sure to conquer – for the rogue is young:
And all that's madly wild, or oddly gay,
We call it only pretty Fanny's way.

Let time, that makes you homely, make you sage,
The sphere of wisdom, is the sphere of age.
'Tis true, when beauty dawns with early fire,
And hears the flattering tongues of soft desire,
If not from virtue, from its gravest ways
The soul with pleasing avocation strays.
But beauty gone, 'tis easier to be wise;
As harpers better by the loss of eyes.
Henceforth retire, reduce your roving airs,
Haunt less the plays, and more the public prayers,
Reject the Mechlin head, and gold brocade,
Go pray, in sober Norwich crepe arrayed.

Thy pendant diamonds let thy Fanny take
(Their trembling lustre shows how much you shake);
Or bid her wear thy necklace rowed with pearl,
You'll find your Fanny an obedient girl.
So for the rest, with less encumbrance hung,
You walk through life, unmingled with the young,
And view the shade and substance, as you pass,
With joint endeavour trifling at the glass,
Or Folly dressed, and rambling all her days,
To meet her counterpart, and grow by praise:
Yet still sedate yourself, and gravely plain,
You neither fret, nor envy at the vain.
'Twas thus, if man with woman we compare,
The wise Athenian crossed a glittering fair,
Unmoved by tongue and sights, he walked the place,
Through tape, toys, tinsel, gimp, perfume, and lace;
Then bends from Mars's hill his awful eyes,
And – 'What a world I never want?' he cries:
But cries unheard: for Folly will be free.
So parts the buzzing gawdy crowd and he:
As careless he for them, as they for him:
He wrapped in wisdom, and they whirled by whim.

THOMAS PARNELL

From *The Rape of the Lock*

Sol through white curtains shot a tim'rous ray,
And oped those eyes that must eclipse the day:
Now lapdogs gave themselves the rousing shake,
And sleepless lovers, just at twelve, awake:
Thrice rung the bell, the slipper knocked the ground,
And the pressed watch returned a silver sound.
Belinda still her downy pillow pressed,
Her guardian sylph prolonged the balmy rest.

*

And now, unveiled, the toilet stands displayed,
Each silver vase in mystic order laid.
First, robed in white, the nymph intent adores,
With head uncovered, the cosmetic powers.
A heav'nly image in the glass appears,
To that she bends, to that her eyes she rears;
Th'inferior priestess, at her altar's side,
Trembling, begins the sacred rites of pride.
Unnumbered treasures ope at once, and here
The various offerings of the world appear;
From each she nicely culls with curious toil,
And decks the goddess with the glittering spoil.
This casket India's glowing gems unlocks,
And all Arabia breathes from yonder box.
The tortoise here and elephant unite,
Transformed to combs, the speckled, and the white.
Here files of pins extend their shining rows,
Puffs, powders, patches, Bibles, billet-doux.
Now awful beauty puts on all its arms;
The fair each moment rises in her charms,
Repairs her smiles, awakens every grace,
And calls forth all the wonders of her face;
Sees by degrees a purer blush arise,
And keener lightnings quicken in her eyes.
The busy sylphs surround their darling care,
These set the head, and those divide the hair,
Some fold the sleeve, while others plait the gown;
And Betty's praised for labours not her own.

*

Not with more glories, in th'ethereal plain,
The sun first rises o'er the purpled main,
Than, issuing forth, the rival of his beams
Launched on the bosom of the silver Thames.
Fair nymphs, and well-dressed youths around her shone,
But every eye was fixed on her alone.
On her white breast a sparkling cross she wore,
Which Jews might kiss, and infidels adore.

Her lively looks a sprightly mind disclose,
Quick as her eyes, and as unfixed as those:
Favours to none, to all she smiles extends;
Oft she rejects, but never once offends.
Bright as the sun, her eyes the gazers strike,
And, like the sun, they shine on all alike.
Yet graceful ease, and sweetness void of pride
Might hide her faults, if belles had faults to hide:
If to her share some female errors fall,
Look on her face, and you'll forget them all.

*

Hither the heroes and the nymphs resort,
To taste awhile the pleasures of a court;
In various talk th'instructive hours they passed,
Who gave the ball, or paid the visit last:
One speaks the glory of the British Queen,
And one describes a charming Indian screen;
A third interprets motions, looks, and eyes;
At every word a reputation dies.
Snuff, or the fan, supply each pause of chat,
With singing, laughing, ogling, *and all that.*

*

'Say why are beauties praised and honoured most,
The wise man's passion, and the vain man's toast?
Why decked with all that land and sea afford,
Why angels called, and angel-like adored?
Why round our coaches crowd the white-gloved beaux?
Why bows the side-box from its inmost rows?
How vain are all these glories, all our pains,
Unless good sense preserve what beauty gains:
That men may say, when we the front-box grace,
"Behold the first in virtue as in face!"
Oh! if to dance all night, and dress all day,
Charmed the small-pox, or chased old age away;
Who would not scorn what housewife's cares produce,
Or who would learn one earthly thing of use?

To patch, nay ogle, might become a saint,
Nor could it sure be such a sin to paint.
But since, alas! frail beauty must decay,
Curled or uncurled, since locks will turn to grey;
Since painted, or not painted, all shall fade,
And she who scorns a man, must die a maid;
What then remains but well our power to use,
And keep good-humour still whate'er we lose?
And trust me, dear! good-humour can prevail,
When airs, and flights, and screams, and scolding fail.
Beauties in vain their pretty eyes may roll;
Charms strike the sight, but merit wins the soul.'
    So spoke the dame, but no applause ensued;
Belinda frowned, Thalestris called her prude.

ALEXANDER POPE

Epigram

ON A LADY WHO SHED HER WATER AT SEEING
THE TRAGEDY OF CATO; OCCASIONED BY AN
EPIGRAM ON A LADY WHO WEPT AT IT

Whilst maudlin Whigs deplore their Cato's fate,
Still with dry eyes the Tory Celia sate:
But though her pride forbade her eyes to flow,
The gushing waters found a vent below.
Though secret, yet with copious streams she mourns,
Like twenty river-gods with all their urns.
Let others screw an hypocritic face,
She shows her grief in a sincerer place!
Here Nature reigns, and passion void of art;
For this road leads directly to the heart.

NICHOLAS ROWE

Venus Attiring the Graces

> ... In naked beauty more adorned,
> More lovely.
>
> *Milton*

As Venus one day, at her toilet affairs,
With the Graces attending, adjusted her airs,
In a negligent way, without bodice or hoop,
As Guido has painted the beautiful group,
(For Guido, no doubt, in idea at least,
Had seen all the Graces and Venus undressed)
Half pensive, half smiling, the goddess of beauty
Looked round on the girls, as they toiled in their duty:
'And surely,' she cried, 'you have strangely miscarried,
That not one of the three should have ever been married.
Let me nicely examine – fair foreheads, straight noses,
And cheeks that might rival Aurora's own roses;
Lips; teeth; and what eyes! that can languish, or roll,
To enliven or soften the elegant whole.
The sweet auburn tresses, that shade what they deck;
The shoulders, that fall from the delicate neck;
The polished round arm, which *my* statues might own,
And the lovely contour which descends from the zone.
Then how it should happen I cannot divine:
Either you are too coy, or the gods too supine.
I believe 'tis the latter; for every soft bosom
Must have its attachments, and wish to disclose 'em.
Some lovers not beauty but novelty warms,
They have seen you so often they're tired of your charms.
But I'll find out a method their languor to move,
And at least make them stare, if I can't make them love.
Come here, you two girls, that look full in my face,
And you that so often are turning your back,
Put on these cork rumps, and then tighten your stays
Till your hips, and your ribs, and the strings themselves crack.
Can ye speak? can ye breathe? – Not a word – then 'twill do.

You have often dressed *me*, and for once I'll dress *you*.
Don't let your curls fall with that natural bend,
But stretch them up tight till each hair stands on end.
One, two, nay three cushions, like Cybele's towers;
Then a few ells of gauze, and some baskets of flowers.
These bottles of nectar will serve for perfumes.
Go pluck the fledged Cupids, and bring me their plumes.
If that's not enough, you may strip all the fowls,
My doves, Juno's peacocks, and Pallas's owls.
And stay, from Jove's eagle, if napping you take him,
You may snatch a few quills – but be sure you don't wake him.
Hold! what are ye doing! I vow and protest,
If I don't watch you closely you'll spoil the whole jest.
What I have disordered you still set to rights,
And seem half unwilling to make yourselves frights,
What I am concealing you want to display;
But it shan't serve the turn, for I will have my way.
Those crimped colet'montés don't reach to your chins,
And the heels of your slippers are broader than pins.
You can stand, you can walk, like the girls in the street;
Those buckles won't do, they scarce cover your feet.
Here, run to the Cyclops, you boys without wings,
And bring up their boxes of contraband things.
Well, now you're bedizened, I'll swear, as ye pass,
I can scarcely help laughing – don't look in the glass.
Those tittering boys shall be whipped if they tease you,
So come away, girls. From your torments to ease you,
We'll haste to Olympus, and get the thing over;
I have *not* the least doubt but you'll each find a lover.
And if it succeeds, with a torrent of mirth
We'll pester their godships again and again;
Then send the receipt to the ladies on earth,
And bid *them* become monsters, till men become men.'

WILLIAM WHITEHEAD

A Beautiful Young Nymph Going to Bed

WRITTEN FOR THE HONOUR OF THE FAIR SEX

Corinna, pride of Drury Lane,
For whom no shepherd sighs in vain;
Never did Covent Garden boast
So bright a battered, strolling toast;
No drunken rake to pick her up,
No cellar where on tick to sup;
Returning at the midnight hour;
Four stories climbing to her bower;
Then, seated on a three-legged chair,
Takes off her artificial hair:
Now, picking out a crystal eye,
She wipes it clean, and lays it by.
Her eye-brows from a mouse's hide,
Stuck on with art on either side,
Pulls off with care, and first displays 'em,
Then in a play-book smoothly lays 'em.
Now dextrously her plumpers draws,
That serve to fill her hollow jaws.
Untwists a wire; and from her gums
A set of teeth completely comes.
Pulls out the rags contrived to prop
Her flabby dugs and down they drop.
Proceeding on, the lovely goddess
Unlaces next her steel-ribbed bodice;
Which by the operator's skill,
Press down the lumps, the hollows fill,
Up goes her hand, and off she slips
The bolsters that supply her hips.
With gentlest touch, she next explores
Her shankers, issues, running sores,
Effects of many a sad disaster;
And then to each applies a plaster.
But must, before she goes to bed,

Rub off the daubs of white and red;
And smooth the furrows in her front,
With greasy paper stuck upon't.
She takes a bolus ere she sleeps;
And then between two blankets creeps.
With pains of love tormented lies;
Or if she chance to close her eyes,
Of Bridewell and the Compter dreams,
And feels the lash, and faintly screams;
Or, by a faithless bully drawn,
At some hedge-tavern lies in pawn;
Or to Jamaica seems transported,
Alone, and by no planter courted;
Or, near Fleet Ditch's oozy brinks,
Surrounded with a hundred stinks,
Belated, seems on watch to lie,
And snap some cully passing by;
Or, struck with fear, her fancy runs
On watchmen, constables and duns,
From whom she meets with frequent rubs;
But, never from religious clubs;
Whose favour she is sure to find,
Because she pays them all in kind.
    Corinna wakes. A dreadful sight!
Behold the ruins of the night!
A wicked rat her plaster stole,
Half ate, and dragged it to his hole.
The crystal eye, alas, was missed;
And puss had on her plumpers pissed.
A pigeon picked her issue-peas;
And Shock her tresses filled with fleas.
    The nymph, though in this mangled plight,
Must every morn her limbs unite.
But how shall I describe her arts
To recollect the scattered parts?
Or show the anguish, toil, and pain,
Of gathering up herself again?
The bashful muse will never bear

In such a scene to interfere.
Corinna in the morning dizened,
Who sees, will spew; who smells, be poisoned.

JONATHAN SWIFT

2

'The proper study of mankind is man.'

The Maid's Husband

Genteel in personage,
Conduct and equipage,
Noble by heritage,
      Generous and free:
Brave, not romantic,
Learn'd, not pedantic,
Frolic, not frantic:
      This must be he.

Honour maintaining,
Meanness disdaining,
Still entertaining,
      Engaging, and new:
Neat, but not finical,
Sage, but not cynical,
Never tyrannical,
      But ever true.

HENRY CAREY

From *Epistle to Dr Arbuthnot*

Yet let me flap this bug with gilded wings,
This painted child of dirt, that stinks and stings;
Whose buzz the witty and the fair annoys,
Yet wit ne'er tastes, and beauty ne'er enjoys:
So well-bred spaniels civilly delight
In mumbling of the game they dare not bite.
Eternal smiles his emptiness betray,
As shallow streams run dimpling all the way.
Whether in florid impotence he speaks,
And, as the prompter breathes, the puppet squeaks;
Or, at the ear of Eve, familiar toad,

Half froth, half venom, spits himself abroad,
In puns, or politics, or tales, or lies,
Or spite, or smut, or rhymes, or blasphemies.
His wit all see-saw, between *that* and *this*,
Now high, now low, now master up, now miss,
And he himself one vile antithesis.
Amphibious thing! that acting either part,
The trifling head, or the corrupted heart,
Fop at the toilet, flatterer at the board,
Now trips a lady, and now struts a lord.
Eve's tempter thus the Rabbins have expressed,
A cherub's face, a reptile all the rest,
Beauty that shocks you, parts that none will trust,
Wit that can creep, and pride that licks the dust.

ALEXANDER POPE

Jupiter and Mercury

A FABLE

Here Hermes, says Jove who with nectar was mellow,
Go fetch me some clay – I will make an odd fellow:
Right and wrong shall be jumbled – much gold and some
    dross;
Without cause be he pleased, without cause be he cross;
Be sure as I work to throw in contradictions,
A great love of truth; yet a mind turned to fictions;
Now mix these ingredients, which warmed in the baking,
Turn to learning, and gaming, religion and raking.
With the love of a wench, let his writings be chaste;
Tip his tongue with strange matter, his pen with fine taste;
That the rake and the poet o'er all may prevail,
Set fire to the head, and set fire to the tale:
For the joy of each sex, on the world I'll bestow it:
This scholar, rake, Christian, dupe, gamester and poet,

Through a mixture so odd, he shall merit great fame,
And among brother mortals – be GOLDSMITH his name!
When on earth this strange meteor no more shall appear,
You, Hermes, shall fetch him – to make us sport here!

DAVID GARRICK

From *Town Eclogues*

SILLIANDER

Ill fates pursue me, may I never find
The dice propitious, or the ladies kind,
If fair Miss Flippy's fan I did not tear,
And one from me she condescends to wear!

PATCH

Women are always ready to receive;
'Tis then a favour when the sex we give.
A lady (but she is too great to name),
Beauteous in person, spotless in her fame,
With gentle strugglings let me force this ring;
Another day may give another thing.

SILLIANDER

I could say something – see this billet-doux –
And as for presents – look upon my shoe –
These buckles were not forced, nor half a theft,
But a young countess fondly made the gift.

PATCH

My countess is more nice, more artful too,
Affects to fly, that I may fierce pursue:
This snuff-box which I begged, she still denied,
And when I strove to snatch it, seemed to hide;
She laughed and fled, and as I sought to seize,

With affectation crammed it down her stays;
Yet hoped she did not place it there unseen,
I pressed her breasts, and pulled it from between.

SILLIANDER

Last night, as I stood ogling of her Grace,
Drinking delicious poison from her face,
The soft enchantress did that face decline,
Nor ever raised her eyes to meet with mine;
With sudden art some secret did pretend,
Leaned cross two chairs to whisper to a friend,
While the stiff whalebone with the motion rose,
And thousand beauties to my sight expose.

PATCH

Early this morn – (but I was asked to come)
I drank bohea in Celia's dressing-room:
Warm from her bed, to me alone within,
Her night-gown fastened with a single pin;
Her night-clothes tumbled with resistless grace,
And her bright hair played careless round her face;
Reaching the kettle made her gown unpin,
She wore no waistcoat, and her shift was thin.

SILLIANDER

See Titiana driving to the park!
Haste! let us follow, 'tis not yet too dark:
In her all beauties of the spring are seen,
Her cheeks are rosy, and her mantle green.

PATCH

See Tintoretta to the opera goes!
Haste! or the crowd will not permit our bows;
In her the glory of the heavens we view,
Her eyes are star-like, and her mantle blue.

SILLIANDER

What colour does in Celia's stockings shine?
Reveal that secret, and the prize is thine.

PATCH

What are her garters? Tell me, if you can;
I'll freely own thee far the happier man.

Thus Patch continued his heroic strain,
While Silliander but contends in vain;

After a contest so important gained,
Unrivalled Patch in every ruelle reigned.

LADY MARY WORTLEY MONTAGU

From *The Modern Fine Gentleman*

WRITTEN IN THE YEAR 1746

Just broke from school, pert, impudent, and raw,
Expert in Latin, more expert in taw,
His Honour posts o'er Italy and France,
Measures St Peter's dome and learns to dance.
Thence, having quick through various countries flown,
Gleaned all their follies, and exposed his own,
He back returns, a thing so strange all o'er,
As never ages past produced before:
A monster of such complicated worth,
As no one single clime could e'er bring forth;
Half atheist, papist, gamester, bubble, rook,
Half fiddler, coachman, dancer, groom, and cook.
Next, because business is now all the vogue,
And who'd be quite polite must be a rogue,
In parliament he purchases a seat,
To make the accomplished gentleman complete.
There safe in self-sufficient impudence,

53

Without experience, honesty, or sense,
Unknowing in her interest, trade, or laws,
He vainly undertakes his country's cause:
Forth from his lips, prepared at all to rail,
Torrents of nonsense burst, like bottled ale,
Though shallow, muddy; brisk, though mighty dull;
Fierce without strength; o'erflowing, though not full.

SOAME JENYNS

The Vanity of Human Wishes

THE TENTH SATIRE OF JUVENAL IMITATED

Let observation with extensive view,
Survey mankind from China to Peru;
Remark each anxious toil, each eager strife,
And watch the busy scenes of crowded life;
Then say how hope and fear, desire and hate,
O'erspread with snares the clouded maze of fate,
Where wavering man, betrayed by venturous pride,
To tread the dreary paths without a guide;
As treacherous phantoms in the mist delude,
Shuns fancied ills, or chases airy good.
How rarely reason guides the stubborn choice,
Rules the bold hand, or prompts the suppliant voice,
How nations sink, by darling schemes oppressed,
When vengeance listens to the fool's request.
Fate wings with every wish th'afflictive dart,
Each gift of nature, and each grace of art,
With fatal heat impetuous courage glows,
With fatal sweetness elocution flows,
Impeachment stops the speaker's powerful breath,
And restless fire precipitates on death.
    But scarce observed the knowing and the bold,
Fall in the general massacre of gold;

Wide-wasting pest! that rages unconfined,
And crowds with crimes the records of mankind,
For gold his sword the hireling ruffian draws,
For gold the hireling judge distorts the laws;
Wealth heaped on wealth, nor truth nor safety buys,
The dangers gather as the treasures rise.

    Let history tell where rival kings command,
And dubious title shakes the madded land,
When statutes glean the refuse of the sword,
How much more safe the vassal than the lord,
Low skulks the hind beneath the rage of power,
And leaves the wealthy traitor in the Tower,
Untouched his cottage, and his slumbers sound,
Though confiscation's vultures hover round.

    The needy traveller, serene and gay,
Walks the wild heath, and sings his toil away.
Does envy seize thee? crush th'upbraiding joy,
Increase his riches and his peace destroy,
Now fears in dire vicissitude invade,
The rustling brake alarms, and quivering shade,
Nor light nor darkness bring his pain relief,
One shows the plunder, and one hides the thief.

    Yet still one general cry the skies assails
And gain and grandeur load the tainted gales;
Few know the toiling statesman's fear or care,
Th'insidious rival and the gaping heir.

    Once more, Democritus, arise on earth,
With cheerful wisdom and instructive mirth,
See motley life in modern trappings dressed,
And feed with varied fools th'eternal jest:
Thou who couldst laugh where want enchained caprice,
Toil crushed conceit, and man was of a piece;
Where wealth unloved without a mourner died;
And scarce a sycophant was fed by pride;
Where ne'er was known the form of mock debate,
Or seen a new-made mayor's unwieldy state;
Where change of favourites made no change of laws,
And senates heard before they judged a cause;

How wouldst thou shake at Britain's modish tribe,
Dart the quick taunt, and edge the piercing gibe?
Attentive truth and nature to descry,
And pierce each scene with philosophic eye.
To thee were solemn toys or empty show,
The robes of pleasure and the veils of woe:
All aid the farce, and all thy mirth maintain,
Whose joys are causeless, or whose griefs are vain.

Such was the scorn that filled the sage's mind,
Renewed at every glance on humankind;
How just that scorn ere yet thy voice declare,
Search every state, and canvass every prayer.

Unnumbered suppliants crowd preferment's gate,
Athirst for wealth, and burning to be great;
Delusive fortune hears th'incessant call,
They mount, they shine, evaporate, and fall.
On every stage the foes of peace attend,
Hate dogs their flight, and insult mocks their end.
Love ends with hope, the sinking statesman's door
Pours in the morning worshipper no more;
For growing names the weekly scribbler lies,
To growing wealth the dedicator flies,
From every room descends the painted face,
That hung the bright Palladium of the place,
And smoked in kitchens, or in auctions sold,
To better features yields the frame of gold;
For now no more we trace in every line
Heroic worth, benevolence divine:
The form distorted justifies the fall,
And detestation rids th'indignant wall.

But will not Britain hear the last appeal,
Sign her foes' doom, or guard her favourites' zeal;
Through freedom's sons no more remonstrance rings,
Degrading nobles and controlling kings;
Our supple tribes repress their patriot throats,
And ask no questions but the price of votes;
With weekly libels and septennial ale,
Their wish is full to riot and to rail.

In full-blown dignity, see Wolsey stand,
Law in his voice, and fortune in his hand:
To him the church, the realm, their powers consign,
Through him the rays of regal bounty shine,
Turned by his nod the stream of honour flows,
His smile alone security bestows:
Still to new heights his restless wishes tower,
Claim leads to claim, and power advances power;
Till conquest unresisted ceased to please,
And rights submitted, left him none to seize.
At length his sovereign frowns – the train of state
Mark the keen glance, and watch the sign to hate.
Where-e'er he turns he meets a stranger's eye,
His suppliants scorn him, and his followers fly;
At once is lost the pride of awful state,
The golden canopy, the glittering plate,
The regal palace, the luxurious board,
The liveried army, and the menial lord.
With age, with cares, with maladies oppressed,
He seeks the refuge of monastic rest.
Grief aids disease, remembered folly stings,
And his last sighs reproach the faith of kings.

Speak thou, whose thoughts at humble peace repine,
Shall Wolsey's wealth, with Wolsey's end be thine?
Or liv'st thou now, with safer pride content,
The wisest justice on the banks of Trent?
For why did Wolsey near the steeps of fate,
On weak foundations raise th'enormous weight?
Why but to sink beneath misfortune's blow,
With louder ruin to the gulfs below?

What gave great Villiers to th'assassin's knife,
And fixed disease on Harley's closing life?
What murdered Wentworth, and what exiled Hyde,
By kings protected and to kings allied?
What but their wish indulged in courts to shine,
And power too great to keep or to resign?

When first the college rolls receive his name,
The young enthusiast quits his ease for fame;

Through all his veins the fever of renown
Burns from the strong contagion of the gown;
O'er Bodley's dome his future labours spread,
And Bacon's mansion trembles o'er his head;
Are these thy views? proceed, illustrious youth,
And virtue guard thee to the throne of truth,
Yet should thy soul indulge the generous heat,
Till captive science yields her last retreat;
Should reason guide thee with her brightest ray,
And pour on misty doubt resistless day;
Should no false kindness lure to loose delight,
Nor praise relax, nor difficulty fright;
Should tempting novelty thy cell refrain,
And sloth effuse her opiate fumes in vain;
Should beauty blunt on fops her fatal dart,
Nor claim the triumph of a lettered heart;
Should no disease thy torpid veins invade,
Nor melancholy's phantoms haunt thy shade;
Yet hope not life from grief or danger free,
Nor think the doom of man reversed for thee:
Deign on the passing world to turn thine eyes,
And pause awhile from letters to be wise;
There mark what ills the scholar's life assail,
Toil, envy, want, the patron, and the jail.
See nations slowly wise, and meanly just,
To buried merit raise the tardy bust.
If dreams yet flatter, once again attend,
Hear Lydiat's life and Galileo's end.

Nor deem, when learning her last prize bestows
The glittering eminence exempt from foes;
See when the vulgar 'scapes, despised or awed,
Rebellion's vengeful talons seize on Laud.
From meaner minds, though smaller fines content
The plundered palace or sequestered rent;
Marked out by dangerous parts he meets the shock,
And fatal learning leads him to the block:
Around his tomb let art and genius weep,
But hear his death, ye blockheads, hear and sleep.

The festal blazes, the triumphal show,
The ravished standard, and the captive foe,
The senate's thanks, the gazette's pompous tale,
With force resistless o'er the brave prevail.
Such bribes the rapid Greek o'er Asia whirled,
For such the steady Romans shook the world;
For such in distant lands the Britons shine,
And stain with blood the Danube or the Rhine;
This power has praise, that virtue scarce can warm,
Till fame supplies the universal charm.
Yet reason frowns on war's unequal game,
Where wasted nations raise a single name,
And mortgaged states their grandsires' wreaths regret
From age to age in everlasting debt;
Wreaths which at last the dear-bought right convey
To rust on medals, or on stones decay.
On what foundation stands the warrior's pride?
How just his hopes let Swedish Charles decide;
A frame of adamant, a soul of fire,
No dangers fright him, and no labours tire;
O'er love, o'er fear, extends his wide domain,
Unconquered lord of pleasure and of pain;
No joys to him pacific sceptres yield,
War sounds the trump, he rushes to the field;
Behold surrounding kings their powers combine,
And one capitulate, and one resign;
Peace courts his hand, but spreads her charms in vain;
'Think nothing gained,' he cries, 'till nought remain,
On Moscow's walls till Gothic standards fly,
And all be mine beneath the polar sky.'
The march begins in military state,
And nations on his eye suspended wait;
Stern famine guards the solitary coast,
And winter barricades the realms of frost;
He comes, nor want nor cold his course delay; —
Hide, blushing glory, hide Pultowa's day:
The vanquished hero leaves his broken bands,
And shows his miseries in distant lands;

Condemned a needy supplicant to wait,
While ladies interpose, and slaves debate.
But did not chance at length her error mend?
Did no subverted empire mark his end?
Did rival monarchs give the fatal wound?
Or hostile millions press him to the ground?
His fall was destined to a barren strand,
A petty fortress, and a dubious hand;
He left the name, at which the world grew pale,
To point a moral, or adorn a tale.

All times their scenes of pompous woes afford,
From Persia's tyrant to Bavaria's lord.
In gay hostility, and barbarous pride,
With half mankind embattled at his side,
Great Xerxes comes to seize the certain prey,
And starves exhausted regions in his way;
Attendant flattery counts his myriads o'er,
Till counted myriads sooth his pride no more;
Fresh praise is tried till madness fires his mind,
The waves he lashes, and enchains the wind;
New powers are claimed, new powers are still bestowed,
Till rude resistance lops the spreading god;
The daring Greeks deride the martial show,
And heap their valleys with the gaudy foe;
Th'insulted sea with humbler thoughts he gains,
A single skiff to speed his flight remains;
Th'incumbered oar scarce leaves the dreaded coast
Through purple billows and a floating host.

The bold Bavarian, in a luckless hour,
Tries the dread summits of Caesarian power,
With unexpected legions bursts away,
And sees defenceless realms receive his sway;
Short sway! fair Austria spreads her mournful charms,
The queen, the beauty, sets the world in arms;
From hill to hill the beacons' rousing blaze
Spreads wide the hope of plunder and of praise;
The fierce Croatian, and the wild Hussar,
With all the sons of ravage crowd the war;

The baffled prince in honour's flattering bloom
Of hasty greatness finds the fatal doom,
His foes' derision, and his subjects' blame,
And steals to death from anguish and from shame.
    Enlarge my life with multitude of days,
In health, in sickness, thus the suppliant prays;
Hides from himself his state, and shuns to know,
That life protracted is protracted woe.
Time hovers o'er, impatient to destroy,
And shuts up all the passages of joy:
In vain their gifts the bounteous seasons pour,
The fruit autumnal, and the vernal flower,
With listless eyes the dotard views the store,
He views, and wonders that they please no more;
Now palls the tasteless meats, and joyless wines,
And luxury with sighs her slave resigns.
Approach, ye minstrels, try the soothing strain,
Diffuse the tuneful lenitives of pain:
No sound alas would touch th'impervious ear,
Though dancing mountains witnessed Orpheus near;
Nor lute nor lyre his feeble powers attend,
Nor sweeter music of a virtuous friend,
But everlasting dictates crowd his tongue,
Perversely grave, or positively wrong.
The still returning tale, and lingering jest,
Perplex the fawning niece and pampered guest,
While growing hopes scarce awe the gathering sneer,
And scarce a legacy can bribe to hear;
The watchful guests still hint the last offence,
The daughter's petulance, the son's expense,
Improve his heady rage with treacherous skill,
And mould his passions till they make his will.
    Unnumbered maladies his joints invade,
Lay siege to life and press the dire blockade;
But unextinguished avarice still remains,
And dreaded losses aggravate his pains;
He turns, with anxious heart and crippled hands,
His bonds of debt, and mortgages of lands;

Or views his coffers with suspicious eyes,
Unlocks his gold, and counts it till he dies.

But grant, the virtues of a temperate prime
Bless with an age exempt from scorn or crime;
An age that melts with unperceived decay,
And glides in modest innocence away;
Whose peaceful day benevolence endears,
Whose night congratulating conscience cheers;
The general favourite as the general friend:
Such age there is, and who shall wish its end?

Yet even on this her load misfortune flings,
To press the weary minutes' flagging wings:
New sorrow rises as the day returns,
A sister sickens, or a daughter mourns.
Now kindred merit fills the sable bier,
Now lacerated friendship claims a tear.
Year chases year, decay pursues decay,
Still drops some joy from withering life away;
New forms arise, and different views engage,
Superfluous lags the veteran on the stage,
Till pitying nature signs the last release,
And bids afflicted worth retire to peace.

But few there are whom hours like these await,
Who set unclouded in the gulfs of fate.
From Lydia's monarch should the search descend,
By Solon cautioned to regard his end,
In life's last scene what prodigies surprise,
Fears of the brave, and follies of the wise?
From Marlborough's eyes the streams of dotage flow,
And Swift expires a driveler and a show.

The teeming mother, anxious for her race,
Begs for each birth the fortune of a face:
Yet Vane could tell what ills from beauty spring;
And Sedley curse the form that pleased a king.
Ye nymphs of rosy lips and radiant eyes,
Whom pleasure keeps too busy to be wise,
Whom joys with soft varieties invite
By day the frolic, and the dance by night,

Who frown with vanity, who smile with art,
And ask the latest fashion of the heart,
What care, what rules your heedless charms shall save,
Each nymph your rival, and each youth your slave?
Against your fame with fondness hate combines,
The rival batters, and the lover mines.
With distant voice neglected virtue calls,
Less heard, and less the faint remonstrance falls;
Tired with contempt, she quits the slippery reign,
And pride and prudence take her seat in vain.
In crowd at once, where none the pass defend,
The harmless freedom, and the private friend.
The guardians yield, by force superior plied;
To interest, prudence; and to flattery, pride.
Here beauty falls betrayed, despised, distressed,
And hissing infamy proclaims the rest.
    Where then shall hope and fear their objects find?
Must dull suspense corrupt the stagnant mind?
Must helpless man, in ignorance sedate,
Roll darkling down the torrent of his fate?
Must no dislike alarm, no wishes rise,
No cries invoke the mercies of the skies?
Enquirer, cease, petitions yet remain,
Which heaven may hear, nor deem religion vain.
Still raise for good the supplicating voice,
But leave to heaven the measure and the choice.
Safe in his power, whose eyes discern afar
The secret ambush of a specious prayer.
Implore his aid, in his decisions rest,
Secure whate'er he gives, he gives the best.
Yet when the sense of sacred presence fires,
And strong devotion to the skies aspires,
Pour forth thy fervours for a healthful mind,
Obedient passions, and a will resigned;
For love, which scarce collective man can fill;
For patience sovereign o'er transmuted ill;
For faith, that panting for a happier seat,
Counts death kind nature's signal of retreat:

These goods for man the laws of heaven ordain,
These goods he grants, who grants the power to gain;
With these celestial wisdom calms the mind,
And makes the happiness she does not find.

SAMUEL JOHNSON

Epitaph

ON DR SAMUEL JOHNSON

Here lies Sam Johnson: – Reader, have a care,
Tread lightly, lest you wake a sleeping bear:
Religious, moral, generous, and humane
He was; but self-sufficient, proud, and vain,
Fond of, and overbearing in dispute,
A Christian, and a scholar – but a brute.

SOAME JENYNS

From *A Familiar Epistle to J.B. Esq.*

An Unworthy Parson

Mark yon round parson, fat and sleek,
Who preaches only once a week,
Whom claret, sloth, and ven'son join
To make an orthodox divine;
Whose holiness receives its beauty
From income large, and little duty;
Who loves the pipe, the glass, the smock,
And keeps – a curate for his flock.
The world, obsequious to his nod,
Shall hail this oily man of God,
While the poor priest, with half a score
Of prattling infants at his door,

Whose sober wishes ne'er regale
Beyond the homely jug of ale,
Is hardly deemed companion fit
For man of wealth, or man of wit,
Though learn'd perhaps and wise as he
Who signs with staring S.T.P.
And full of sacerdotal pride,
Lays God and duty both aside.
 'This curate, say you, learn'd and wise!
Why does not then this curate rise?'
 This curate then, at forty-three,
(Years which become a curacy)
At no great mart of letters bred,
Had strange odd notions in his head,
That parts, and books, and application,
Furnished all means of education;
And that a pulpiteer should know
More than his gaping flock below;
That learning was not got with pain,
To be forgotten all again;
That Latin words, and rumbling Greek,
However charming sounds to speak,
Apt or unapt in each quotation,
Were insults on a congregation,
Who could not understand one word
Of all the learned stuff they heard;
That something more than preaching fine,
Should go to make a sound divine;
That church and prayer, and holy Sunday,
Were no excuse for sinful Monday;
That pious doctrine, pious life,
Should both make one, as man and wife.
 Thinking in this uncommon mode,
So out of all the priestly road,
What man alive can e'er suppose,
Who marks the way Preferment goes,
That she should ever find her way
To this poor curate's house of clay?

Such was the priest, so strangely wise!
He could not bow – how should he rise?
Learned he was, and deeply read;
– But what of that? – not duly bred.
For he had sucked no grammar rules
From royal founts, or public schools,
Nor gained a single corn of knowledge
From that vast granary – a college.
A granary, which food supplies
To vermin of uncommon size.

ROBERT LLOYD

From *Of the Use of Riches*

At Timon's villa let us pass a day,
Where all cry out, 'What sums are thrown away!'
So proud, so grand, of that stupendous air,
Soft and agreeable come never there.
Greatness, with Timon, dwells in such a draught
As brings all Brobdingnag before your thought.
To compass this, his building is a town,
His pond an ocean, his parterre a down:
Who but must laugh, the master when he sees?
A puny insect, shivering at a breeze.
Lo, what huge heaps of littleness around!
The whole, a laboured quarry above ground.
Two cupids squirt before: a lake behind
Improves the keenness of the northern wind.
His gardens next your admiration call,
On every side you look, behold the wall!
No pleasing intricacies intervene,
No artful wildness to perplex the scene;
Grove nods at grove, each alley has a brother,
And half the platform just reflects the other.
The suffering eye inverted Nature sees,

Trees cut to statues, statues thick as trees,
With here a fountain, never to be played,
And there a summer-house, that knows no shade.
Here Amphitrite sails through myrtle bowers;
There gladiators fight, or die, in flowers;
Unwatered see the drooping sea-horse mourn,
And swallows roost in Nilus' dusty urn.

My Lord advances with majestic mien,
Smit with the mighty pleasure, to be seen:
But soft – by regular approach – not yet –
First through the length of yon hot terrace sweat,
And when up ten steep slopes you've dragged your thighs,
Just at his study-door he'll bless your eyes.

His study! with what authors is it stored?
In books, not authors, curious is my Lord;
To all their dated backs he turns you round:
These Aldus printed, those Du Sueïl has bound.
Lo some are vellum, and the rest as good
For all his Lordship knows, but they are wood.
For Locke or Milton 'tis in vain to look,
These shelves admit not any modern book.

And now the chapel's silver bell you hear,
That summons you to all the pride of prayer:
Light quirks of music, broken and uneven,
Make the soul dance upon a jig to Heaven.
On painted ceilings you devoutly stare,
Where sprawl the saints of Verrio or Laguerre,
Or gilded clouds in fair expansion lie,
And bring all Paradise before your eye.
To rest, the cushion and soft Dean invite,
Who never mentions Hell to ears polite.

ALEXANDER POPE

Verses

ADDRESSED TO THE IMITATOR OF THE FIRST SATIRE OF THE SECOND BOOK OF HORACE

An Attack on Pope

In two large columns on thy motley page,
Where Roman wit is striped with English rage;
Where ribaldry to satire makes pretence,
And modern scandal rolls with ancient sense:
Whilst on one side we see how Horace thought,
And on the other how he never wrote;
Who can believe, who view the bad, the good,
That the dull copyist better understood
That spirit he pretends to imitate,
Than heretofore that Greek he did translate?

Thine is just such an image of his pen,
As thou thyself art of the sons of men,
Where our own species in burlesque we trace,
A sign-post likeness of the human race,
That is at once resemblance and disgrace.

Horace can laugh, is delicate, is clear,
You only coarsely rail, or darkly sneer;
His style is elegant, his diction pure,
Whilst none thy crabbed numbers can endure;
Hard as thy heart, and as thy birth obscure.

If he has thorns, they all on roses grow;
Thine like thistles, and mean brambles show;
With this exception, that, though rank the soil,
Weeds as they are, they seem produced by toil.

Satire should, like a polished razor, keen,
Wound with a touch, that's scarcely felt or seen:
Thine is an oyster-knife, that hacks and hews;
The rage, but not the talent to abuse;
And is in hate, what love is in the stews.
'Tis the gross lust of hate, that still annoys,

Without distinction, as gross love enjoys:
Neither to folly, nor to vice confined,
The object of thy spleen is humankind:
It preys on all who yield, or who resist:
To thee 'tis provocation to exist.

But if thou seest a great and generous heart,
Thy bow is doubly bent to force a dart.
Nor dignity nor innocence is spared,
Nor age, nor sex, nor thrones, nor graves, revered.
Nor only justice vainly we demand,
But even benefits can't rein thy hand;
To this or that alike in vain we trust,
Nor find thee less ungrateful than unjust.

Not even youth and beauty can control
The universal rancour of thy soul;
Charms that might soften superstition's rage,
Might humble pride, or thaw the ice of age.
But how should'st thou by beauty's force be moved,
No more for loving made than to be loved?
It was the equity of righteous Heaven,
That such a soul to such a form was given;
And shows the uniformity of fate,
That one so odious should be born to hate.

When God created thee, one would believe
He said the same as to the snake of Eve;
To human race antipathy declare,
'Twixt them and thee be everlasting war.
But oh! the sequel of the sentence dread,
And whilst you bruise their heel, beware your head.
Nor think thy weakness shall be thy defence,
The female scold's protection in offence.
Sure 'tis as fair to beat who cannot fight,
As 'tis to libel those who cannot write.
And if thou drawest thy pen to aid the law,
Others a cudgel, or a rod, may draw.
If none with vengeance yet thy crimes pursue,
Or give thy manifold affronts their due;
If limbs unbroken, skin without a stain,

Unwhipped, unblanketed, unkicked, unslain,
That wretched little carcase you retain,
The reason is, not that the world wants eyes,
But thou'rt so mean, they see, and they despise:
When fretful porcupine, with rancorous will,
From mounted back shoots forth a harmless quill,
Cool the spectators stand; and all the while
Upon the angry little monster smile.
Thus 'tis with thee: — while impotently safe,
You strike unwounding, we unhurt can laugh.
Who but must laugh, this bully when he sees,
A puny insect shivering at a breeze?
One over-matched by every blast of wind,
Insulting and provoking all mankind.

Is this the thing to keep mankind in awe,
To make those tremble who escape the law?
Is this the ridicule to live so long,
The deathless satire and immortal song?
No: like the self-blown praise, thy scandal flies;
And, as we're told of wasps, it stings and dies.

If none do yet return th'intended blow,
You all your safety to your dulness owe:
But whilst that armour thy poor corpse defends,
'Twill make thy readers few, as are thy friends:
Those, who thy nature loathed, yet loved thy art,
Who liked thy head, and yet abhorred thy heart:
Chose thee to read, but never to converse,
And scorned in prose him whom they prized in verse:
Even they shall now their partial error see,
Shall shun thy writings like thy company;
And to thy books shall ope their eyes no more
Than to thy person they would do their door.

Nor thou the justice of the world disown,
That leaves thee thus an outcast and alone;
For though in law to murder be to kill,
In equity the murder's in the will:
Then whilst with coward-hand you stab a name,
And try at least t'assassinate our fame,

Like the first bold assassin's be thy lot,
Ne'er be thy guilt forgiven, or forgot;
But, as thou hatest, be hated by mankind,
And with the emblem of thy crooked mind
Marked on thy back, like Cain by God's own hand,
Wander, like him, accurséd through the land.

LADY MARY WORTLEY MONTAGU

The Inquisitive Bridegroom

A TALE

Frank Plume, a spark about the town,
Now weary of intriguing grown,
Thought it advisable to wed,
And choose a partner of his bed,
Virtuous and chaste – Aye, right – but where
Is there a nymph that's chaste as fair;
A blessing to be prized, but rare.
For continence penurious Heaven
With a too sparing hand has given;
A plant but seldom to be found,
And thrives but ill on British ground.
Should our adventurer haste on board,
And see what foreign soils afford?
Where watchful dragons guard the prize,
And jealous dons have Argus' eyes,
Where the rich casket, close immured,
Is under lock and key secured?
No – Frank, by long experience wise,
Had known these forts took by surprise.
Nature in spite of art prevailed,
And all their vigilance had failed.
The youth was puzzled – should he go
And scale a convent? would that do?
Is nun's-flesh always good and sweet?

Fly-blown sometimes, not fit to eat.
Well – he resolves to do his best,
And prudently contrives this test;
If the last favour I obtain,
And the nymph yield, the case is plain:
Married, she'll play the same odd prank
With others – she's no wife for Frank.
But, could I find a female heart
Impregnable to force or art,
That all my batteries could withstand,
The sap, and even sword in hand;
Ye gods! how happy should I be,
From each perplexing thought set free,
From cuckoldom, and jealousy!
The project pleased. He now appears,
And shines in all his killing airs,
And every useful toy prepares,
New opera tunes, and billet-doux,
The clouded cane, and red-heeled shoes;
Nor the clock-stocking was forgot,
Th'embroidered coat, and shoulder-knot:
All that a woman's heart might move,
The potent trumpery of love.
Here importunity prevails,
There tears in floods, or sighs in gales.
Now, in the lucky moment tried,
Low at his feet the fair one died,
For Strephon would not be denied.
Then, if no motives could persuade,
A golden shower debauched the maid,
The mistress truckled, and obeyed.
To modesty a sham pretence
Gained some, others impertinence;
But most, plain downright impudence.
Like Caesar, now he conquered all,
The vassal sex before him fall;
Where'er he marched, slaughter ensued,
He came, he saw, and he subdued.

At length a stubborn nymph he found,
For bold Camilla stood her ground;
Parried his thrusts with equal art,
And had him both in tierce and quart:
She kept the hero still in play,
And still maintained the doubtful day.
Here he resolves to make a stand,
Take her, and marry out of hand,
The jolly priest soon tied the knot,
The luscious tale was not forgot,
Then emptied both his pipe and pot.
The posset drunk, the stocking thrown,
The candles out, the curtains drawn,
And sir and madam all alone;
'My dear,' said he, 'I strove, you know,
To taste the joys you now bestow,
All my persuasive arts I tried,
But still relentless you denied;
Tell me, inexorable fair,
How could you, thus attacked, forbear?'
'Swear to forgive what's past,' she cried;
'The naked truth shan't be denied.'
He did; the baggage thus replied:
'Deceived so many times before
By your false sex, I rashly swore,
To trust deceitful man no more.'

WILLIAM SOMERVILLE

A Letter from a Captain in Country Quarters to his Corinna in Town

My earliest flame, to whom I owe
All that a captain needs to know;
Dress, and quadrille, and air, and chat,
Lewd songs, loud laughter, and all that;

Arts that have widows oft subdued,
And never failed to win a prude;
Think, charmer, how I live forlorn
At quarters, from Corinna torn.
When thou, my fair one, art away,
How shall I kill that foe, the day?
The landed squire, and dull freeholder,
Are sure no comrades for a soldier;
To drink with parsons all day long,
Misaubin tells me would be wrong:
And nunnery tales and Curl's *Dutch Whore*
I've read, till I can read no more.
At noon I rise, and straight alarm
The sempstress' shop, or country farm;
Repulsed, my next pursuit is a'ter
The parson's wife, or landlord's daughter:
Oft at the ball for game I search,
At market oft, sometimes at church,
And plight my faith and gold to boot;
Yet demme if a soul will do't –
In short our credit's sunk so low,
Since troops were kept o'foot for show,
All that for soldiers once ran mad,
Are now turned patriots, egad!
And when I boast my feats, the shrew
Asks who was slain the last review.
Know then, that I and captain Trueman
Resolve to keep a miss – in common:
Not her, among the buttered lasses,
Such as our friend Toupet caresses,
But her, a nymph of polished sense,
Which pedants call impertinence;
Trained up to laugh, and drink, and swear,
And rally with the prettiest air –
Come dimpled smiles, and stealing sighs,
The lisp, the luscious ecstasies,
The sidelong glance, the feeble trip,
The head inclined, the pouting lip

Come, decked in colours, which may vie
With Iris, when she paints the sky.
Amidst our frolics and carouses
How shall we pity wretched spouses!
But where can this dear soul be found,
In garret high, or under ground?
If so divine a fair there be,
Charming Corinna, thou art she.
'But oh! what motives can persuade
Belles, to prefer a rural shade,
In this gay month, when pleasures bloom,
The park, the play – the drawing room –
Lo! birthnights upon birthnights tread,
Term is begun, the lawyer fee'd;
My friend the merchant, let me tell ye,
Calls on his way to Farinelli;
What if my satin gown and watch
Some unfledged booty squire may catch,
Who, charmed with his delicious quarry,
May first debauch me, and then marry?
Never was season more befitting
Since convocations last were sitting.
And shall I leave dear Charing Cross,
And let two boys my charms engross?
Leave temple, playhouse, rose and rummer,
A country friend might serve in summer!'

The town's your choice – yet, charming fair,
Observe what ills attend you there.
Captains, that once admired your beauty,
Are kept by quality on – duty;
Cits, half a crown for alms disburse,
From templars look for something worse:
My lord may take you to his bed,
But then he sends you back unpaid;
And all you gain from generous cully,
Must go to keep some Irish bully.
Pinchfeet demands the tweezer case,

And Monmouth Street the gown and stays;
More mischiefs yet come crowding on,
Bridewell, – West Indies – and Sir John –
Then oh! to lewdness bid adieu
And chastely live, confined to two.

ISAAC HAWKINS BROWNE

From *The Task*

Effeminate Englishmen

England, with all thy faults, I love thee still –
My country! and, while yet a nook is left
Where English minds and manners may be found,
Shall be constrained to love thee. Though thy clime
Be fickle, and thy year most part deformed
With dripping rains, or withered by a frost,
I would not yet exchange thy sullen skies,
And fields without a flower, for warmer France
With all her vines; nor for Ausonia's groves
Of golden fruitage, and her myrtle bowers.
To shake thy senate, and from heights sublime
Of patriot eloquence to flash down fire
Upon thy foes, was never meant my task:
But I can feel thy fortunes, and partake
Thy joys and sorrows, with as true a heart
As any thunderer there. And I can feel
Thy follies, too; and with a just disdain
Frown at effeminates, whose very looks
Reflect dishonour on the land I love.
How, in the name of soldiership and sense,
Should England prosper, when such things, as smooth
And tender as a girl, all essenced o'er
With odours, and as profligate as sweet;
Who sell their laurel for a myrtle wreath,
And love when they should fight; when such as these

Presume to lay their hand upon the ark
Of her magnificent and awful cause?

WILLIAM COWPER

From *Adriano*, or *The First of June*

The Student

So joyful he to Alma Mater went
A sturdy freshman. See him just arrived,
Received, matriculated, and resolved
To drown his freshness in a pipe of port.
'Quick, Mr Vintner, twenty dozen more;
Some claret too. Here's to our friends at home.
There let 'em doze. Be it our nobler aim
To live – where stands the bottle?' Then to town
Hies the gay spark for futile purposes,
And deeds my bashful muse disdains to name.
From town to college, till a fresh supply
Sends him again from college up to town.
The tedious interval the mace and cue,
The tennis court and raquette, the slow lounge
From street to street, the badger-hunt, the race,
The raffle, the excursion, and the dance,
Ices and soups, dice, and the bet at whist,
Serve well enough to fill. Grievous accounts
The weekly post to the vexed parent brings
Of college impositions, heavy dues,
Demands enormous, which the wicked son
Declares he does his utmost to prevent.
So, blaming with good cause the vast expense,
Bill after bill he sends, and pens the draft
Till the full ink-horn fails.

JAMES HURDIS

The Sluggard

'Tis the voice of the sluggard; I heard him complain,
'You have waked me too soon, I must slumber again.'
As the door on its hinges, so he on his bed,
Turns his sides and his shoulders and his heavy head.

'A little more sleep, and a little more slumber;'
Thus he wastes half his days and his hours without number;
And when he gets up, he sits folding his hands,
Or walks about sauntering, or trifling he stands.

I passed by his garden, and saw the wild brier,
The thorn and the thistle grow broader and higher;
The clothes that hang on him are turning to rags;
And his money still wastes, till he starves or he begs.

I made him a visit, still hoping to find
He had took better care for improving his mind:
He told me his dreams, talked of eating and drinking;
But he scarce reads his bible, and never loves thinking.

Said I then to my heart, 'Here's a lesson for me;
That man's but a picture of what I might be:
But thanks to my friends for their care in my breeding,
Who taught me betimes to love working and reading.'

ISAAC WATTS

Peter Grimes

Old Peter Grimes made fishing his employ,
His wife he cabined with him and his boy,
And seemed that life laborious to enjoy:
To town came quiet Peter with his fish,
And had of all a civil word and wish.

He left his trade upon the sabbath-day,
And took young Peter in his hand to pray:
But soon the stubborn boy from care broke loose,
At first refused, then added his abuse:
His father's love he scorned, his power defied,
But being drunk, wept sorely when he died.

Yes! then he wept, and to his mind there came
Much of his conduct, and he felt the shame, –
How he had oft the good old man reviled,
And never paid the duty of a child;
How, when the father in his Bible read,
He in contempt and anger left the shed:
'It is the word of life,' the parent cried;
– 'This is the life itself,' the boy replied;
And while old Peter in amazement stood,
Gave the hot spirit to his boiling blood: –
How he, with oath and furious speech, began
To prove his freedom and assert the man;
And when the parent checked his impious rage,
How he had cursed the tyranny of age, –
Nay, once had dealt the sacrilegious blow
On his bare head, and laid his parent low;
The father groaned – 'If thou art old,' said he,
'And hast a son – thou wilt remember me:
Thy mother left me in a happy time,
Thou killedst not her – Heaven spares the double crime.'

On an inn-settle, in his maudlin grief,
This he revolved, and drank for his relief.

Now lived the youth in freedom, but debarred
From constant pleasure, and he thought it hard;
Hard that he could not every wish obey,
But must awhile relinquish ale and play;
Hard! that he could not to his cards attend,
But must acquire the money he would spend.

With greedy eye he looked on all he saw,
He knew not justice, and he laughed at law;
On all he marked he stretched his ready hand;
He fished by water, and he filched by land:

Oft in the night has Peter dropped his oar,
Fled from his boat and sought for prey on shore;
Oft up the hedge-row glided, on his back
Bearing the orchard's produce in a sack,
Or farm-yard load, tugged fiercely from the stack;
And as these wrongs to greater numbers rose,
The more he looked on all men as his foes.

He built a mud-walled hovel, where he kept
His various wealth, and there he oft-times slept;
But no success could please his cruel soul,
He wished for one to trouble and control;
He wanted some obedient boy to stand
And bear the blow of his outrageous hand;
And hoped to find in some propitious hour
A feeling creature subject to his power.

Peter had heard there were in London then, –
Still have they being! – workhouse-clearing men,
Who, undisturbed by feelings just or kind,
Would parish-boys to needy tradesmen bind:
They in their want a trifling sum would take,
And toiling slaves of piteous orphans make.

Such Peter sought, and when a lad was found,
The sum was dealt him, and the slave was bound.
Some few in town observed in Peter's trap
A boy, with jacket blue and woollen cap;
But none inquired how Peter used the rope,
Or what the bruise, that made the stripling stoop;
None could the ridges on his back behold,
None sought him shivering in the winter's cold;
None put the question, – 'Peter, dost thou give
The boy his food? – What, man! the lad must live:
Consider, Peter, let the child have bread,
He'll serve thee better if he's stroked and fed.'
None reasoned thus – and some, on hearing cries,
Said calmly, 'Grimes is at his exercise.'

Pinned, beaten, cold, pinched, threatened, and abused –
His efforts punished and his food refused, –
Awake tormented, – soon aroused from sleep, –

Struck if he wept, and yet compelled to weep,
The trembling boy dropped down and strove to pray,
Received a blow, and trembling turned away,
Or sobbed and hid his piteous face; – while he,
The savage master, grinned in horrid glee:
He'd now the power he ever loved to show,
A feeling being subject to his blow.

Thus lived the lad, in hunger, peril, pain,
His tears despised, his supplications vain:
Compelled by fear to lie, by need to steal,
His bed uneasy and unblessed his meal,
For three sad years the boy his tortures bore,
And then his pains and trials were no more.

'How died he, Peter?' when the people said,
He growled – 'I found him lifeless in his bed;'
Then tried for softer tone, and sigh'd, 'Poor Sam is dead.'
Yet murmurs were there, and some questions asked, –
How he was fed, how punished, and how tasked?
Much they suspected, but they little proved,
And Peter passed untroubled and unmoved.

Another boy with equal ease was found,
The money granted, and the victim bound;
And what his fate? – One night it chanced he fell
From the boat's mast and perished in her well,
Where fish were living kept, and where the boy
(So reasoned men) could not himself destroy: –
'Yes! so it was,' said Peter, 'in his play,
(For he was idle both by night and day),
He climbed the main-mast and then fell below:' –
Then showed his corpse and pointed to the blow:
What said the jury? – they were long in doubt,
But sturdy Peter faced the matter out:
So they dismissed him, saying at the time,
'Keep fast your hatchway when you've boys who climb.'
This hit the conscience, and he coloured more
Than for the closest questions put before.

Thus all his fears the verdict set aside,
And at the slave-shop Peter still applied.

Then came a boy, of manners soft and mild, –
Our seamen's wives with grief beheld the child;
All thought (the poor themselves) that he was one
Of gentle blood, some noble sinner's son,
Who had, belike, deceived some humble maid,
Whom he had first seduced and then betrayed: –
However this, he seemed a gracious lad,
In grief submissive and with patience sad.

Passive he laboured, till his slender frame
Bent with his loads, and he at length was lame:
Strange that a frame so weak could bear so long
The grossest insult and the foulest wrong;
But there were causes – in the town they gave
Fire, food, and comfort, to the gentle slave;
And though stern Peter, with a cruel hand,
And knotted rope, enforced the rude command,
Yet he considered what he'd lately felt,
And his vile blows with selfish pity dealt.

One day such draughts the cruel fisher made,
He could not vend them in his borough-trade,
But sailed for London-mart: the boy was ill,
But ever humbled to his master's will;
And on the river, where they smoothly sailed,
He strove with terror and awhile prevailed;
But new to danger on the angry sea,
He clung affrightened to his master's knee:
The boat grew leaky and the wind was strong,
Rough was the passage and the time was long;
His liquor failed, and Peter's wrath arose, –
No more is known – the rest we must suppose,
Or learn of Peter; – Peter says, he 'spied
The stripling's danger and for harbour tried;
'Meantime the fish, and then the apprentice died.'

The pitying women raised a clamour round,
And weeping said, 'Thou hast thy prentice drowned.'

Now the stern man was summoned to the hall,
To tell his tale before the burghers all:
He gave the account; professed the lad he loved,

And kept his brazen features all unmoved.
    The mayor himself with tone severe replied, —
'Henceforth with thee shall never boy abide;
Hire thee a freeman, whom thou durst not beat,
But who, in thy despite, will sleep and eat:
Free thou art now! — again shouldst thou appear,
Thou'lt find thy sentence, like thy soul, severe.'
    Alas! for Peter, not a helping hand,
So he was hated, could he now command;
Alone he rowed his boat, alone he cast
His nets beside, or made his anchor fast;
To hold a rope or hear a curse was none, —
He toiled and railed; he groaned and swore alone.
    Thus by himself compelled to live each day,
To wait for certain hours the tide's delay;
At the same times the same dull views to see,
The bounding marsh-bank and the blighted tree;
The water only, when the tides were high,
When low, the mud half-covered and half-dry;
The sun-burnt tar that blisters on the planks,
And bank-side stakes in their uneven ranks;
Heaps of entangled weeds that slowly float,
As the tide rolls by the impeded boat.
    When tides were neap, and, in the sultry day,
Through the tall bounding mud-banks made their way,
Which on each side rose swelling, and below
The dark warm flood ran silently and slow;
There anchoring, Peter chose from man to hide,
There hang his head, and view the lazy tide
In its hot slimy channel slowly glide;
Where the small eels that left the deeper way
For the warm shore, within the shallows play;
Where gaping mussels, left upon the mud,
Slope their slow passage to the fallen flood; —
Here dull and hopeless he'd lie down and trace
How sidelong crabs had scrawled their crooked race;
Or sadly listen to the tuneless cry
Of fishing gull or clanging golden-eye;

What time the sea-birds to the marsh would come,
And the loud bittern, from the bull-rush home,
Gave from the salt-ditch side the bellowing boom:
He nursed the feelings these dull scenes produce,
And loved to stop beside the opening sluice;
Where the small stream, confined in narrow bound,
Ran with a dull, unvaried, saddening sound;
Where all, presented to the eye or ear,
Oppressed the soul with misery, grief, and fear.

Besides these objects, there were places three,
Which Peter seemed with certain dread to see;
When he drew near them he would turn from each,
And loudly whistle till he passed the reach.

A change of scene to him brought no relief;
In town, 'twas plain, men took him for a thief:
The sailors' wives would stop him in the street,
And say, 'Now, Peter, thou'st no boy to beat:'
Infants at play, when they perceived him, ran,
Warning each other – 'That's the wicked man:'
He growled an oath, and in an angry tone
Cursed the whole place and wished to be alone.

Alone he was, the same dull scenes in view,
And still more gloomy in his sight they grew:
Though man he hated, yet employed alone
At bootless labour, he would swear and groan,
Cursing the shoals that glided by the spot,
And gulls that caught them when his arts could not.

Cold nervous tremblings shook his sturdy frame,
And strange disease – he couldn't say the name;
Wild were his dreams, and oft he rose in fright,
Waked by his view of horrors in the night, –
Horrors that would the sternest minds amaze,
Horrors that demons might be proud to raise:
And though he felt forsaken, grieved at heart,
To think he lived from all mankind apart;
Yet, if a man approached, in terrors he would start.

A winter passed since Peter saw the town,
And summer-lodgers were again come down;

These, idly curious, with their glasses spied
The ships in bay as anchored for the tide, –
The river's craft, – the bustle of the quay, –
And sea-port views, which landmen love to see.

One, up the river, had a man and boat
Seen day by day, now anchored, now afloat;
Fisher he seemed, yet used no net nor hook;
Of sea-fowl swimming by no heed he took,
But on the gliding waves still fixed his lazy look:
At certain stations he would view the stream,
As if he stood bewildered in a dream,
Or that some power had chained him for a time,
To feel a curse or meditate on crime.

This known, some curious, some in pity went,
And others questioned – 'Wretch, dost thou repent?'
He heard, he trembled, and in fear resigned
His boat: new terror filled his restless mind;
Furious he grew, and up the country ran,
And there they seized him – a distempered man: –
Him we received, and to a parish-bed,
Followed and cursed, the groaning man was led.

Here, when they saw him, whom they used to shun,
A lost, lone man, so harassed and undone;
Our gentle females, ever prompt to feel,
Perceived compassion on their anger steal;
His crimes they could not from their memories blot,
But they were grieved, and trembled at his lot.

A priest too came, to whom his words are told;
And all the signs they shuddered to behold.

'Look! look!' they cried; 'his limbs with horror shake,
And as he grinds his teeth, what noise they make!
How glare his angry eyes, and yet he's not awake:
See! what cold drops upon his forehead stand,
And how he clenches that broad bony hand.'

The priest attending, found he spoke at times
As one alluding to his fears and crimes:
'It was the fall,' he muttered, 'I can show
The manner how – I never struck a blow:' –

And then aloud – 'Unhand me, free my chain;
On oath, he fell – it struck him to the brain: –
Why ask my father? – that old man will swear
Against my life; besides, he wasn't there: –
What, all agreed? – Am I to die to-day? –
My Lord, in mercy, give me time to pray.'

Then, as they watched him, calmer he became,
And grew so weak he couldn't move his frame,
But murmuring spake, – while they could see and hear
The start of terror and the groan of fear;
See the large dew-beads on his forehead rise,
And the cold death-drop glaze his sunken eyes;
Nor yet he died, but with unwonted force
Seemed with some fancied being to discourse:
He knew not us, or with accustomed art
He hid the knowledge, yet exposed his heart;
'Twas part confession and the rest defence,
A madman's tale, with gleams of waking sense.

'I'll tell you all,' he said, 'the very day
When the old man first placed them in my way:
My father's spirit – he who always tried
To give me trouble, when he lived and died –
When he was gone, he could not be content
To see my days in painful labour spent,
But would appoint his meetings, and he made
Me watch at these, and so neglect my trade.

''Twas one hot noon, all silent, still, serene,
No living being had I lately seen;
I paddled up and down and dipped my net,
But (such his pleasure) I could nothing get, –
A father's pleasure, when his toil was done,
To plague and torture thus an only son!
And so I sat and looked upon the stream,
How it ran on, and felt as in a dream:
But dream it was not; no! – I fixed my eyes
On the mid stream and saw the spirits rise;
I saw my father on the water stand,
And hold a thin pale boy in either hand;

And there they glided ghastly on the top
Of the salt flood, and never touched a drop:
I would have struck them, but they knew the intent,
And smiled upon the oar, and down they went.
　'Now, from that day, whenever I began
To dip my net, there stood the hard old man –
He and those boys: I humbled me and prayed
They would be gone; – they heeded not, but stayed:
Nor could I turn, nor would the boat go by,
But gazing on the spirits, there was I:
They bade me leap to death, but I was loth to die:
And every day, as sure as day arose,
Would these three spirits meet me ere the close;
To hear and mark them daily was my doom,
And "Come," they said, with weak, sad voices, "come."
To row away with all my strength I tried,
But there were they, hard by me in the tide,
The three unbodied forms – and "Come," still "come," they
　　cried.
　'Fathers should pity – but this old man shook
His hoary locks, and froze me by a look:
Thrice, when I struck them, through the water came
A hollow groan, that weakened all my frame:
"Father!" said I, "have mercy:" – He replied,
I know not what – the angry spirit lied, –
"Didst thou not draw thy knife?" said he: – 'Twas true,
But I had pity and my arm withdrew:
He cried for mercy which I kindly gave,
But he has no compassion in his grave.
　'There were three places, where they ever rose, –
The whole long river has not such as those, –
Places accursed, where, if a man remain,
He'll see the things which strike him to the brain;
And there they made me on my paddle lean,
And look at them for hours; – accursed scene!
When they would glide to that smooth eddy-space,
Then bid me leap and join them in the place;
And at my groans each little villain sprite

Enjoyed my pains and vanished in delight.
  'In one fierce summer-day, when my poor brain
Was burning hot and cruel was my pain,
Then came this father-foe, and there he stood
With his two boys again upon the flood;
There was more mischief in their eyes, more glee
In their pale faces when they glared at me:
Still did they force me on the oar to rest,
And when they saw me fainting and oppressed,
He, with his hand, the old man, scooped the flood,
And there came flame about him mixed with blood;
He bade me stoop and look upon the place,
Then flung the hot-red liquor in my face;
Burning it blazed, and then I roared for pain,
I thought the demons would have turned my brain.
  'Still there they stood, and forced me to behold
A place of horrors – they cannot be told –
Where the flood opened, there I heard the shriek
Of tortured guilt – no earthly tongue can speak:
"All days alike! for ever!" did they say,
"And unremitted torments every day" –
Yes, so they said:' – But here he ceased and gazed
On all around, affrightened and amazed;
And still he tried to speak, and looked in dread
Of frightened females gathering round his bed;
Then dropped exhausted and appeared at rest,
Till the strong foe the vital powers possessed;
Then with an inward, broken voice he cried,
'Again they come,' and muttered as he died.

GEORGE CRABBE

3

'Dear, damned, distracting town,
Farewell!'

From *The Art of Preserving Health*

Urban Pollution

Ye who amid this feverish world would wear
A body free of pain, of cares a mind;
Fly the rank city, shun its turbid air;
Breathe not the chaos of eternal smoke
And volatile corruption, from the dead,
The dying, sickening, and the living world
Exhaled, to sully Heaven's transparent dome
With dim mortality. It is not air
That from a thousand lungs reeks back to thine,
Sated with exhalations rank and fell,
The spoil of dunghills, and the putrid thaw
Of nature; when from shape and texture she
Relapses into fighting elements:
It is not air, but floats a nauseous mass
Of all obscene, corrupt, offensive things.

JOHN ARMSTRONG

From *The Fleece*

Urban Progress

Thus all is here in motion, all is life:
The creaking wain brings copious store of corn:
The grazier's sleeky kine obstructs the roads;
The neat-dressed housewives, for the festal board
Crowned with full baskets, in the field-way paths
Come tripping on; th'echoing hills repeat
The stroke of axe and hammer; scaffolds rise,
And growing edifices; heaps of stone,
Beneath the chisel, beauteous shapes assume
Of frieze and column. Some, with even line,

New streets are marking in the neighbouring fields,
And sacred domes of worship. Industry,
Which dignifies the artist, lifts the swain,
And the straw cottage to a palace turns,
Over the work presides. Such was the scene
Of hurrying Carthage, when the Trojan chief
First viewed her growing turrets. So appear
Th'increasing walls of busy Manchester,
Sheffield, and Birmingham, whose reddening fields
Rise and enlarge their suburbs.

JOHN DYER

A Description of the Morning

Now hardly here and there a hackney-coach
Appearing, showed the ruddy morn's approach.
Now Betty from her master's bed had flown,
And softly stole to discompose her own.
The slipshod prentice from his master's door,
Had pared the dirt, and sprinkled round the floor.
Now Moll had whirled her mop with dexterous airs,
Prepared to scrub the entry and the stairs.
The youth with broomy stumps began to trace
The kennel-edge, where wheels had worn the place.
The smallcoal-man was heard with cadence deep,
'Till drowned in shriller notes of chimney-sweep.
Duns at his lordship's gate began to meet,
And Brickdust Moll had screamed through half a street.
The turnkey now his flock returning sees,
Duly let out a-nights to steal for fees.
The watchful bailiffs take their silent stands,
And school-boys lag with satchels in their hands.

JONATHAN SWIFT

From *The First Epistle of the First Book of Horace*

Profiteers

Well, if a king's a lion, at the least
The people are a many-headed beast:
Can they direct what measures to pursue,
Who know themselves so little what to do?
Alike in nothing but one lust of gold,
Just half the land would buy, and half be sold:
Their country's wealth our mightier misers drain,
Or cross, to plunder provinces, the main;
The rest, some farm the poor-box, some the pews;
Some keep assemblies, and would keep the stews;
Some with fat bucks on childless dotards fawn;
Some win rich widows by their chine and brawn;
While with the silent growth of ten per cent,
In dirt and darkness hundreds stink content.

ALEXANDER POPE

Newgate's Garland;

BEING A NEW BALLAD,
SHOWING HOW MR JONATHAN WILD'S THROAT
WAS CUT FROM EAR TO EAR WITH A PENKNIFE,
BY MR BLAKE, ALIAS BLUESKIN, THE BOLD
HIGHWAYMAN, AS HE STOOD AT HIS TRIAL IN
THE OLD-BAILEY, 1725

To the tune of – The Cut-purse

Ye gallants of Newgate, whose fingers are nice,
In diving in pockets, or cogging of dice;
Ye sharpers so rich, who can buy off the noose;

93

JOHN GAY

Ye honester poor rogues, who die in your shoes;
  Attend and draw near,
  Good news ye shall hear,
  How Jonathan's throat was cut from ear to ear;
How Blueskin's sharp penknife hath set you at ease,
And every man round me may rob, if he please.

When to the Old Bailey this Blueskin was led,
He held up his hand, his indictment was read,
Loud rattled his chains, near him Jonathan stood,
For full forty pounds was the price of his blood.
  Then, hopeless of life,
  He drew his penknife,
  And made a sad widow of Jonathan's wife.
But forty pounds paid her, her grief shall appease,
And every man round me may rob, if he please.

Some say there are courtiers of highest renown,
Who steal the king's gold, and leave him but a crown;
Some say there are peers, and some parliament-men,
Who meet once a year, to rob courtiers again:
  Let them all take their swing,
  To pillage the king,
  And get a blue ribbon instead of a string.
Now Blueskin's sharp penknife hath set you at ease,
And every man round me may rob, if he please.

Knaves of old, to hide guilt by their cunning inventions,
Called briberies grants, and plain robberies pensions;
Physicians and lawyers (who take their degrees
To be learnéd rogues) called their pilfering, fees:
  Since this happy day,
  Now every man may
  Rob (as safe as in office) upon the highway.
For Blueskin's sharp penknife hath set you at ease,
And every man round me may rob, if he please.

Some cheat in the customs, some rob the excise,
But he who robs both is esteeméd most wise.

Churchwardens, too prudent to hazard the halter,
As yet only venture to steal from the altar:
  But now to get gold,
  They may be more bold,
  And rob on the highway, since Jonathan's cold.
For Blueskin's sharp penknife hath set you at ease,
And every man round me may rob, if he please.

JOHN GAY

From *The New Bath Guide*

Letter VI

IN WHICH MR S. BLUNDERHEAD GIVES A
DESCRIPTION OF THE BATHING

This morning, dear mother, as soon as 'twas light,
I was waked by a noise that astonished me quite,
For in Tabitha's chamber I heard such a clatter,
I could not conceive what the deuce was the matter:
And, would you believe it? I went up and found her
In a blanket, with two lusty fellows around her,
Who both seemed a-going to carry her off in
A little black box just the size of a coffin:
Pray tell me, says I, what ye're doing of there?
'Why, master, 'tis hard to be bilked of our fare,
And so we were thrusting her into a chair:
We don't see no reason for using us so,
For she bade us come hither, and now she won't go;
We've earned all the fare, for we both came and knocked her
Up, as soon as 'twas light, by advice of the doctor;
And this is a job that we often go after
For ladies that choose to go into the water.'
  'But pray,' says I, 'Tabitha, what is your drift
To be covered in flannel instead of a shift?
'Tis all by the doctor's advice, I suppose,

That nothing is left to be seen but your nose:
I think if you really intend to go in,
'Twould do you more good if you stripped to the skin,
And if you've a mind for a frolic, i'faith
I'll just step and see you jump into the bath.'
So they hoisted her down just as safe and as well
And as snug as a Hod'mandod rides in his shell:
I fain would have gone to see Tabitha dip,
But they turned at a corner and gave me the slip,
Yet in searching about I had better success,
For I got to a place where the ladies undress;
Thinks I to myself they are after some fun,
And I'll see what they're doing as sure as a gun:
So I peeped at the door, and I saw a great mat
That covered a table, and got under that,
And laid myself down there, as snug and as still
(As a body may say) like a thief in a mill:
And of all the fine sights I have seen, my dear mother,
I never expect to behold such another:
How the ladies did giggle and set up their clacks,
All the while an old woman was rubbing their backs!
Oh! 'twas pretty to see them all put on their flannels,
And then take the water like so many spaniels,
And though all the while it grew hotter and hotter,
They swam just as if they were hunting an otter;
'Twas a glorious sight to behold the fair sex
All wading with gentlemen up to their necks,
And view them so prettily tumble and sprawl
In a great smoking kettle as big as our hall:
And today many persons of rank and condition
Were boiled by command of an able physician:
Dean Spavin, Dean Mangey, and Doctor de Squirt,
Were all sent from Cambridge to rub off their dirt;
Judge Scrub, and the worthy old Councillor Pest
Joined issue at once and went in with the rest:
And this they all said was exceedingly good
For strengthening the spirits, and mending the blood.
It pleased me to see how they all were inclined

To lengthen their lives for the good of mankind;
For I ne'er would believe that a bishop or judge
Can fancy old Satan may owe him a grudge,
Though some think the lawyer may choose to demur,
And the priest till another occasion defer,
And both to be better prepared for herea'ter,
Take a smack of the brimstone contained in the water.
But, what is surprising, no mortal e'er viewed
Any one of the physical gentlemen stewed;
Since the day that King Bladud first found out the bogs,
And thought them so good for himself and his hogs,
Not one of the faculty ever has tried
These excellent waters to cure his own hide:
Though many a skilful and learned physician,
With candour, good sense, and profound erudition,
Obliges the world with the fruits of his brain
Their nature and hidden effects to explain:
Thus Chiron advised Madam Thetis to take
And dip her poor child in the Stygian Lake,
But the worthy old doctor was not such an elf
As ever to venture his carcase himself:
So Jason's good wife used to set on a pot,
And put in at once all the patients she got,
But thought it sufficient to give her direction,
Without being coddled to mend her complexion:
And I never have heard that she wrote any treatise
To tell what the virtue of water and heat is.
You cannot conceive what a number of ladies
Were washed in the water the same as our maid is:
Old Baron Vanteazer, a man of great wealth,
Brought his lady the Baroness here for her health;
The Baroness bathes, and she says that her case
Has been hit to a hair, and is mending apace:
And this is a point all the learned agree on,
The Baron has met with the fate of Acteon;
Who while he peeped into the bath had the luck
To find himself suddenly changed to a buck.
Miss Scratchit went in and the Countess of Scales,

Both ladies of very great fashion in Wales;
Then all of a sudden two persons of worth
My Lady Pandora MacScurvey came forth,
With General Sulphur arrived from the north.
So Tabby, you see, had the honour of washing
With folk of distinction and very high fashion,
But in spite of good company, poor little soul,
She shook both her ears like a mouse in a bowl.

Odds bobs! how delighted I was unawares
With the fiddles I heard in the room above stairs,
For music is wholesome the doctors all think
For ladies that bathe, and for ladies that drink;
And that's the opinion of Robin our driver,
Who whistles his nags while they stand at the river:
They say it is right that for every glass
A tune you should take, that the water may pass:
So while little Tabby was washing her rump,
The ladies kept drinking it out of a pump.
  I've a deal more to say, but am loath to intrude
On your time, my dear mother, so now I'll conclude.

Bath, 1766   Simkin Blunderhead

                                         CHRISTOPHER ANSTEY

From *Trivia*

OR, THE ART OF WALKING THE STREETS OF LONDON

If clothed in black you tread the busy town,
Or if distinguished by the reverend gown,
Three trades avoid: oft in the mingling press
The barber's apron soils the sable dress;
Shun the perfumer's touch with cautious eye,
Nor let the baker's step advance too nigh.
Ye walkers too, that youthful colours wear,

Three sullying trades avoid with equal care:
The little chimney-sweeper skulks along,
And marks with sooty stains the heedless throng;
When small-coal murmurs in the hoarser throat,
From smutty dangers guard thy threatened coat;
The dustman's cart offends thy clothes and eyes,
When through the street a cloud of ashes flies;
But, whether black or lighter dyes are worn,
The chandler's basket, on his shoulder borne,
With tallow spots thy coat; resign the way,
To shun the surly butcher's greasy tray,
Butchers, whose hands are died with blood's foul stain,
And always foremost in the hangman's train.

Let due civilities be strictly paid;
The wall surrender to the hooded maid;
Nor let thy sturdy elbow's hasty rage
Jostle the feeble steps of trembling age:
And when the porter bends beneath his load,
And pants for breath, clear thou the crowded road.
But, above all, the groping blind direct;
And from the pressing throng the lame protect.

You'll sometimes meet a fop, of nicest tread,
Whose mantling peruke veils his empty head;
At every step he dreads the wall to lose,
And risks, to save a coach, his red-heeled shoes;
Him, like the miller, pass with caution by,
Lest from his shoulder clouds of powder fly.
But, when the bully, with assuming pace,
Cocks his broad hat, edged round with tarnished lace,
Yield not the way, defy his strutting pride,
And thrust him to the muddy kennel's side;
He never turns again, nor dares oppose,
But mutters coward curses as he goes.

*

The thoughtless wits shall frequent forfeits pay,
Who 'gainst the sentry's box discharge their tea,

Do thou some court or secret corner seek,
Nor flush with shame the passing virgin's cheek.

*

Winter Sports

Winter my theme confines; whose nitry wind
Shall crust the slabby mire, and kennels bind;
She bids the snow descend in flaky sheets,
And in her hoary mantle clothe the streets.
Let not the virgin tread these slippery roads,
The gathering fleece the hollow patten loads;
But if thy footstep slide with clotted frost,
Strike off the breaking balls against the post.
On silent wheels the passing coaches roll;
Oft look behind, and ward the threatening pole.
In hardened orbs the school-boy moulds the snow,
To mark the coachman with a dexterous throw.
Why do ye, boys, the kennel's surface spread,
To tempt with faithless pass the matron's tread?
How can you laugh to see the damsel spurn,
Sink in your frauds, and her green stocking mourn?
At White's the harnessed chairman idly stands,
And swings around his waist his tingling hands;
The sempstress speeds to Change with red-tipped nose;
The Belgian stove beneath her footstool glows;
In half-whipped muslin needles useless lie,
And shuttlecocks across the counter fly.
These sports warm harmless; why then will ye prove,
Deluded maids, the dangerous flame of love?
    Where Covent-garden's famous temple stands,
That boasts the work of Jones' immortal hands;
Columns with plain magnificence appear,
And graceful porches lead along the square:
Here oft my course I bend; when, lo! from far
I spy the furies of the football war:
The 'prentice quits his shop, to join the crew,
Increasing crowds the flying game pursue.
Thus, as you roll the ball o'er snowy ground,

The gathering globe augments with every round.
But whither shall I run? the throng draws nigh,
The ball now skims the street, now soars on high;
The dexterous glazier strong returns the bound,
And jingling sashes on the pent-house sound.

O, roving Muse! recall that wondrous year,
When winter reigned in bleak Britannia's air;
When hoary Thames, with frosted osiers crowned,
Was three long moons in icy fetters bound.
The waterman, forlorn, along the shore,
Pensive reclines upon his useless oar;
See harnessed steeds desert the stony town,
And wander roads unstable, not their own;
Wheels o'er the hardened waters smoothly glide,
And raze with whitened tracks the slippery tide;
Here the fat cook piles high the blazing fire,
And scarce the spit can turn the steer entire;
Booths sudden hide the Thames, long streets appear,
And numerous games proclaim the crowded fair.

*

Pickpockets

Where the mob gathers, swiftly shoot along,
Nor idly mingle in the noisy throng:
Lured by the silver hilt, amid the swarm,
The subtle artist will thy side disarm.
Nor is the flaxen wig with safety worn;
High on the shoulder, in a basket borne,
Lurks the sly boy, whose hand, to rapine bred,
Plucks off the curling honours of thy head.
Here dives the skulking thief, with practised sleight,
And unfelt fingers make thy pocket light.
Where's now the watch, with all its trinkets, flown?
And thy late snuff-box is no more thy own.
But, lo! his bolder thefts some tradesman spies,
Swift from his prey the scudding lurcher flies;
Dexterous he 'scapes the coach with nimble bounds,
Whilst every honest tongue 'stop thief!' resounds.

So speeds the wily fox, alarmed by fear,
Who lately filched the turkey's callow care;
Hounds following hounds grow louder as he flies,
And injured tenants join the hunter's cries.
Breathless, he stumbling falls. Ill-fated boy!
Why did not honest work thy youth employ?
Seized by rough hands, he's dragged amid the rout,
And stretched beneath the pump's incessant spout:
Or, plunged in miry ponds, he gasping lies,
Mud chokes his mouth, and plasters o'er his eyes.

*

Where Lincoln's Inn, wide space, is railed around,
Cross not with venturous step; there oft is found
The lurking thief, who, while the daylight shone,
Made the walls echo with his begging tone:
That crutch, which late compassion moved, shall wound
Thy bleeding head, and fell thee to the ground.
Though thou art tempted by the link-man's call,
Yet trust him not along the lonely wall;
In the mid-way he'll quench the flaming brand,
And share the booty with the pilfering band.
Still keep the public streets, where oily rays,
Shot from the crystal lamp, o'erspread the ways.

*

Thieves and Whores

Who can the various city frauds recite,
With all the petty rapines of the night?
Who now the guinea-dropper's bait regards,
Tricked by the sharper's dice, or juggler's cards?
Why should I warn thee, ne'er to join the fray,
Where the sham quarrel interrupts the way?
Lives there in these our days so soft a clown,
Braved by the bully's oaths, or threatening frown?
I need not strict enjoin the pocket's care,
When from the crowded play thou lead'st the fair;

Who has not here or watch or snuff-box lost,
Or handkerchiefs that India's shuttle boast?
O! may thy virtue guard thee through the roads
Of Drury's mazy courts, and dark abodes!
The harlots' guileful paths, who nightly stand
Where Catharine Street descends into the Strand!
Say, vagrant Muse, their wiles and subtle arts,
To lure the strangers' unsuspecting hearts:
So shall our youth on healthful sinews tread,
And city cheeks grow warm with rural red.

   'Tis she who nightly strolls with sauntering pace,
No stubborn stays her yielding shape embrace;
Beneath the lamp her tawdry ribbons glare,
The new-scoured manteau, and the slattern air;
High-draggled petticoats her travels show,
And hollow cheeks with artful blushes glow;
With flattering sounds she soothes the credulous ear,
'My noble captain! charmer! love! my dear!'
In riding-hood near tavern-doors she plies,
Or muffled pinners hide her livid eyes.
With empty bandbox she delights to range,
And feigns a distant errand from the 'Change;
Nay, she will oft the quaker's hood profane,
And trudge demure the rounds of Drury Lane.
She darts from sarsenet ambush wily leers,
Twitches thy sleeve, or with familiar airs
Her fan will pat thy cheek; these snares disdain,
Nor gaze behind thee, when she turns again.

JOHN GAY

From *The Grave*

   But see! the well-plumed hearse comes nodding on
Stately and slow, and properly attended
By the whole sable tribe, that painful watch
The sick man's door, and live upon the dead,

By letting out their persons by the hour,
To mimic sorrow when the heart's not sad.
How rich the trappings! now they're all unfurled,
And glittering in the sun; triumphant entries
Of conquerors, and coronation pomps,
In glory scarce exceed. Great gluts of people
Retard th'unwieldy show: whilst from the casements,
And houses' tops, ranks behind ranks, close wedged,
Hang bellying o'er. But tell us why this waste,
Why this ado in earthing up a carcase
That's fall'n into disgrace, and in the nostril
Smells horrible? – Ye undertakers, tell us,
'Midst all the gorgeous figures you exhibit,
Why is the principal concealed, for which
You make this mighty stir? – 'Tis wisely done:
What would offend the eye in a good picture,
The painter casts discreetly into shades.

ROBERT BLAIR

From *Of Taste*

The Englishman at the Table

Time was, a wealthy Englishman would join
A rich plum-pudding to a fat sirloin;
Or bake a pasty, whose enormous wall
Took up almost the area of his hall:
But now, as art improves, and life refines,
The demon Taste attends him when he dines;
Serves on his board an elegant regale,
Where three stewed mushrooms flank a larded quail;
Where infant turkeys, half a month resigned
To the soft breathings of a southern wind,
And smothered in a rich ragout of snails,
Outstink a lenten supper at Versailles.
Is there a saint that would not laugh to see

The good man piddling with his fricassee;
Forced by the luxury of taste to drain
A flask of poison, which he calls champagne!
While he, poor idiot! though he dare not speak,
Pines all the while for porter and ox-cheek.
   Sure 'tis enough to starve for pomp and show,
To drink, and curse the clarets of Bordeaux:
Yet such our humour, such our skill to hit
Excess of folly through excess of wit,
We plant the garden, and we build the seat,
Just as absurdly as we drink and eat.

JAMES CAWTHORN

Sunday

A FRAGMENT

TRANSCRIBED FROM A MS. IN CHATTERTON'S HANDWRITING

Hervenis, harping on the hackneyed text,
By disquisitions is so sore perplexed,
He stammers, instantaneously is drawn,
A bordered piece of inspiration lawn,
Which being thrice unto his nose applied,
Into his pineal gland the vapours glide;
And now again we hear the doctor roar
On subjects he dissected thrice before;
I own at church I very seldom pray,
For vicars, strangers to devotion, bray.
Sermons, though flowing from the sacred lawn,
Are flimsy wires from reason's ingot drawn;
And to confess the truth, another cause
My every prayer and adoration draws;
In all the glaring tinctures of the bow,
The ladies front me in celestial row;

(Though when black melancholy damps my joys,
I call them Nature's trifles, airy toys;
Yet when the goddess Reason guides the strain,
I think them, what they are, a heavenly train;)
The amorous rolling, the black sparkling eye,
The gentle hazel, and the optic sly;
The easy shape, the panting semi-globes,
The frankness which each latent charm disrobes;
The melting passions, and the sweet severe,
The easy amble, the majestic air;
The tapering waist, the silver-mantled arms,
All is one vast variety of charms.
Say, who but sages stretched beyond their span,
Italian singers, or an unmanned man,
Can see Elysium spread upon their brow,
And to a drowsy curate's sermon bow.
If (but 'tis seldom) no fair female face
Attracts my notice by some glowing grace,
Around the monuments I cast my eyes,
And see absurdities and nonsense rise.
Here rueful-visaged angels seem to tell
With weeping eyes, a soul is gone to Hell;
There a child's head supported by duck's wings,
With toothless mouth a hallelujah sings:
In funeral pile eternal marble burns,
And a good Christian seems to sleep in urns.
A self-drawn curtain bids the reader see
An honourable Welshman's pedigree;
A rock of porphyry darkens half the place,
And virtues blubber with no awkward grace;
Yet, strange to tell, in all the dreary gloom
That makes the sacred honours of the tomb,
No quartered coats above the bell appear,
No battered arms, or golden corsets there.

*

THOMAS CHATTERTON

From *Epistle III*

French Fops

What peer of France would let his duchess rove,
Where Boulogne's closest woods invite to love?
But here no wife can blast her husband's fame,
Cuckold is grown an honourable name.
Stretched on the grass, the shepherd sighs his pain;
And on the grass what shepherd sighs in vain?
On Chloe's lap here Damon, laid along,
Melts with the languish of her amorous song;
There Iris flies Palæmon through the glade,
Nor trips by chance – till in the thickest shade;
Here Celimene defends her lips and breast,
For kisses are by struggling closer pressed:
Alexis there with eager flame grows bold,
Nor can the nymph his wanton fingers hold:
Be wise, Alexis; what, so near the road!
Hark, a coach rolls, and husbands are abroad!
Such were our pleasures in the days of yore,
When amorous Charles Britannia's sceptre bore;
The nightly scene of joy the Park was made,
And Love in couples peopled every shade.
But, since at court the rural taste is lost,
What mighty sums have velvet couches cost!
Sometimes the Tuilleries' gaudy walk I love,
Where I through crowds of rustling mantuas rove.
As here from side to side my eyes I cast,
And gazed on all the glittering train that passed,
Sudden a fop steps forth before the rest;
I knew the bold embroidery of his vest.
He thus accosts me with familiar air,
'Parbleu! on a fait cet habit en Angleterre!
Quelle manche! ce galon est grossièrement rangé;
Voilà quelque chose de fort beau et dégagé!'
This said: on his red heel he turns, and then

Hums a soft minuet, and proceeds again:
'Well; now you've Paris seen, you'll frankly own
Your boasted London seems a country town.
Has Christianity yet reached your nation?
Are churches built? Are masquerades in fashion?
Do daily soups your dinners introduce?
Are music, snuff, and coaches, yet in use?'
'Pardon me, sir; we know the Paris mode,
And gather *politesse* from courts abroad.
Like you, our courtiers keep a numerous train
To load their coach, and tradesmen dun in vain.
Nor has religion left us in the lurch;
And, as in France, our vulgar crowd the church:
Our ladies too support the masquerade;
The sex by nature love th'intriguing trade.'
Straight the vain fop in ignorant raptures cries,
'Paris the barbarous world will civilize!'
'Pray, sir, point out among the passing band
The present beauties who the town command.'
'See yonder dame; strict virtue chills her breast,
Mark in her eye demure the prude professed;
That frozen bosom native fire must want,
Which boasts of constancy to one gallant!
This next the spoils of fifty lovers wears,
Rich Dandin's brilliant favours grace her ears;
The necklace Florio's generous flame bestowed,
Clitander's sparkling gems her finger load;
But now her charms grow cheap by constant use,
She sins for scarfs, clocked-stockings, knots, and shoes.
This next, with sober gait and serious leer,
Wearies her knees with morn and evening prayer;
She scorns th'ignoble love of feeble pages,
But with three abbots in one night engages.
This with the cardinal her nights employs,
Where holy sinews consecrate her joys.
Why have I promised things beyond my power?
Five assignations wait me at this hour!
The sprightly countess first my visit claims,

Tomorrow shall indulge inferior dames.
Pardon me, sir, that thus I take my leave;
Gay Florimella slily twitched my sleeve.'
'Adieu, Monsieur!' – The opera hour draws near.
Not see the opera! all the world is there;
Where on the stage th'embroidered youth of France
In bright array attract the female glance;
This languishes, this struts, to show his mien,
And not a gold-clocked stocking moves unseen.
But hark! the full orchestra strike the strings,
The hero struts, and the whole audience sings.
My jarring ear harsh grating murmurs wound,
Hoarse and confused, like Babel's mingled sound.
Hard chance had placed me near a noisy throat,
That in rough quavers bellowed every note.
'Pray, sir,' says I, 'suspend awhile your song;
The opera's drowned; your lungs are wondrous strong;
I wish to hear your Roland's ranting strain,
While he with rooted forests strews the plain.'
Sudden he shrugs surprise, and answers quick,
'Monsieur apparemment n'aime pas la musique!'
Then turning round, he joined th'ungrateful noise:
And the loud chorus thundered with his voice.

JOHN GAY

Visit of Hope to Sydney Cove, near Botany Bay

Where Sydney Cove her lucid bosom swells,
And with wide arms the indignant storm repels;
High on a rock amid the troubled air
Hope stood sublime, and waved her golden hair;
Calmed with her rosy smile the tossing deep,
And with sweet accents charmed the winds to sleep;
To each wild plain she stretched her snowy hand,

High-waving wood, and sea-encircled strand.
'Hear me,' she cried, 'ye rising realms! record
Time's opening scenes, and Truth's prophetic word.
There shall broad streets their stately walls extend,
The circus widen, and the crescent bend;
There, rayed from cities o'er the cultured land,
Shall bright canals, and solid roads expand.
There the proud arch, colossus-like, bestride
Yon glittering streams, and bound the chasing tide;
Embellished villas crown the landscape-scene,
Farms wave with gold, and orchards blush between.
There shall tall spires, and dome-capped towers ascend,
And piers and quays their massy structures blend;
While with each breeze approaching vessels glide,
And northern treasures dance on every tide!'
Then ceased the nymph – tumultuous echoes roar,
And Joy's loud voice was heard from shore to shore –
Her graceful steps descending pressed the plain,
And Peace, and Art, and Labour, joined her train.

ERASMUS DARWIN

4

*'And yet my numbers please the
rural throng.'*

From *The Country Walk*

I am resolved, this charming day,
In the open field to stray;
And have no roof above my head,
But that whereon the gods do tread.
Before the yellow barn I see
A beautiful variety
Of strutting cocks, advancing stout,
And flirting empty chaff about,
Hens, ducks, and geese, and all their brood,
And turkeys gobbling for their food;
While rustics thrash the wealthy floor,
And tempt them all to crowd the door.

JOHN DYER

From *Winter*

The Ploughman's Horse

Sweet then the ploughman's slumbers, hale and young,
When the last topic dies upon his tongue;
Sweet then the bliss his transient dreams inspire,
Till chilblains wake him, or the snapping fire.
He starts, and ever thoughtful of his team,
Along the glittering snow a feeble gleam
Shoots from his lantern, as he yawning goes
To add fresh comforts to their night's repose;
Diffusing fragrance as their food he moves,
And pats the jolly sides of those he loves.
Thus full replenished, perfect ease possessed,
From night till morn alternate food and rest,
No rightful cheer withheld, no sleep debarred,
Their each day's labour brings its sure reward.
Yet when from plough or lumbering cart set free,

They taste awhile the sweets of liberty:
E'en sober Dobbin lifts his clumsy heel
And kicks, disdainful of the dirty wheel;
But soon, his frolic ended, yields again
To trudge the road, and wear the clinking chain.
    Short-sighted Dobbin! . . . thou canst only see
The trivial hardships that encompass thee:
Thy chains were freedom, and thy toils repose,
Could the poor post-horse tell thee all his woes;
Show thee his bleeding shoulders, and unfold
The dreadful anguish he endures for gold:
Hired at each call of business, lust, or rage,
That prompts the traveller on from stage to stage,
Still on his strength depends their boasted speed;
For them his limbs grow weak, his bare ribs bleed;
And though he groaning quickens at command,
Their extra shilling in the rider's hand
Becomes his bitter scourge; . . . 'tis he must feel
The double efforts of the lash and steel;
Till when, up hill, the destined inn he gains,
And trembling under complicated pains,
Prone from his nostrils, darting on the ground,
His breath emitted floats in clouds around,
Drops chase each other down his chest and sides,
And spattered mud his native colour hides:
Through his swoln veins the boiling torrent flows,
And every nerve a separate torture knows.
His harness loosed, he welcomes eager-eyed
The pail's full draught that quivers by his side;
And joys to see the well-known stable door,
As the starved mariner the friendly shore.
    Ah, well for him if here his sufferings ceased,
And ample hours of rest his pains appeased!
But roused again, and sternly bade to rise,
And shake refreshing slumber from his eyes,
Ere his exhausted spirits can return,
Or through his frame reviving ardour burn,
Come forth he must, though limping, maimed, and sore;

He hears the whip; the chaise is at the door: ...
The collar tightens, and again he feels
His half-healed wounds inflamed; again the wheels
With tiresome sameness in his ears resound,
O'er blinding dust, or miles of flinty ground.
Thus nightly robbed, and injured day by day,
His piece-meal murderers wear his life away.

ROBERT BLOOMFIELD

From *Agriculture*

Rustic Courtship

When Patty, lovely Patty, graced the crowd,
Pride of the neighbouring plains. Who hath not heard
Of Patty, the fair milkmaid? Beautiful
As an Arcadian nymph, upon her brow
Sat virgin Modesty, while in her eyes
Young Sensibility began to play
With Innocence. Her waving locks fell down
On either side her face in careless curls,
Shading the tender blushes in her cheek.
Her breath was sweeter than the morning gale,
Stolen from the rose or violet's dewy leaves.
Her ivory teeth appeared in even rows,
Through lips of living coral. When she spoke
Her features wore intelligence: her words
Were soft, with such a smile accompanied,
As lighted in her face resistless charms.
Her polished neck rose rounding from her breast,
With pleasing elegance: – That lovely breast! –
Ah! Fancy, dwell not there, lest gay Desire,
Who smiling hovers o'er th'enchanting place,
Tempt thy wild thoughts to dangerous ecstasy.
Her shape was moulded by the hand of Ease;
Exact-proportion harmonized her frame;

While Grace, following her steps, with secret art
Stole into all her motions. Thus she walked
In sweet simplicity; a snow-white pail
Hung on her arm, the symbol of her skill
In that fair province of the rural state,
The dairy: source of more delicious bowls
Than Bacchus from his choicest vintage boasts.

   How great the power of beauty! The rude swains
Grew civil at her sight; and gaping crowds
Rapt in astonishment, with transport gaze,
Whispering her praises in each other's ear.
As when a gentle breeze, borne through the grove,
With quick vibration shakes the trembling leaves,
And hushing murmurs run from tree to tree;
So ran a spreading whisper through the crowd.
Young Thyrsis hearing, turned aside his head,
And soon the pleasing wonder caught his eye.
Full in the prime of youth, the joyful heir
Of numerous acres, a large freehold farm,
Thyrsis as yet from beauty felt no pain,
Had seen no virgin he could wish to make
His wedded partner. Now his beating heart
Feels new emotion; now his fixéd eye
With fervent rapture dwelling on her charms,
Drinks in delicious draughts of new-born love.
No rest the night, no peace the following day
Brought to his struggling heart: her beauteous form,
Her fair perfections playing on his mind,
With pleasing anguish torture him. In vain
He strives to tear her image from his breast;
Each little grace, each dear bewitching look,
Returns triumphant, breaking his resolves,
And binding all his soul a slave to love.

   Ah! little did he know, alas, the while,
Poor Patty's tender heart, in mutual pain,
Long, long for him had heaved the secret sigh.
For him she dressed, for him the pleasing arts
She studied, and for him she wished to live.

But her low fortunes, nursing sad despair,
Checked the young hope; nor durst her modest eyes
Indulge the smallest glances of her flame,
Lest curious malice, like a watchful spy,
Should catch the secret, and with taunts reveal.
   Judge then the sweet surprise when she at length
Beheld him, all irresolute, approach;
And gently taking her fair trembling hand,
Breathe these soft words into her listening ear:
'O Patty! dearest maid! whose beauteous form
Dwells in my breast, and charms my soul to love,
Accept my vows; accept a faithful heart,
Which from this hour devotes itself to thee:
Wealth has no relish, life can give no joy,
If you forbid my hopes to call you mine.'
Ah! who the sudden tumult can describe
Of struggling passions rising in her breast?
Hope, fear, confusion, modesty, and love
Oppress her labouring soul: – She strove to speak,
But the faint accents died upon her tongue:
Her fears prevented utterance. – At length –
'Can Thyrsis mock my poverty? can he
Be so unkind? O no! yet I, alas,
Too humble even to hope' – No more she said;
But gently, as if half unwilling, stole
Her hand from his; and, with sweet modesty,
Casting a look of diffidence and fear,
To hide her blushes, silently withdrew.
But Thyrsis read, with rapture, in her eyes
The language of her soul. He followed, wooed,
And won her for his wife. His lowing herds
Soon call her mistress; soon their milky streams
Coagulated, rise in circling piles
Of hardened curd; and all the dairies round,
To her sweet butter yield superior praise.

ROBERT DODSLEY

From *An Epistle*

Written in the Country

TO THE RIGHT HON. THE LORD LOVELACE
THEN IN TOWN. SEPTEMBER 1735

Nor can I for my soul delight
In the dull feast of neighbouring knight,
Who, if you send three days before,
In white gloves meets you at the door,
With superfluity of breeding
First makes you sick, and then with feeding:
Or if, with ceremony cloyed,
You would next time such plagues avoid,
And visit without previous notice,
'John, John, a coach! – I can't think who 'tis,'
My lady cries, who spies your coach,
Ere you the avenue approach;
'Lord, how unlucky! – washing day!
And all the men are in the hay!'
Entrance to gain is something hard,
The dogs all bark, the gates are barred;
The yard's with lines of linen crossed,
The hall door's locked, the key is lost:
These difficulties all o'ercome,
We reach at length the drawing-room;
Then there's such trampling overhead,
Madam you'd swear was brought to bed;
Miss in a hurry bursts her lock,
To get clean sleeves to hide her smock;
The servants run, the pewter clatters,
My lady dresses, calls, and chatters;
The cook-maid raves for want of butter,
Pigs squeak, fowls scream, and green geese flutter.
Now after three hours tedious waiting,
On all our neighbours' faults debating,

And having nine times viewed the garden,
In which there's nothing worth a farthing,
In comes my lady and the pudden:
'You will excuse, sir, – on a sudden' –
Then, that we may have four and four,
The bacon, fowls, and cauliflower
Their ancient unity divide,
The top one graces, one each side;
And by and by, the second course
Comes lagging like a distanced horse;
A salver then to church and king,
The butler swears, the glasses ring;
The cloth removed, the toasts go round,
Bawdy and politics abound;
And as the knight more tipsy waxes,
We damn all ministers and taxes.
At last the ruddy sun quite sunk,
The coachman tolerably drunk,
Whirling o'er hillocks, ruts, and stones,
Enough to dislocate one's bones,
We home return, a wondrous token
Of Heaven's kind care, with limbs unbroken.
Afflict us not, ye gods, though sinners,
With many days like this, or dinners!

SOAME JENYNS

Holiday Gown

In holiday gown, and my new-fangled hat,
    Last Monday I tripped to the fair;
I held up my head, and I'll tell you for what,
    Brisk Roger I guessed would be there:
He woos me to marry whenever we meet,
    There's honey sure dwells on his tongue!
He hugs me so close, and he kisses so sweet,
    I'd wed – if I were not too young.

Fond Sue, I'll assure you, laid hold on the boy,
  (The vixen would fain be his bride)
Some token she claimed, either ribbon or toy,
  And swore that she'd not be denied:
A top-knot he bought her, and garters of green,
  Pert Susan was cruelly stung;
I hate her so much, that, to kill her with spleen,
  I'd wed – if I were not too young.

He whispered such soft pretty things in mine ear!
  He flattered, he promised, and swore!
Such trinkets he gave me, such laces and gear,
  That, trust me, – my pockets ran o'er:
Some ballads he bought me, the best he could find,
  And sweetly their burthen he sung;
Good faith! he's so handsome, so witty, and kind,
  I'd wed – if I were not too young.

The sun was just setting, 'twas time to retire,
  (Our cottage was distant a mile)
I rose to be gone – Roger bowed like a squire,
  And handed me over the stile:
His arms he threw round me – love laughed in his eye,
  He led me the meadows among,
There pressed me so close, I agreed, with a sigh,
  To wed – for I was not too young.

JOHN CUNNINGHAM

From *The Chase*

    ... See! there she goes,
She reels along, and by her gait betrays
Her inward weakness. See, how black she looks!
The sweat, that clogs th'obstructed pores, scarce leaves
A languid scent. And now in open view

See, see, she flies! each eager hound exerts
His utmost speed, and stretches every nerve.
How quick she turns! their gaping jaws eludes,
And yet a moment lives; till, round enclosed
By all the greedy pack, with infant screams
She yields her breath, and there reluctant dies.
So when the furious Bacchanals assailed
Thracian Orpheus, poor ill-fated bard!
Loud was the cry; hills, woods, and Hebrus' banks,
Returned their clamorous rage; distressed he flies,
Shifting from place to place, but flies in vain;
For eager they pursue, till panting, faint,
By noisy multitudes o'erpowered, he sinks
To the relentless crowd a bleeding prey.

The huntsman now, a deep incision made,
Shakes out with hands impure, and dashes down
Her reeking entrails and yet quivering heart.
These claim the pack, the bloody perquisite
For all their toils. Stretched on the ground she lies
A mangled corpse; in her dim glaring eyes
Cold Death exults, and stiffens every limb.
Awed by the threatening whip, the furious hounds
Around her bay; or at their master's foot,
Each happy favourite courts his kind applause,
With humble adulation cowering low.
All now is joy.

WILLIAM SOMERVILLE

From *A Fragment of a Poem on Hunting*

Such be the dog, I charge, thou mean'st to train,
His back is crooked, and his belly plain,
Of fillet stretched, and huge of haunch behind,
A tapering tail, that nimbly cuts the wind;
Truss-thighed, straight-hammed, and fox-like formed his paw,

Large-legged, dry-soled, and of protended claw.
His flat, wide nostrils snuff the savory steam,
And from his eyes he shoots pernicious gleam;
Middling his head, and prone to earth his view,
With ears and chest that dash the morning dew:
He best to stem the flood, to leap the bound,
And charm the dryads with his voice profound;
To pay large tribute to his weary lord,
And crown the sylvan hero's plenteous board.

   The matron bitch whose womb shall best produce
The hopes and fortune of th'illustrious house,
Derived from noble, but from foreign seed,
For various nature loaths incestuous breed,
Is like the sire throughout. Nor yet displease
Large flanks, and ribs, to give the teemer ease.

THOMAS TICKELL

The Beggar Woman

   A gentleman in hunting rode astray,
More out of choice, than that he lost his way:
He let his company the hare pursue,
For he himself had other game in view:
A beggar by her trade; yet not so mean,
But that her cheeks were fresh, and linen clean.
'Mistress,' quoth he, 'and what if we two should
Retire a little way into the wood?'
   She needed not much courtship to be kind,
He ambles on before, she trots behind;
For little Bobby, to her shoulders bound,
Hinders the gentle dame from ridding ground.
He often asked her to expose; but she
Still feared the coming of his company.
Says she, 'I know an unfrequented place,
To the left hand, where we our time may pass,

And the meanwhile your horse may find some grass.'
Thither they come, and both the horse secure;
Then thinks the squire, I have the matter sure.
She's asked to sit: but then excuse is made,
'Sitting,' says she, ''s not usual in my trade:
Should you be rude, and then should throw me down,
I might perhaps break more backs than my own.'
He smiling cries, 'Come, I'll the knot untie,
And, if you mean the child's, we'll lay it by.'
Says she, 'That can't be done, for then 'twill cry.
I'd not have us, but chiefly for your sake,
Discovered by the hideous noise 'twould make.
Use is another nature, and 'twould lack,
More than the breast, its custom to the back.'
'Then,' says the gentleman, 'I should be loth
To come so far and disoblige you both:
Were the child tied to me, d'ye think 'twould do?'
'Mighty well, sir! Oh, Lord! if tied to you!'

   With speed incredible to work she goes,
And from her shoulder soon the burthen throws;
Then mounts the infant with a gentle toss
Upon her generous friend, and, like a cross,
The sheet she with a dextrous motion winds,
Till a firm knot the wandering fabric binds.
   The gentleman had scarce got time to know
What she was doing; she, about to go,
Cries, 'Sir, good bye; ben't angry that we part,
I trust the child to you with all my heart:
But, ere you get another, 'ten't amiss
To try a year or two how you'll keep this.'

WILLIAM KING

The Miller

A BALLAD

In a plain pleasant cottage, conveniently neat,
With a mill and some meadows – a freehold estate,
A well-meaning miller by labour supplies
Those blessings, that grandeur to great ones denies:
No passions to plague him, no cares to torment,
His constant companions are Health and Content;
Their lordships in lace may remark, if they will,
He's honest, though daubed with the dust of his mill.

Ere the lark's early carols salute the new day,
He springs from his cottage as jocund as May;
He cheerfully whistles, regardless of care,
Or sings the last ballad he bought at the fair:
While courtiers are toiled in the cobwebs of state,
Or bribing elections, in hopes to be great,
No fraud or ambition his bosom e'er fill,
Contented he works, if there's grist for his mill.

On Sunday, bedecked in his homespun array,
At church he's the loudest to chant or to pray;
He sits to a dinner of plain English food,
Though simple the pudding, his appetite's good.
At night, when the priest and exciseman are gone,
He quaffs at the alehouse with Roger and John,
Then reels to his pillow, and dreams of no ill;
No monarch more blest than the man of the mill.

JOHN CUNNINGHAM

From *The Country Justice*

A Warning against the Gypsies

But, ah! ye maids, beware the gipsy's lures!
She opens not the womb of time, but yours.
Oft has her hands the hapless Marian wrung,
Marian, whom Gay in sweetest strains has sung!
The parson's maid – sore cause had she to rue
The gipsy's tongue; the parson's daughter too,
Long had that anxious daughter sighed to know
What Vellum's sprucy clerk, the valley's beau,
Meant by those glances, which at church he stole,
Her father nodding to the psalms' slow drawl;
Long had she sighed, at length a prophet came,
By many a sure prediction known to fame,
To Marian known, and all she told, for true:
She knew the future, for the past she knew.

Where, in the darkling shed, the moon's dim rays
Beamed on the ruins of a one-horse chaise,
Villaria sat, while faithful Marian brought
The wayward prophet of the woe she sought.
Twice did her hands, the income of the week,
On either side, the crooked sixpence seek;
Twice were those hands withdrawn from either side,
To stop the tittering laugh, the blush to hide.
The wayward prophet made no long delay,
No novice she in Fortune's devious way!
'Ere yet,' she cried, 'ten rolling months are o'er,
Must ye be mothers; maids at least no more.
With you shall soon, O lady fair, prevail
A gentle youth, the flower of this fair vale.
To Marian, once of Colin Clout the scorn,
Shall bumpkin come, and bumpkinets be born.'

Smote to the heart, the maidens marvelled sore,
That ten short months had such events in store;
But holding firm, what village-maids believe,

'That strife with fate is milking in a sieve;'
To prove their prophet true, though to their cost,
They justly thought no time was to be lost.

    These foes to youth, that seek, with dangerous art,
To aid the native weakness of the heart;
These miscreants from thy harmless village drive,
As wasps felonious from the labouring hive.

JOHN LANGHORNE

Inscriptions

III

Tragedy of a Shepherd

Whoe'er thou art whose path, in summer, lies
Through yonder village, turn thee where the grove
Of branching oaks a rural palace old
Embosoms. There dwells Albert, generous lord
Of all the harvest round. And onward thence
A low plain chapel fronts the morning light
Fast by a silent rivulet. Humbly walk,
O stranger, o'er the consecrated ground;
And on that verdant hillock, which thou seest
Beset with osiers, let thy pious hand
Sprinkle fresh water from the brook, and strew
Sweet-smelling flowers. For there doth Edmund rest,
The learned shepherd; for each rural art
Famed, and for songs harmonious, and the woes
Of ill-requited love. The faithless pride
Of fair Matilda sank him to the grave
In manhood's prime. But soon did righteous Heaven
With tears, with sharp remorse, and pining care,
Avenge her falsehood. Nor could all the gold,
And nuptial pomp, which lured her plighted faith
From Edmund to a loftier husband's home,

Relieve her breaking heart, or turn aside
The strokes of Death. Go, traveller; relate
The mournful story. Haply some fair maid
May hold it in remembrance, and be taught
That riches cannot pay for truth or love.

MARK AKENSIDE

The Deserted Village

Sweet Auburn, loveliest village of the plain,
Where health and plenty cheered the labouring swain,
Where smiling spring its earliest visit paid,
And parting summer's lingering blooms delayed:
Dear lovely bowers of innocence and ease,
Seats of my youth, when every sport could please,
How often have I loitered o'er thy green,
Where humble happiness endeared each scene;
How often have I paused on every charm,
The sheltered cot, the cultivated farm,
The never-failing brook, the busy mill,
The decent church that topped the neighbouring hill,
The hawthorn bush, with seats beneath the shade,
For talking age and whispering lovers made.
How often have I blessed the coming day,
When toil remitting lent its turn to play,
And all the village train, from labour free,
Led up their sports beneath the spreading tree,
While many a pastime circled in the shade,
The young contending as the old surveyed;
And many a gambol frolicked o'er the ground,
And sleights of art and feats of strength went round.
And still as each repeated pleasure tired,
Succeeding sports the mirthful band inspired;
The dancing pair that simply sought renown,
By holding out to tire each other down;

The swain mistrustless of his smutted face,
While secret laughter tittered round the place;
The bashful virgin's sidelong looks of love,
The matron's glance that would those looks reprove.
These were thy charms, sweet village; sports like these,
With sweet succession, taught even toil to please;
These round thy bowers their cheerful influence shed,
These were thy charms – but all these charms are fled.

Sweet smiling village, loveliest of the lawn,
Thy sports are fled and all thy charms withdrawn;
Amidst thy bowers the tyrant's hand is seen,
And desolation saddens all thy green:
One only master grasps the whole domain,
And half a tillage stints thy smiling plain:
No more thy glassy brook reflects the day,
But, choked with sedges, works its weedy way.
Along thy glades, a solitary guest,
The hollow-sounding bittern guards its nest;
Amidst thy desert walks the lapwing flies,
And tires their echoes with unvaried cries.
Sunk are thy bowers in shapeless ruin all,
And the long grass o'ertops the mouldering wall;
And trembling, shrinking from the spoiler's hand,
Far, far away, thy children leave the land.

Ill fares the land, to hastening ills a prey,
Where wealth accumulates and men decay:
Princes and lords may flourish or may fade;
A breath can make them, as a breath has made;
But a bold peasantry, their country's pride,
When once destroyed, can never be supplied.

A time there was, ere England's griefs began,
When every rood of ground maintained its man;
For him light labour spread her wholesome store,
Just gave what life required, but gave no more:
His best companions, innocence and health;
And his best riches, ignorance of wealth.

But times are altered; trade's unfeeling train
Usurp the land and dispossess the swain;
Along the lawn, where scattered hamlets rose,
Unwieldy wealth and cumbrous pomp repose;
And every want to opulence allied,
And every pang that folly pays to pride.
These gentle hours that plenty bade to bloom,
Those calm desires that asked but little room,
Those healthful sports that graced the peaceful scene,
Lived in each look and brightened all the green;
These, far departing, seek a kinder shore,
And rural mirth and manners are no more.

Sweet Auburn! parent of the blissful hour,
Thy glades forlorn confess the tyrant's power.
Here as I take my solitary rounds,
Amidst thy tangling walks and ruined grounds,
And, many a year elapsed, return to view
Where once the cottage stood, the hawthorn grew,
Remembrance wakes with all her busy train,
Swells at my breast and turns the past to pain.

In all my wanderings round this world of care,
In all my griefs – and God has given my share –
I still had hopes my latest hours to crown,
Amidst these humble bowers to lay me down;
To husband our life's taper at the close
And keep the flame from wasting by repose.
I still had hopes, for pride attends us still,
Amidst the swains to show my book-learned skill,
Around my fire an evening group to draw,
And tell of all I felt and all I saw;
And, as a hare, whom hounds and horns pursue,
Pants to the place from whence at first she flew,
I still had hopes, my long vexations past,
Here to return – and die at home at last.

O blest retirement, friend to life's decline,
Retreats from care, that never must be mine,
How happy he who crowns in shades like these
A youth of labour with an age of ease;
Who quits a world where strong temptations try
And, since 'tis hard to combat, learns to fly.
For him no wretches, born to work and weep,
Explore the mine or tempt the dangerous deep;
No surly porter stands in guilty state
To spurn imploring famine from the gate;
But on he moves to meet his latter end,
Angels around befriending virtue's friend;
Bends to the grave with unperceived decay,
While resignation gently slopes the way;
And, all his prospects brightening to the last,
His Heaven commences ere the world be past!

Sweet was the sound, when oft at evening's close
Up yonder hill the village murmur rose;
There, as I passed with careless steps and slow,
The mingling notes came softened from below;
The swain responsive as the milkmaid sung,
The sober herd that lowed to meet their young;
The noisy geese that gabbled o'er the pool,
The playful children just let loose from school;
The watchdog's voice that bayed the whispering wind,
And the loud laugh that spoke the vacant mind;
These all in sweet confusion sought the shade,
And filled each pause the nightingale had made.
But now the sounds of population fail,
No cheerful murmurs fluctuate in the gale,
No busy steps the grassgrown foot-way tread,
For all the bloomy flush of life is fled.
All but yon widowed, solitary thing
That feebly bends beside the plashy spring;
She, wretched matron, forced, in age, for bread,
To strip the brook with mantling cresses spread,
To pick her wintry faggot from the thorn,

To seek her nightly shed and weep till morn;
She only left of all the harmless train,
The sad historian of the pensive plain.

Near yonder copse, where once the garden smiled,
And still where many a garden flower grows wild;
There, where a few torn shrubs the place disclose,
The village preacher's modest mansion rose.
A man he was to all the country dear,
And passing rich with forty pounds a year;
Remote from towns he ran his godly race,
Nor e'er had changed, nor wished to change, his place;
Unpractised he to fawn, or seek for power,
By doctrines fashioned to the varying hour;
Far other aims his heart had learned to prize,
More skilled to raise the wretched than to rise.
His house was known to all the vagrant train,
He chid their wanderings, but relieved their pain;
The long-remembered beggar was his guest,
Whose beard descending swept his aged breast;
The ruined spendthrift, now no longer proud,
Claimed kindred there and had his claims allowed;
The broken soldier, kindly bade to stay,
Sat by his fire and talked the night away;
Wept o'er his wounds or tales of sorrow done,
Shouldered his crutch and showed how fields were won.
Pleased with his guests, the good man learned to glow,
And quite forgot their vices in their woe;
Careless their merits or their faults to scan,
His pity gave ere charity began.

Thus to relieve the wretched was his pride,
And even his failings leaned to virtue's side;
But in his duty prompt at every call,
He watched and wept, he prayed and felt, for all.
And, as a bird each fond endearment tries
To tempt its new-fledged offspring to the skies,
He tried each art, reproved each dull delay,
Allured to brighter worlds and led the way.

Beside the bed where parting life was laid,
And sorrow, guilt, and pain by turns dismayed,
The reverend champion stood. At his control,
Despair and anguish fled the struggling soul;
Comfort came down the trembling wretch to raise,
And his last faltering accents whispered praise.

At church, with meek and unaffected grace,
His looks adorned the venerable place;
Truth from his lips prevailed with double sway,
And fools, who came to scoff, remained to pray.
The service past, around the pious man,
With steady zeal, each honest rustic ran;
Even children followed with endearing wile,
And plucked his gown, to share the good man's smile.
His ready smile a parent's warmth expressed,
Their welfare pleased him and their cares distressed;
To them his heart, his love, his griefs were given,
But all his serious thoughts had rest in Heaven.
As some tall cliff, that lifts its awful form,
Swells from the vale and midway leaves the storm,
Though round its breast the rolling clouds are spread,
Eternal sunshine settles on its head.

Beside yon straggling fence that skirts the way,
With blossomed furze unprofitably gay,
There, in his noisy mansion, skilled to rule,
The village master taught his little school;
A man severe he was and stern to view;
I knew him well, and every truant knew;
Well had the boding tremblers learned to trace
The day's disasters in his morning face;
Full well they laughed, with counterfeited glee,
At all his jokes, for many a joke had he;
Full well the busy whisper, circling round,
Conveyed the dismal tidings when he frowned;
Yet he was kind, or, if severe in aught,
The love he bore to learning was in fault;

The village all declared how much he knew;
'Twas certain he could write and cipher too;
Lands he could measure, terms and tides presage,
And even the story ran that he could gauge.
In arguing too, the parson owned his skill,
For even though vanquished, he could argue still;
While words of learned length and thundering sound
Amazed the gazing rustics ranged around,
And still they gazed, and still the wonder grew,
That one small head could carry all he knew.

But past is all his fame. The very spot,
Where many a time he triumphed, is forgot.
Near yonder thorn, that lifts its head on high,
Where once the signpost caught the passing eye,
Low lies that house where nutbrown draughts inspired,
Where greybeard mirth and smiling toil retired,
Where village statesmen talked with looks profound,
And news much older than their ale went round.
Imagination fondly stoops to trace
The parlour splendours of that festive place;
The white-washed wall, the nicely sanded floor,
The varnished clock that clicked behind the door;
The chest contrived a double debt to pay,
A bed by night, a chest of drawers by day;
The pictures placed for ornament and use,
The twelve good rules, the royal game of goose;
The hearth, except when winter chilled the day,
With aspen boughs and flowers and fennel gay;
While broken teacups, wisely kept for show,
Ranged o'er the chimney, glistened in a row.

Vain, transitory splendours! Could not all
Reprieve the tottering mansion from its fall!
Obscure it sinks, nor shall it more impart
An hour's importance to the poor man's heart;
Thither no more the peasant shall repair
To sweet oblivion of his daily care;

No more the farmer's news, the barber's tale,
No more the woodman's ballad shall prevail;
No more the smith his dusky brow shall clear,
Relax his ponderous strength and lean to hear;
The host himself no longer shall be found
Careful to see the mantling bliss go round;
Nor the coy maid, half willing to be pressed,
Shall kiss the cup to pass it to the rest.

Yes! let the rich deride, the proud disdain,
These simple blessings of the lowly train;
To me more dear, congenial to my heart,
One native charm than all the gloss of art;
Spontaneous joys, where nature has its play,
The soul adopts and owns their firstborn sway;
Lightly they frolic o'er the vacant mind,
Unenvied, unmolested, unconfined:
But the long pomp, the midnight masquerade,
With all the freaks of wanton wealth arrayed,
In these, ere triflers half their wish obtain,
The toiling pleasure sickens into pain;
And, even while fashion's brightest arts decoy,
The heart distrusting asks, if this be joy.

Ye friends to truth, ye statesmen, who survey
The rich man's joys increase, the poor's decay,
'Tis yours to judge how wide the limits stand
Between a splendid and an happy land.
Proud swells the tide with loads of freighted ore,
And shouting Folly hails them from her shore;
Hoards, even beyond the miser's wish abound,
And rich men flock from all the world around.
Yet count our gains. This wealth is but a name
That leaves our useful products still the same.
Not so the loss. The man of wealth and pride
Takes up a space that many poor supplied;
Space for his lake, his park's extended bounds,
Space for his horses, equipage and hounds;

The robe that wraps his limbs in silken sloth
Has robbed the neighbouring field of half their growth;
His seat, where solitary sports are seen,
Indignant spurns the cottage from the green;
Around the world each needful product flies,
For all the luxuries the world supplies:
While thus the land, adorned for pleasure all,
In barren splendour feebly waits the fall.

As some fair female unadorned and plain,
Secure to please while youth confirms her reign,
Slights every borrowed charm that dress supplies,
Nor shares with art the triumph of her eyes;
But when those charms are passed, for charms are frail,
When time advances and when lovers fail,
She then shines forth, solicitous to bless,
In all the glaring impotence of dress:
Thus fares the land, by luxury betrayed,
In nature's simplest charms at first arrayed;
But verging to decline, its splendours rise,
Its vistas strike, its palaces surprise;
While scourged by famine from the smiling land,
The mournful peasant leads his humble band;
And while he sinks, without one arm to save,
The country blooms – a garden and a grave.

Where then, ah where, shall poverty reside,
To 'scape the pressure of contiguous pride?
If to some common's fenceless limits strayed,
He drives his flock to pick the scanty blade,
Those fenceless fields the sons of wealth divide,
And even the bare-worn common is denied.

If to the city sped – what waits him there?
To see profusion that he must not share;
To see ten thousand baneful arts combined
To pamper luxury and thin mankind;
To see those joys the sons of pleasure know

Extorted from his fellow creature's woe.
Here, while the courtier glitters in brocade,
There the pale artist plies the sickly trade;
Here, while the proud their long-drawn pomps display,
There the black gibbet glooms beside the way.
The dome where Pleasure holds her midnight reign
Here, richly decked, admits the gorgeous train;
Tumultuous grandeur crowds the blazing square,
The rattling chariots clash, the torches glare.
Sure scenes like these no troubles e'er annoy!
Sure these denote one universal joy!
Are these thy serious thoughts? – Ah, turn thine eyes
Where the poor, houseless, shivering female lies.
She once, perhaps, in village plenty blest,
Has wept at tales of innocence distressed;
Her modest looks the cottage might adorn,
Sweet as the primrose peeps beneath the thorn;
Now lost to all; her friends, her virtue fled,
Near her betrayer's door she lays her head,
And, pinched with cold and shrinking from the shower,
With heavy heart deplores that luckless hour,
When idly first, ambitious of the town,
She left her wheel and robes of country brown.

Do thine, sweet Auburn, thine, the loveliest train,
Do thy fair tribes participate her pain?
Even now, perhaps, by cold and hunger led,
At proud men's doors they ask a little bread!

Ah, no. To distant climes, a dreary scene,
Where half the convex world intrudes between,
Through torrid tracts with fainting steps they go,
Where wild Altama murmurs to their woe.
Far different there from all that charmed before
The various terrors of that horrid shore:
Those blazing suns that dart a downward ray,
And fiercely shed intolerable day;
Those matted woods where birds forget to sing,

But silent bats in drowsy clusters cling;
Those poisonous fields with rank luxuriance crowned,
Where the dark scorpion gathers death around;
Where at each step the stranger fears to wake
The rattling terrors of the vengeful snake;
Where crouching tigers wait their hapless prey,
And savage men more murderous still than they;
While oft in whirls the mad tornado flies,
Mingling the ravaged landscape with the skies.
Far different these from every former scene,
The cooling brook, the grassy-vested green,
The breezy covert of the warbling grove,
That only sheltered thefts of harmless love.

Good Heaven! what sorrows gloomed that parting day,
That called them from their native walks away;
When the poor exiles, every pleasure past,
Hung round their bowers and fondly looked their last,
And took a long farewell and wished in vain
For seats like these beyond the western main;
And shuddering still to face the distant deep,
Returned and wept, and still returned to weep.
The good old sire the first prepared to go
To new-found worlds, and wept for others' woe;
But for himself, in conscious virtue brave,
He only wished for worlds beyond the grave.
His lovely daughter, lovelier in her tears,
The fond companion of his helpless years,
Silent went next, neglectful of her charms,
And left a lover's for a father's arms.
With louder plaints the mother spoke her woes,
And blessed the cot where every pleasure rose;
And kissed her thoughtless babes with many a tear,
And clasped them close, in sorrow doubly dear;
Whilst her fond husband strove to lend relief
In all the silent manliness of grief.

O luxury! thou cursed by Heaven's decree,
How ill exchanged are things like these for thee!

How do thy potions with insidious joy
Diffuse their pleasures only to destroy!
Kingdoms, by thee to sickly greatness grown,
Boast of a florid vigour not their own.
At every draught more large and large they grow,
A bloated mass of rank unwieldy woe;
Till sapped their strength and every part unsound,
Down, down they sink and spread a ruin round.

Even now the devastation is begun,
And half the business of destruction done;
Even now, methinks, as pondering here I stand
I see the rural virtues leave the land.
Down where yon anchoring vessel spreads the sail,
That idly waiting flaps with every gale,
Downward they move, a melancholy band,
Pass from the shore and darken all the strand.
Contented toil and hospitable care,
And kind connubial tenderness are there;
And piety, with wishes placed above,
And steady loyalty and faithful love.
And thou, sweet Poetry, thou loveliest maid,
Still first to fly where sensual joys invade;
Unfit, in these degenerate times of shame,
To catch the heart or strike for honest fame;
Dear charming nymph, neglected and decried,
My shame in crowds, my solitary pride;
Thou source of all my bliss and all my woe,
That found'st me poor at first and keep'st me so;
Thou guide by which the nobler arts excel,
Thou nurse of every virtue, fare thee well!
Farewell, and oh, where'er thy voice be tried,
On Torno's cliffs or Pambamarca's side,
Whether where equinoctial fervours glow,
Or winter wraps the polar world in snow,
Still let thy voice, prevailing over time,
Redress the rigours of the inclement clime;
Aid slighted truth; with thy persuasive strain

Teach erring man to spurn the rage of gain;
Teach him that states of native strength possessed,
Though very poor, may still be very blest;
That trade's proud empire hastes to swift decay,
As ocean sweeps the laboured mole away;
While self-dependent power can time defy,
As rocks resist the billows and the sky.

OLIVER GOLDSMITH

From *Hobbinol*

On the Village Green

See on yon verdant lawn, the gathering crowd
Thickens amain; the buxom nymphs advance
Ushered by jolly clowns: distinctions cease,
Lost in the common joy, and the bold slave
Leans on his wealthy master, unreproved:
The sick no pains can feel, no wants the poor.
Round his fond mother's neck the smiling babe
Exulting clings; hard by, decrepit age,
Propped on his staff, with anxious thought revolves
His pleasures past, and casts his grave remarks
Among the heedless throng. The vigorous youth
Strips for the combat, hopeful to subdue
The fair-one's long disdain, by valour now
Glad to convince her coy erroneous heart,
And prove his merit equal to her charms.
Soft pity pleads his cause; blushing she views
His brawny limbs, and his undaunted eye,
That looks a proud defiance on his foes.
Resolved and obstinately firm he stands;
Danger nor death he fears, while the rich prize
Is victory and love. On the large bough
Of a thick-spreading elm Twangdillo sits:
One leg on Ister's banks the hardy swain

Left undismayed, Bellona's lightning scorched
His manly visage, but in pity left
One eye secure. He many a painful bruise
Intrepid felt, and many a gaping wound,
For brown Kate's sake, and for his country's weal:
Yet still the merry bard without regret
Bears his own ills, and with his sounding shell,
And comic phiz, relieves his drooping friends.
Hark, from aloft his tortured cat-gut squeals,
He tickles every string, to every note
He bends his pliant neck, his single eye
Twinkles with joy, his active stump beats time:
Let but this subtle artist softly touch
The trembling chords, the faint expiring swain
Trembles no less, and the fond yielding maid
Is tweedled into love. See with what pomp
The gaudy bands advance in trim array!
Love beats in every vein, from every eye
Darts his contagious flames. They frisk, they bound
Now to brisk airs, and to the speaking strings:
Attentive, in mid-way the sexes meet;
Joyous their adverse fronts they close, and press
To strict embrace, as resolute to force
And storm a passage to each other's heart:
Till by the varying notes forewarned back they
Recoil disparted: each with longing eyes
Pursues his mate retiring, till again
The blended sexes mix; then hand in hand
Fast locked, around they fly, or nimbly wheel
In mazes intricate. The jocund troop,
Pleased with their grateful toil, incessant shake
Their uncouth brawny limbs, and knock their heels
Sonorous; down each brow the trickling balm
In torrents flows, exhaling sweets refresh
The gazing crowd, and heavenly fragrance fills
The circuit wide.

WILLIAM SOMERVILLE

From *The Village Curate*

The Village Fair

Now comes the happy morning long desired
By rural lads and lasses. Light appears.
The swain is ready in his Sunday frock,
And calls on Nell to trip it to the fair.
The village bells are up, and jangling loud
Proclaim the holiday. The clamorous drum
Calls to the puppet-show. The groaning horn
And twanging trumpet speak the sale begun,
Of articles most rare and cheap. Dogs bark,
Boys shout, and the grave Doctor mounts sublime
His crowded scaffold, struts, and makes a speech,
Maintains the virtue of his salve for corns,
His worm-cake and his pills, puffs his known art,
And shows his kettle, silver knives and forks,
Ladle and cream-pot, and, to crown the bait,
The splendid tankard. Andrew grins, and courts
The gaping multitude, till Tom and Sue
And Abigail and Ned their shoulders shrug,
And laugh and whisper, and resolve to sport
The solitary shilling. Simple swains
And silly maids, you laugh, but Andrew wins:
And what for you but sorrow and remorse,
Or box of salve to plaster disappointment?
Unless the smart of folly may be soothed
By Andrew's cheerful pranks, the dancing girl,
And frolic tumbler. Now the street is filled
With stalls and booths for gingerbread and beer,
Reared by enchantment, finished in a trice.
Amusement here for children old and young;
For little master's pence, a coach, a drum,
A horse, a wife, a trumpet; dolls for miss,
Fans, cups and saucers, kettles, maids, and churns.
For idle schoolboys Punchinello rants,

The juggler shuffles, and the artful dame
Extends her lucky-bag. For infants tall,
Of twenty years and upwards, rueful games,
To whirl the horse-shoe, bowl at the nine pins,
Game at the dial-plate, drink beer and gin,
Vapour and swear, cudgel, get drunk and fight.

JAMES HURDIS

From *The Village*

The Poor-house

Theirs is yon house that holds the parish poor,
Whose walls of mud scarce bear the broken door;
There, where the putrid vapours flagging, play,
And the dull wheel hums doleful through the day; —
There children dwell who know no parents' care;
Parents, who know no children's love, dwell there;
Heart-broken matrons on their joyless bed,
Forsaken wives and mothers never wed;
Dejected widows with unheeded tears,
And crippled age with more than childhood-fears;
The lame, the blind, and, far the happiest they!
The moping idiot and the madman gay.

Here too the sick their final doom receive,
Here brought amid the scenes of grief, to grieve;
Where the loud groans from some sad chamber flow,
Mixed with the clamours of the crowd below;
Here sorrowing, they each kindred sorrow scan,
And the cold charities of man to man:
Whose laws indeed for ruined age provide,
And strong compulsion plucks the scrap from pride;
But still that scrap is bought with many a sigh,
And pride embitters what it can't deny.

Say ye, oppressed by some fantastic woes,

Some jarring nerve that baffles your repose;
Who press the downy couch, while slaves advance
With timid eye, to read the distant glance;
Who with sad prayers the weary doctor tease,
To name the nameless ever-new disease;
Who with mock patience dire complaints endure,
Which real pain and that alone can cure;
How would ye bear in real pain to lie,
Despised, neglected, left alone to die?
How would ye bear to draw your latest breath,
Where all that's wretched paves the way for death?

Such is that room which one rude beam divides,
And naked rafters form the sloping sides;
Where the vile bands that bind the thatch are seen,
And lath and mud are all that lie between;
Save one dull pane, that, coarsely patched, gives way
To the rude tempest, yet excludes the day:
Here, on a matted flock, with dust o'erspread,
The drooping wretch reclines his languid head;
For him no hand the cordial cup applies,
Or wipes the tear that stagnates in his eyes;
No friends with soft discourse his pain beguile,
Or promise hope till sickness wears a smile.

But soon a loud and hasty summons calls,
Shakes the thin roof, and echoes round the walls;
Anon, a figure enters, quaintly neat,
All pride and business, bustle and conceit;
With looks unaltered by these scenes of woe,
With speed that, entering, speaks his haste to go;
He bids the gazing throng around him fly,
And carries Fate and Physic in his eye;
A potent quack, long versed in human ills,
Who first insults the victim whom he kills;
Whose murderous hand a drowsy Bench protect,
And whose most tender mercy is neglect.

Paid by the parish for attendance here,
He wears contempt upon his sapient sneer;
In haste he seeks the bed where misery lies,

Impatience marked in his averted eyes;
And, some habitual queries hurried o'er,
Without reply, he rushes on the door;
His drooping patient, long inured to pain,
And long unheeded, knows remonstrance vain;
He ceases now the feeble help to crave
Of man; and silent sinks into the grave.

GEORGE CRABBE

Soliloquy
Of a Beauty in the Country

WRITTEN AT ETON SCHOOL

'Twas night; and Flavia, to her room retired,
With evening chat and sober reading tired;
There, melancholy, pensive, and alone,
She meditates on the forsaken town:
On her raised arm reclined her drooping head,
She sighed, and thus in plaintive accents said:
  'Ah! what avails it to be young and fair;
To move with negligence, to dress with care?
What worth have all the charms our pride can boast,
If all in envious solitude are lost?
Where none admire, 'tis useless to excel;
Where none are beaux, 'tis vain to be a belle;
Beauty, like wit, to judges should be shown;
Both most are valued, where they best are known.
With every grace of Nature or of Art,
We cannot break one stubborn country heart:
The brutes, insensible, our power defy:
To love, exceeds a squire's capacity.
The town, the court, is Beauty's proper sphere;
That is our Heaven, and we are angels there:
In that gay circle thousand Cupids rove,

The court of Britain is the court of Love.
How has my conscious heart with triumph glowed,
How have my sparkling eyes their transport showed,
At each distinguished birth-night ball, to see
The homage, due to empire, paid to me!
When every eye was fixed on me alone,
And dreaded mine more than the monarch's frown;
When rival statesmen for my favour strove,
Less jealous in their power than in their love.
Changed is the scene; and all my glories die,
Like flowers transplanted to a colder sky:
Lost is the dear delight of giving pain,
The tyrant joy of hearing slaves complain.
In stupid indolence my life is spent,
Supinely calm, and dully innocent:
Unblessed I wear my useless time away;
Sleep (wretched maid!) all night, and dream all day;
Go at set hours to dinner and to prayer
(For dullness ever must be regular.)
Now with mamma at tedious whist I play;
Now without scandal drink insipid tea;
Or in the garden breathe the country air,
Secure from meeting any tempter there;
From books to work, from work to books, I rove,
And am, alas! at leisure to improve! –
Is this the life a beauty ought to lead?
Were eyes so radiant only made to read?
These fingers, at whose touch even age would glow,
Are these of use for nothing but to sew?
Sure erring Nature never could design
To form a housewife in a mould like mine!
O Venus, queen and guardian of the fair,
Attend propitious to thy votary's prayer:
Let me revisit the dear town again:
Let me be seen! – could I that wish obtain,
All other wishes my own power would gain.'

LORD GEORGE LYTTELTON

Verses

WRITTEN IN THE CHIOSK OF THE BRITISH PALACE, AT PERA, OVERLOOKING THE CITY OF CONSTANTINOPLE, DEC. 26, 1717

Give me, great God! said I, a little farm,
In summer shady, and in winter warm;
Where a clear spring gives birth to murmuring brooks,
By nature gliding down the mossy rocks.
Not artfully by leaden pipes conveyed,
Or greatly falling in a forced cascade,
Pure and unsullied winding through the shade.
All bounteous Heaven has added to my prayer,
A softer climate and a purer air.

   Our frozen isle now chilling winter binds,
Deformed by rains, and rough with blasting winds;
The withered woods grow white with hoary frost,
By driving storms their verdant beauty lost;
The trembling birds their leafless covert shun,
And seek in distant climes a warmer sun:
The water-nymphs their silent urns deplore,
Even Thames, benumbed, 's a river now no more:
The barren meads no longer yield delight,
By glistening snows made painful to the sight.

   Here summer reigns with one eternal smile,
Succeeding harvests bless the happy soil;
Fair fertile fields, to whom indulgent Heaven
Has every charm of every season given.
No killing cold deforms the beauteous year,
The springing flowers no coming winter fear.
But as the parent rose decays and dies,
The infant buds with brighter colours rise,
And with fresh sweets the mother's scent supplies.

   Near them the violet grows with odours blest,
And blooms in more than Tyrian purple dressed;
The rich jonquils their golden beams display,
And shine in glory's emulating day;
The peaceful groves their verdant leaves retain,

The streams still murmur undefiled with rain,
And towering greens adorn the fruitful plain.
The warbling kind uninterrupted sing,
Warmed with enjoyments of perpetual spring.
   Here, at my window, I at once survey
The crowded city and resounding sea;
In distant views the Asian mountains rise,
And lose their snowy summits in the skies;
Above these mountains proud Olympus towers,
The parliamental seat of heavenly powers!
New to the sight my ravished eyes admire
Each gilded crescent and each antique spire,
The marble mosques, beneath whose ample domes
Fierce warlike sultans sleep in peaceful tombs;
Those lofty structures, once the Christian's boast,
Their names, their beauty, and their honours lost;
Those altars bright with gold and sculpture graced,
By barbarous zeal of savage foes defaced;
Sophia alone, her ancient name retains,
Though th'unbeliever now her shrine profanes;
Where holy saints have died in sacred cells,
Where monarchs prayed, the frantic dervish dwells.
How art thou fallen, imperial city, low!
Where are thy hopes of Roman glory now?
Where are thy palaces by prelates raised?
Where Grecian artists all their skill displayed,
Before the happy sciences decayed;
So vast, that youthful kings might here reside,
So splendid, to content a patriarch's pride;
Convents where emperors professed of old,
The laboured pillars that their triumphs told;
Vain monuments of them that once were great,
Sunk undistinguished by one common fate;
One little spot the tenure small contains,
Of Greek nobility the poor remains;
Where other Helens, with like powerful charms,
Had once engaged the warring world in arms;
Those names which royal ancestors can boast,
In mean mechanic arts obscurely lost;

Those eyes a second Homer might inspire,
Fixed at the loom, destroy their useless fire:
Grieved at a view, which struck upon my mind
The short-lived vanity of humankind.

    In gaudy objects I indulge my sight,
And turn where Eastern pomp gives gay delight;
See the vast train in various habits dressed,
By the bright scimitar and sable vest
The proud vizier distinguished o'er the rest!
Six slaves in gay attire his bridle hold,
His bridle rich with gems, and stirrups gold;
His snowy steed adorned with costly pride,
Whole troops of soldiers mounted by his side,
These top the plumy crest Arabian courtiers guide.
With artful duty all decline their eyes,
No bellowing shouts of noisy crowds arise;
Silence, in solemn state, the march attends,
Till at the dread divan the slow procession ends.

    Yet not these prospects all profusely gay,
The gilded navy that adorns the sea,
The rising city in confusion fair,
Magnificently formed, irregular,
Where woods and palaces at once surprise,
Gardens on gardens, domes on domes arise,
And endless beauties tire the wandering eyes,
So soothe my wishes, or so charm my mind,
As this retreat secure from humankind.
No knave's successful craft does spleen excite,
No coxcomb's tawdry splendour shocks my sight,
No mob-alarm awakes my female fear,
No praise my mind, nor envy hurts my ear,
Even fame itself can hardly reach me here;
Impertinence, with all her tattling train,
Fair-sounding flattery's delicious bane;
Censorious folly, noisy party rage,
The thousand tongues with which she must engage
Who dares have virtue in a vicious age.

LADY MARY WORTLEY MONTAGU

5

*'Blest with each talent, and each
art to please.'*

From *The Gymnasiad*

The Boxers

Incessant now their hollow sides they pound,
Loud on each breast the bounding bangs resound;
Their flying fists around the temples glow,
And the jaws crackle with the massy blow.
The raging combat every eye appals,
Strokes following strokes, and falls succeeding falls.
Now drooped the youth, yet, urging all his might,
With feeble arm still vindicates the fight,
Till on the part where heaved the panting breath,
A fatal blow impressed the seal of death.
Down dropped the hero, weltering in his gore,
And his stretched limbs lay quivering on the floor.
So, when a falcon skims the airy way,
Stoops from the clouds, and pounces on his prey;
Dashed on the earth the feathered victim lies,
Expands its feeble wings, and, fluttering, dies.
His faithful friends their dying hero reared,
O'er his broad shoulders dangling hung his head;
Dragging its limbs, they bear the body forth,
Mashed teeth and clotted blood came issuing from his mouth.

PAUL WHITEHEAD

The Playhouse

Where gentle Thames through stately channels glides,
And England's proud metropolis divides;
A lofty fabric does the sight invade,
And stretches o'er the waves a pompous shade;
Whence sudden shouts the neighbourhood surprise,
And thundering claps and dreadful hissings rise.
  Here thrifty R— hires monarchs by the day,

And keeps his mercenary kings in pay;
With deep-mouthed actors fills the vacant scenes,
And rakes the stews for goddesses and queens:
Here the lewd punk, with crowns and sceptres graced,
Teaches her eyes a more majestic cast;
And hungry monarchs with a numerous train
Of suppliant slaves, like Sancho, starve and reign.

But enter in, my Muse; the stage survey,
And all its pomp and pageantry display;
Trap-doors and pit-falls, form th'unfaithful ground,
And magic walls encompass it around:
On either side maimed temples fill our eyes,
And intermixed with brothel-houses rise;
Disjointed palaces in order stand,
And groves obedient to the mover's hand
O'ershade the stage, and flourish at command.
A stamp makes broken towns and trees entire:
So when Amphion struck the vocal lyre,
He saw the spacious circuit all around,
With crowding woods and rising cities crowned.

But next the tiring-room survey, and see
False titles, and promiscuous quality,
Confus'dly swarm, from heroes and from queens,
To those that swing in clouds and fill machines.
Their various characters they choose with art,
The frowning bully fits the tyrant's part:
Swoll'n cheeks and swaggering belly make an host,
Pale meagre looks and hollow voice a ghost;
From careful brows and heavy downcast eyes,
Dull cits and thick-skulled aldermen arise:
The comic tone, inspired by Congreve, draws
At every word, loud laughter and applause:
The whining dame continues as before,
Her character unchanged, and acts a whore.

Above the rest, the prince with haughty stalks
Magnificent in purple buskins walks:
The royal robes his awful shoulders grace,
Profuse of spangles and of copper-lace:

Officious rascals to his mighty thigh,
Guiltless of blood, th'unpointed weapon tie:
Then the gay glittering diadem put on,
Ponderous with brass, and starred with Bristol-stone.
His royal consort next consults her glass,
And out of twenty boxes culls a face;
The whitening first her ghastly looks besmears,
All pale and wan th'unfinished form appears;
Till on her cheeks the blushing purple glows,
And a false virgin-modesty bestows.
Her ruddy lips the deep vermilion dyes;
Length to her brows the pencil's art supplies,
And with black bending arches shades her eyes.
Well pleased at length the picture she beholds,
And spots it o'er with artificial moulds;
Her countenance complete, the beaux she warms
With looks not hers: and, spite of nature, charms.

Thus artfully their persons they disguise,
Till the last flourish bids the curtain rise.
The prince then enters on the stage in state;
Behind, a guard of candle-snuffers wait:
There swoll'n with empire, terrible and fierce,
He shakes the dome, and tears his lungs with verse:
His subjects tremble; the submissive pit,
Wrapped up in silence and attention, sit;
Till, freed at length, he lays aside the weight
Of public business and affairs of state:
Forgets his pomp, dead to ambitious fires,
And to some peaceful brandy-shop retires;
Where in full gills his anxious thoughts he drowns,
And quaffs away the care that waits on crowns.

The princess next her painted charms displays,
Where every look the pencil's art betrays;
The callow squire at distance feeds his eyes,
And silently for paint and washes dies:
But if the youth behind the scenes retreat,
He sees the blended colours melt with heat,
And all the trickling beauty run in sweat.

The borrowed visage he admires no more,
And nauseates every charm he loved before:
So the famed spear, for double force renowned,
Applied the remedy that gave the wound.

In tedious lists 'twere endless to engage,
And draw at length the rabble of the stage,
Where one for twenty years has given alarms,
And called contending monarchs to their arms;
Another fills a more important post,
And rises every other night a ghost;
Through the cleft stage his mealy face he rears,
Then stalks along, groans thrice, and disappears;
Others, with swords and shields, the soldier's pride,
More than a thousand times have changed their side,
And in a thousand fatal battles died.

Thus several persons several parts perform;
Soft lovers whine, and blustering heroes storm.
The stern exasperated tyrants rage,
Till the kind bowl of poison clears the stage.
Then honours vanish, and distinctions cease;
Then, with reluctance, haughty queens undress.
Heroes no more their fading laurels boast,
And mighty kings in private men are lost.
He, whom such titles swelled, such power made proud,
To whom whole realms and vanquished nations bowed,
Throws off the gaudy plume, the purple train,
And in his own vile tatters stinks again.

JOSEPH ADDISON

From *The Actor*

ADDRESSED TO
BONNEL THORNTON, ESQ.

Acting, dear Thornton, its perfection draws,
From no observance of mechanic laws:

No settled maxims of a favourite stage,
No rules delivered down from age to age,
Let players nicely mark them as they will,
Can e'er entail hereditary skill.
If, 'mongst the humble hearers of the pit,
Some curious veteran critic chance to sit,
Is he pleased more because 'twas acted so
By Booth and Cibber thirty years ago?
The mind recalls an object held more dear,
And hates the copy, that it comes so near.
Why loved he Wilks's air, Booth's nervous tone
In them 'twas natural, 'twas all their own.
A Garrick's genius must our wonder raise,
But gives his mimic no reflected praise.

Thrice happy genius, whose unrivalled name
Shall live for ever in the voice of Fame!
'Tis thine to lead with more than magic skill,
The train of captive passions at thy will;
To bid the bursting tear spontaneous flow
In the sweet sense of sympathetic woe:
Through every vein I feel a chillness creep,
When horrors such as thine *have murdered sleep*;
And at the old man's look and frantic stare
'Tis Lear alarms me, for I see him there.
Nor yet confined to tragic walks alone,
The comic Muse too claims thee for her own.
With each delightful requisite to please,
Taste, spirit, judgment, elegance, and ease,
Familiar Nature forms thy only rule,
From Ranger's rake to Drugger's vacant fool.
With powers so pliant, and so various blessed,
That what we see the last, we like the best.
Not idly pleased at judgment's dear expense,
But burst outrageous with the laugh of sense.

Perfection's top, with weary toil and pain,
'Tis genius only that can hope to gain.
The player's profession (though I hate the phrase,
'Tis so *mechanic* in these modern days)

Lies not in trick, or attitude, or start,
Nature's true knowledge is the only art.
The strong-felt passion bolts into his face,
The mind untouched, what is it but grimace!
To this one standard make your just appeal,
Here lies the golden secret; learn to *feel*.
Or fool, or monarch, happy, or distressed,
No actor pleases that is not *possessed*.

ROBERT LLOYD

Prologue

ON THE OLD WINCHESTER PLAYHOUSE OVER THE OLD BUTCHERS' SHAMBLES

Whoe'er our stage examines, must excuse
The wondrous shifts of the dramatic Muse;
Then kindly listen, while the prologue rambles
From wit to beef, from Shakespeare to the shambles!
Divided only by one flight of stairs,
The monarch swaggers, and the butcher swears!
Quick the transition when the curtain drops,
From meek Monimia's moans to mutton-chops!
While for Lothario's loss Lavinia cries,
Old women scold, and dealers d–n your eyes!
Here Juliet listens to the gentle lark,
There in harsh chorus hungry bulldogs bark.
Cleavers and scimitars give blow for blow,
And heroes bleed above, and sheep below!
While tragic thunders shake the pit and box,
Rebellows to the roar the staggering ox.
Cow-horns and trumpets mix their martial tones,
Kidneys and kings, mouthing and marrow-bones.
Suet and sighs, blank verse and blood abound,
And form a tragi-comedy around.
With weeping lovers, dying calves complain,

Confusion reigns – chaos is come again!
Hither your steelyards, butchers, bring, to weigh
The pound of flesh, Antonio's bond must pay!
Hither your knives, ye Christians, clad in blue,
Bring to be whetted by the ruthless Jew!
Hard is our lot, who, seldom doomed to eat,
Cast a sheep's-eye on this forbidden meat –
Gaze on sirloins, which, ah! we cannot carve,
And in the midst of legs of mutton – starve!
But would you to our house in crowds repair,
Ye generous captains, and ye blooming fair,
The fate of Tantalus we should not fear,
Nor pine for a repast that is so near.
Monarchs no more would supperless remain,
Nor pregnant queens for cutlets long in vain.

THOMAS WARTON

On the Masquerades

Si Natura negat, facit indignatio
versum

Well – we have reached the precipice at last;
The present age of vice obscures the past.
Our dull forefathers were content to stay,
Nor sinned till Nature pointed out the way:
No arts they practised to forestall delight,
But stopped, to wait the calls of appetite.
Their top-debauches were at best precise,
An unimproved simplicity of vice.

But this blest age has found a fairer road,
And left the paths their ancestors have trod.
Nay, we could wear (our taste so very nice is)
Their old cast-fashions sooner than their vices.
Whoring till now a common trade has been,
But masquerades refine upon the sin:

An higher taste to wickedness impart,
And second Nature with the helps of art.
New ways and means to pleasure we devise,
Since pleasure looks the lovelier in disguise.
The stealth and frolic give a smarter gust,
Add wit to vice, and eloquence to lust.
In vain the modish evil to redress,
At once conspire the pulpit and the press:
Our priests and poets preach and write in vain;
All satire's lost both sacred and profane.
So many various changes to impart,
Would tire an Ovid's or a Proteus' art;
Where lost in one promiscuous whim we see,
Sex, age, condition, quality, degree.
Where the facetious crowd themselves lay down,
And take up every person but their own.
Fools, dukes, rakes, cardinals, fops, Indian queens,
Belles in tie-wigs, and lords in harlequins;
Troops of right-honourable porters come,
And gartered small-coal-merchants crowd the room:
Valets adorned with coronets appear,
Lackeys of state, and footmen with a star:
Sailors of quality with judges mix,
And chimney-sweepers drive their coach and six.
Statesmen so used at court the mask to wear,
With less disguise assume the visor here.
Officious Heydegger deceives our eyes,
For his own person is his best disguise:
And half the reigning toasts of equal grace,
Trust to the natural visor of the face.
Idiots turn conjurors; and courtiers clowns;
And sultans drop their handkerchiefs to nuns.
Starched Quakers glare in furbelows and silk;
Beaux deal in sprats, and duchesses cry milk.
But guard thy fancy, Muse, nor stain thy pen
With the lewd joys of this fantastic scene;
Where sexes blend in one confused intrigue,
Where the girls ravish, and the men grow big:

Nor credit what the idle world has said,
Of lawyers forced, and judges brought to bed:
Or that to belles their brothers breathe their vows,
Or husbands through mistake gallant a spouse.
Such dire disasters, and a numerous throng
Of like enormities, require the song:
But the chaste Muse, with blushes covered o'er,
Retires confused, and will reveal no more.

CHRISTOPHER PITT

From *An Essay on Criticism*

The Art of Poetry

Words are like leaves; and where they most abound,
Much fruit of sense beneath is rarely found.
False eloquence, like the prismatic glass,
Its gaudy colours spreads on every place;
The face of Nature we no more survey,
All glares alike, without distinction gay:
But true expression, like th'unchanging sun,
Clears, and improves whate'er it shines upon,
It gilds all objects, but it alters none.
Expression is the dress of thought, and still
Appears more decent, as more suitable;
A vile conceit in pompous words expressed,
Is like a clown in regal purple dressed:
For different styles with different subjects sort,
As several garbs, with country, town, and court.

*

But most by numbers judge a poet's song,
And smooth or rough, with them, is right or wrong;
In the bright Muse though thousand charms conspire,
Her voice is all these tuneful fools admire;
Who haunt Parnassus but to please their ear,

Not mend their minds; as some to church repair,
Not for the doctrine, but the music there.
These equal syllables alone require,
Though oft the ear the open vowels tire;
While expletives their feeble aid do join;
And ten low words oft creep in one dull line;
While they ring round the same unvaried chimes,
With sure returns of still expected rhymes.
Where'er you find 'the cooling western breeze',
In the next line, it 'whispers through the trees':
If crystal streams 'with pleasing murmurs creep',
The reader's threatened (not in vain) with 'sleep'.
Then, at the last and only couplet fraught
With some unmeaning thing they call a thought,
A needless Alexandrine ends the song,
That, like a wounded snake, drags its slow length along.

ALEXANDER POPE

From *Wit and Learning*

Whoever looks on life will see
How strangely mortals disagree:
This reprobates what that approves,
And Tom dislikes what Harry loves;
The soldier's witty on the sailor,
The barber drolls upon the tailor;
And he who makes the nation's wills,
Laughs at the doctor and his pills.
    Yet this antipathy we find
Not to the sons of Earth confined;
Each schoolboy sees, with half an eye,
The quarrels of the pagan sky:
For all the poets fairly tell us,
That gods themselves are proud and jealous;
And will, like mortals, swear and hector,

When mellowed with a cup of nectar.
    But waiving these, and such like fancies,
We meet with in the Greek romances,
Say, shall th'historic Muse retail
A little allegoric tale?
Nor stole from Plato's mystic tome, nor
Translated from the verse of Homer,
But copied, in a modern age,
From Nature, and her fairest page.
    Olympian Jove, whose idle trade is
Employed too much among the ladies,
Though not of manners mighty chaste,
Was certainly a god of taste;
Would often to his feasts admit
A deity, whose name was Wit;
And, to amuse the more discerning,
Would ask the company of Learning.
    Learning was born, as all agree,
Of Truth's half-sister, Memory;
A nymph who rounded in her shape was
By that great artist Esculapius.
    Euphrosine, the younger Grace,
Matchless in feature, mien, and face,
Who, like the beauties of these late days,
Was fond of operas and cantatas,
Would often to a grot retire
To listen to Apollo's lyre;
And thence became, so Ovid writ,
A mother to the god of wit.
    Wit was a strange unlucky child,
Exceeding sly, and very wild;
Too volatile for truth or law,
He minded but his top or taw;
And, ere he reached the age of six,
Had played a thousand waggish tricks. —
He drilled a hole in Vulcan's kettles,
He strewed Minerva's bed with nettles,
Climbed up the solar car to ride in't,

Broke off a prong from Neptune's trident,
Stole Amphitrite's favourite sea-knot,
And urined in Astrea's teapot.

JAMES CAWTHORN

From *The Poetry Professors*

Old England has not lost her prayer,
And George, (thank Heaven!) has got an heir.
A royal babe, a Prince of Wales.
– Poets! I pity all your nails –
What reams of paper will be spoiled!
What graduses be daily soiled
By inky fingers, greasy thumbs,
Hunting the word that never comes!
  Now academics pump their wits,
And lash in vain their lazy tits;
In vain they whip, and slash, and spur,
The callous jades will never stir;
Nor can they reach Parnassus' hill,
Try every method which they will.
Nay, should the tits get on for once,
Each rider is so grave a dunce,
That, as I've heard good judges say,
'Tis ten to one they'd lose their way;
Though not one wit bestrides the back
Of useful drudge, ycleped hack,
But fine bred things of mettled blood,
Picked from Apollo's royal stud.
Greek, Roman, nay Arabian steeds,
Or those our mother country breeds;
Some ride ye in, and ride ye out
And to come home go round about,
Nor on the green sward, nor the road,
And that I think they call an Ode.
Some take the pleasant country air,

And smack their whips and drive a pair,
Each horse with bells which clink and chime,
And so they march – and that is rhyme.
Some copy with prodigious skill
The figures of a buttery-bill,
Which, with great folks of erudition,
Shall pass for Coptic or Phœnician.
While some, as patriot love prevails,
To compliment a prince of Wales,
Salute the royal babe in Welsh,
And send forth gutturals like a belch.

*

Yet matter must be gravely planned,
And syllables on fingers scanned,
And racking pangs rend labouring head,
Till lady Muse is brought to bed:
What hunting, changing, toiling, sweating,
To bring the usual epithet in!
Where the cramped measure kindly shows
It will be verse, but should be prose.
So, when it's neither light nor dark,
To 'prentice spruce, or lawyer's clerk,
The nymph, who takes her nightly stand,
At some sly corner in the Strand,
Plump in the chest, tight in the bodice,
Seems to the eye a perfect goddess;
But canvassed more minutely o'er,
Turns out an old, stale, battered whore.

ROBERT LLOYD

From *A Charge to the Poets*

A life of writing, unless wondrous short,
No wit can brave, no genius can support.
Some soberer province for your business choose,

Be that your helmet, and your plume the Muse.
Through Fame's long rubric, down from Chaucer's time,
Few fortunes have been raised by lofty rhyme.
And, when our toils success no longer crowns,
What shelter find we from a world in frowns?
O'er each distress, which vice or folly brings,
Though charity extend her healing wings,
No maudlin hospitals are yet assigned
For slipshod Muses of the vagrant kind;
Where anthems might succeed to satires keen,
And hymns of penitence to songs obscene.

What refuge then remains? – with gracious grin
Some practised bookseller invites you in.
Where luckless bards, condemned to court the town,
(Not for their parents' vices, but their own!)
Write gay conundrums with an aching head,
Or earn by defamation daily bread,
Or, friendless, shirtless, pennyless, complain,
Not of the world's, but 'Celia's cold disdain'.

Lords of their workhouse see the tyrants sit,
Brokers in books, and stock-jobbers in wit,
Beneath whose lash, obliged to write or fast,
Our confessors and martyrs breathe their last!

And can ye bear such insolence? – away,
For shame; plough, dig, turn pedlars, drive the dray;
With minds indignant each employment suits,
Our fleets want sailors, and our troops recruits;
And many a dirty street, on Thames's side,
Is yet by stool and brush unoccupied.

Time was when poets played the thorough game,
Swore, drank, and blustered, and blasphemed for fame.
The first in brothels with their punk and Muse;
Your toast, ye bards? 'Parnassus and the stews!'
Thank Heaven the times are changed; no poet now
Need roar for Bacchus, or to Venus bow.
'Tis our own fault if Fielding's lash *we* feel,
Or, like French wits, begin with the Bastille.

WILLIAM WHITEHEAD

From *Epilogue to the Satires*

The Art of Satire

P. Ask you what provocation I have had?
The strong antipathy of good to bad.
When truth or virtue an affront endures,
Th'affront is mine, my friend, and should be yours.
Mine, as a foe professed to false pretence,
Who think a coxcomb's honour like his sense;
Mine, as a friend to every worthy mind;
And mine as man, who feels for all mankind.
    F. You're strangely proud.
             P. So proud, I am no slave:
So impudent, I own myself no knave:
So odd, my country's ruin makes me grave.
Yes, I am proud; I must be proud to see
Men not afraid of God, afraid of me:
Safe from the bar, the pulpit, and the throne,
Yet touched and shamed by ridicule alone.

  O sacred weapon! left for Truth's defence,
Sole dread of folly, vice, and insolence!
To all but Heaven-directed hands denied,
The Muse may give thee, but the gods must guide:
Reverent I touch thee! but with honest zeal;
To rouse the watchmen of the public weal,
To virtue's work provoke the tardy Hall,
And goad the prelate slumbering in his stall.
Ye tinsel insects! whom a Court maintains,
That counts your beauties only by your stains,
Spin all your cobwebs o'er the eye of day!
The Muse's wing shall brush you all away:
All his Grace preaches, all his lordship sings,
All that makes saints of queens, and gods of kings,
All, all but truth, drops dead-born from the press,
Like the last Gazette, or the last address.

ALEXANDER POPE

Ode XIV

WRITTEN AFTER READING SOME
MODERN LOVE-VERSES

Take hence this tuneful trifler's lays!
I'll hear no more the unmeaning strain
Of Venus' doves, and Cupid's darts,
And killing eyes, and wounded hearts;
All Flattery's round of fulsome praise,
All Falsehood's cant of fabled pain.

Bring me the Muse whose tongue has told
Love's genuine plaintive tender tale;
Bring me the Muse whose sounds of woe
Midst Death's dread scenes so sweetly flow,
When Friendship's faithful breast lies cold,
When Beauty's blooming cheek is pale:
Bring these – I like their grief sincere;
It soothes my sympathetic gloom:
For, oh! Love's genuine pains I've borne,
And Death's dread rage has made me mourn;
I've wept o'er Friendship's early bier,
And dropped the tear on Beauty's tomb.

JOHN SCOTT

The Passive Participle's Petition

TO THE PRINTER OF THE GENTLEMAN'S
MAGAZINE

Urban, or Sylvan, or whatever name
Delight thee most, thou foremost in the fame
Of magazining chiefs, whose rival page
With monthly medley courts the curious age;

Hear a poor Passive Participle's case,
And if thou can'st, restore me to my place.

Till just of late, good English has thought fit
To call me *written*, or to call me *writ*;
But what is writ or written, by the vote
Of writers now, hereafter must be *wrote*;
And what is *spoken*, too, hereafter *spoke*;
And measures never to be *broken*, *broke*.

I never could be *driven*, but, in spite
Of grammar, they have *drove* me from my right.
None could have *risen* to become my foes;
But what a world of enemies have *rose*!
Who have not *gone*, but they have *went* about,
And, *torn* as I have been, have *tore* me out.

Passive I am, and would be, and implore
That such abuse may be henceforth *forbore*,
If not *forborn*, for by all spelling book,
If not *mistaken*, they are all *mistook*:
And, in plain English, it had been as well
If what had *fall'n* upon me, had not *fell*.

Since this attack upon me has *began*,
Who knows what lengths in language may be *ran*?
For if it once be *grew* into a law,
You'll see such work as never has been *saw*;
Part of our speech and sense, perhaps beside
Shakes when I'm *shook*, and dies when I am *died*.

Then let the preter and imperfect tense
Of my own words to me remit the sense;
Or since we two are oft enough agreed,
Let all the learned take some better heed;
And leave the vulgar to confound the due
Of preter tense, and participle too.

JOHN BYROM

From *The Art of Cookery*

Far from the parlour have your kitchen placed,
Dainties may in their working be disgraced.
In private draw your poultry, clean your tripe,
And from your eels their slimy substance wipe.
Let cruel offices be done by night,
For they who like the thing abhor the sight.

Next, let discretion moderate your cost,
And, when you treat, three courses be the most.
Let never fresh machines your pastry try,
Unless grandees or magistrates are by:
Then you may put a dwarf into a pie.
Or, if you'd fright an alderman and mayor,
Within a pasty lodge a living hare;
Then midst their gravest furs shall mirth arise,
And all the Guild pursue with joyful cries.

'Tis the dessert that graces all the feast,
For an ill end disparages the rest:
A thousand things well done, and one forgot,
Defaces obligation by that blot.
Make your transparent sweet-meats truly nice,
With Indian sugar and Arabian spice:
And let your various creams encircled be
With swelling fruit just ravished from the tree.
Let plates and dishes be from China brought,
With lively paint and earth transparent wrought.
The feast now done, discourses are renewed,
And witty arguments with mirth pursued.
The cheerful master, midst his jovial friends,
His glass 'to their best wishes' recommends.
The grace-cup follows to his sovereign's health,
And to his country, 'plenty, peace, and wealth'.
Performing then the piety of grace,
Each man that pleases re-assumes his place;
While at his gate, from such abundant store,
He showers his god-like blessings on the poor.

WILLIAM KING

6

*'Explore the thought, explain
the asking eye.'*

From *Edge Hill*

Sage Philosophy

The vulgar race of men, like herds that graze,
On instinct live, not knowing how they live;
While reason sleeps, or waking stoops to sense.
But sage philosophy explores the cause
Of each phenomenon of sight, or sound,
Taste, touch, or smell; each organ's inmost frame,
And correspondence with external things:
Explains how different texture of their parts
Excites sensations different, rough, or smooth,
Bitter, or sweet, fragrance, or noisome scent:
How various streams of undulating air,
Through the ear's winding labyrinth conveyed,
Cause all the vast variety of sounds.
Hence too the subtle properties of light,
And seven-fold colour are distinctly viewed
In the prismatic glass, and outward forms
Shown fairly drawn, in miniature divine,
On the transparent eye's membraneous cell.

RICHARD JAGO

Know Yourself

What am I? how produced? and for what end?
Whence drew I being? to what period tend?
Am I the abandoned orphan of blind chance,
Dropped by wild atoms in disordered dance?
Or from an endless chain of causes wrought?
And of unthinking substance, born with thought?
By motion which began without a cause,
Supremely wise, without design or laws.
Am I but what I seem, mere flesh and blood;

A branching channel, with a mazy flood?
The purple stream that through my vessels glides,
Dull and unconscious flows like common tides:
The pipes through which the circling juices stray,
Are not that thinking I, no more than they:
This frame, compacted, with transcendent skill,
Of moving joints obedient to my will;
Nursed from the fruitful glebe, like yonder tree,
Waxes and wastes; I call it mine, not me:
New matter still the mouldering mass sustains,
The mansion changed, the tenant still remains:
And from the fleeting stream repaired by food,
Distinct, as is the swimmer from the flood.
What am I then? sure, of a nobler birth.
Thy parent's right I own, O mother earth;
But claim superior lineage by my Sire,
Who warmed the unthinking clod with heavenly fire:
Essence divine, with lifeless clay allayed,
By double nature, double instinct swayed,
With look erect, I dart my longing eye,
Seem winged to part, and gain my native sky;
I strive to mount, but strive, alas! in vain,
Tied to this massy globe with magic chain.
Now with swift thought I range from pole to pole,
View worlds around their flaming centres roll:
What steady powers their endless motions guide,
Through the same trackless paths of boundless void!
I trace the blazing comet's fiery trail,
And weigh the whirling planets in a scale;
Those godlike thoughts, while eager I pursue,
Some glittering trifle offered to my view,
A gnat, an insect, of the meanest kind,
Erase the new-born image from my mind;
Some beastly want, craving, importunate,
Vile as the grinning mastiffs at my gate,
Calls off from heavenly truth this reasoning me,
And tells me I'm a brute as much as he.
If on sublimer wings of love and praise

My soul above the starry vault I raise,
Lured by some vain conceit, or shameful lust,
I flag, I drop, and flutter in the dust.
The towering lark thus from her lofty strain
Stoops to an emmet, or a barley grain.
By adverse gusts of jarring instincts tossed,
I rove to one, now to the other coast;
To bliss unknown my lofty soul aspires,
My lot unequal to my vast desires.
As 'mongst the hinds a child of royal birth
Finds his high pedigree by conscious worth,
So man, amongst his fellow brutes exposed,
Sees he's a king, but 'tis a king deposed.
Pity him, beasts! you by no law confined,
Are barred from devious paths by being blind;
Whilst man, through opening views of various ways,
Confounded, by the aid of knowledge strays;
Too weak to choose, yet choosing still in haste,
One moment gives the pleasure and distaste;
Bilked by past minutes, while the present cloy,
The flattering future still must give the joy.
Not happy, but amused upon the road,
And like you thoughtless of his last abode,
Whether next sun his being shall restrain
To endless nothing, happiness, or pain.

Around me, lo, the thinking thoughtless crew,
(Bewildered each) their different paths pursue;
Of them I ask the way; the first replies,
Thou art a god; and sends me to the skies.
Down on this turf (the next) thou two-legged beast,
There fix thy lot, thy bliss, and endless rest;
Between those wide extremes the length is such,
I find I know too little or too much.

'Almighty power, by whose most wise command,
Helpless, forlorn, uncertain here I stand;
Take this faint glimmering of thyself away,
Or break into my soul with perfect day!'
This said, expanded lay the sacred text,

The balm, the light, the guide of souls perplexed:
Thus the benighted traveller that strays
Through doubtful paths, enjoys the morning rays;
The nightly mist, and thick descending dew,
Parting, unfold the fields, and vaulted blue.
'O truth divine! enlightened by thy ray,
I grope and guess no more, but see my way;
Thou clear'dst the secret of my high descent,
And told me what those mystic tokens meant;
Marks of my birth, which I had worn in vain,
Too hard for worldly sages to explain;
Zeno's were vain, vain Epicurus' schemes,
Their systems false, delusive were their dreams;
Unskilled my twofold nature to divide,
One nursed by pleasure, and one nursed by pride;
Those jarring truths which human art beguile,
Thy sacred page thus bid me reconcile.'
Offspring of God, no less thy pedigree,
What thou once wert, art now, and still may be,
Thy God alone can tell, alone decree;
Faultless thou dropped from His unerring skill,
With the bare power to sin, since free of will;
Yet charge not with thy guilt His bounteous love;
For who has power to walk, has power to rove,
Who acts by force impelled, can nought deserve;
And wisdom short of infinite, may swerve.
Born on thy new-imped wings, thou took'st thy flight,
Left thy Creator, and the realms of light;
Disdained His gentle precept to fulfil;
And thought to grow a god by doing ill:
Though by foul guilt thy heavenly form defaced,
In nature changed, from happy mansions chased,
Thou still retain'st some sparks of heavenly fire,
Too faint to mount, yet restless to aspire;
Angel enough to seek thy bliss again,
And brute enough to make thy search in vain.
The creatures now withdraw their kindly use,
Some fly thee, some torment, and some seduce;

Repast ill-suited to such different guests,
For what thy sense desires, thy soul distastes;
Thy lust, thy curiosity, thy pride,
Curbed, or deferred, or balked, or gratified,
Rage on, and make thee equally unblessed
In what thou want'st, and what thou hast possessed;
In vain thou hop'st for bliss on this poor clod,
Return, and seek thy father, and thy God:
Yet think not to regain thy native sky,
Born on the wings of vain philosophy;
Mysterious passage! hid from human eyes;
Soaring you'll sink, and sinking you will rise:
Let humble thoughts thy wary footsteps guide,
Regain by meekness what you lost by pride.

JOHN ARBUTHNOT

From *Essay on Man*

Far as creation's ample range extends,
The scale of sensual, mental powers ascends:
Mark how it mounts to man's imperial race,
From the green myriads in the peopled grass:
What modes of sight betwixt each wide extreme,
The mole's dim curtain, and the lynx's beam:
Of smell, the headlong lioness between,
And hound sagacious on the tainted green:
Of hearing, from the life that fills the flood,
To that which warbles through the vernal wood:
The spider's touch, how exquisitely fine!
Feels at each thread, and lives along the line:
In the nice bee, what sense so subtly true
From poisonous herbs extracts the healing dew:
How instinct varies in the groveling swine,
Compared, half-reasoning elephant, with thine:
'Twixt that, and reason, what a nice barrier;

For ever separate, yet for ever near!
Remembrance and reflection how allied;
What thin partitions sense from thought divide:
And middle natures, how they long to join,
Yet never pass th'insuperable line!
Without this just gradation could they be
Subjected these to those, or all to thee?
The powers of all subdued by thee alone,
Is not thy reason all these powers in one?

*

All Nature is but art, unknown to thee;
All chance, direction, which thou canst not see;
All discord, harmony, not understood;
All partial evil, universal good:
And, spite of pride, in erring reason's spite,
One truth is clear, 'Whatever is, is right.'

*

Know then thyself, presume not God to scan;
The proper study of mankind is man.
Placed on this isthmus of a middle state,
A being darkly wise, and rudely great:
With too much knowledge for the sceptic side,
With too much weakness for the stoic's pride,
He hangs between; in doubt to act, or rest,
In doubt to deem himself a god, or beast;
In doubt his mind or body to prefer,
Born but to die, and reasoning but to err;
Alike in ignorance, his reason such,
Whether he thinks too little, or too much:
Chaos of thought and passion, all confused;
Still by himself abused, or disabused;
Created half to rise, and half to fall;
Great lord of all things, yet a prey to all;
Sole judge of truth, in endless error hurled:
The glory, jest, and riddle of the world!

*

Behold the child, by Nature's kindly law,
Pleased with a rattle, tickled with a straw:
Some livelier plaything gives his youth delight,
A little louder, but as empty quite:
Scarfs, garters, gold, amuse his riper stage;
And beads and prayer-books are the toys of age:
Pleased with this bauble still, as that before;
Till tired he sleeps, and life's poor play is o'er!

*

  For forms of government let fools contest;
Whate'er is best administered is best:
For modes of faith let graceless zealots fight;
His can't be wrong whose life is in the right:
In faith and hope the world will disagree,
But all mankind's concern is charity:
All must be false that thwart this one great end,
And all of God, that bless mankind or mend.
  Man, like the generous vine, supported lives;
The strength he gains is from th'embrace he gives.
On their own axis as the planets run,
Yet make at once their circle round the sun:
So two consistent motions act the soul;
And one regards itself, and one the whole.
  Thus God and Nature linked the general frame,
And bade self-love and social be the same.

ALEXANDER POPE

From *The Grasshopper and the Glowworm*

True Knowledge

  When ignorance possessed the schools,
  And reigned by Aristotle's rules,
  Ere Verulam, like dawning light,
  Rose to dispel the Gothic night:

A man was taught to shut his eyes,
And grow abstracted to be wise.
Nature's broad volume fairly spread,
Where all true science might be read
The wisdom of th'Eternal Mind,
Declared and published to mankind,
Was quite neglected, for the whims
Of mortals and their airy dreams:
By narrow principles and few,
By hasty maxims, oft untrue,
By words and phrases ill-defined,
Evasive truth they hoped to bind;
Which still escaped them, and the elves
At last caught nothing but themselves.
Nor is this folly modern quite,
'Tis ancient too: the Stagirite
Improved at first, and taught his school
By rules of art to play the fool.
Ev'n Plato, from example bad,
Would oft turn sophist and run mad;
Make Socrates himself discourse
Like Clarke and Leibnitz, oft-times worse;
'Bout quirks and subtleties contending,
Beyond all human comprehending.
From some strange bias men pursue
False knowledge still in place of true,
Build airy systems of their own,
This moment raised, the next pulled down;
While few attempt to catch those rays
Of truth which nature still displays
Throughout the universal plan,
From moss and mushrooms up to man.

WILLIAM WILKIE

An Elegy Wrote in a Country Church Yard

The curfew tolls the knell of parting day,
The lowing herd winds slowly o'er the lea,
The plough-man homeward plods his weary way,
And leaves the world to darkness, and to me.

Now fades the glimmering landscape on the sight,
And all the air a solemn stillness holds;
Save where the beetle wheels his droning flight,
And drowsy tinklings lull the distant folds.

Save that from yonder ivy-mantled tower
The moping owl does to the moon complain
Of such, as wandering near her sacred bower,
Molest her ancient solitary reign.

Beneath those rugged elms, that yew-tree's shade,
Where heaves the turf in many a mouldering heap,
Each in his narrow cell for ever laid,
The rude forefathers of the hamlet sleep.

The breezy call of incense-breathing morn,
The swallow twittering from the straw-built shed,
The cock's shrill clarion, or the echoing horn,
No more shall wake them from their lowly bed.

For them no more the blazing hearth shall burn,
Or busy housewife ply her evening care:
No children run to lisp their sire's return,
Or climb his knees the envied kiss to share.

Oft did the harvest to their sickle yield,
Their furrow oft the stubborn glebe has broke;
How jocund did they drive their team afield!
How bowed the woods beneath their sturdy stroke!

Let not ambition mock their useful toil,
Their homely joys and destiny obscure;
Nor grandeur hear with a disdainful smile,
The short and simple annals of the poor.

The boast of heraldry, the pomp of power,
And all that beauty, all that wealth e'er gave,
Awaits alike th'inevitable hour.

The paths of glory lead but to the grave.

    Forgive, ye proud, th'involuntary fault,
If memory to these no trophies raise,
Where through the long-drawn aisle and fretted vault
The pealing anthem swells the note of praise.

    Can storied urn or animated bust
Back to its mansion call the fleeting breath?
Can honour's voice provoke the silent dust,
Or flattery sooth the dull cold ear of death?

    Perhaps in this neglected spot is laid
Some heart once pregnant with celestial fire,
Hands that the reins of empire might have swayed,
Or waked to ecstasy the living lyre.

    But knowledge to their eyes her ample page
Rich with the spoils of time did ne'er unroll;
Chill penury repressed their noble rage,
And froze the genial current of the soul.

    Full many a gem of purest ray serene,
The dark unfathomed caves of ocean bear:
Full many a flower is born to blush unseen,
And waste its sweetness on the desert air.

    Some village-Hampden that with dauntless breast
The little tyrant of his fields withstood;
Some mute inglorious Milton here may rest,
Some Cromwell guiltless of his country's blood.

    Th'applause of listening senates to command,
The threats of pain and ruin to despise,
To scatter plenty o'er a smiling land,
And read their history in a nation's eyes

    Their lot forbade: nor circumscribed alone
Their growing virtues, but their crimes confined;
Forbade to wade through slaughter to a throne,
And shut the gates of mercy on mankind,

    The struggling pangs of conscious truth to hide,
To quench the blushes of ingenuous shame,
Or heap the shrine of luxury and pride
With incense, kindled at the muse's flame.

    Far from the madding crowd's ignoble strife,

Their sober wishes never learned to stray;
Along the cool sequestered vale of life
They kept the noiseless tenor of their way.

    Yet ev'n these bones from insult to protect
Some frail memorial still erected nigh,
With uncouth rhymes and shapeless sculpture decked,
Implores the passing tribute of a sigh.

    Their name, their years, spelt by the unlettered muse,
The place of fame and elegy supply:
And many a holy text around she strews,
That teach the rustic moralist to die.

    For who to dumb forgetfulness a prey,
This pleasing anxious being e'er resigned,
Left the warm precincts of the cheerful day,
Nor cast one longing lingering look behind?

    On some fond breast the parting soul relies,
Some pious drops the closing eye requires;
Ev'n from the tomb the voice of nature cries
Awake, and faithful to her wonted fires.

    For thee, who mindful of the unhonoured dead
Dost in these lines their artless tale relate;
If chance, by lonely contemplation led,
Some hidden spirit shall inquire thy fate,

    Haply some hoary-headed swain may say,
'Oft have we seen him at the peep of dawn
Brushing with hasty steps the dews away
To meet the sun upon the upland lawn.

    'There at the foot of yonder nodding beech
That wreathes its old fantastic roots so high,
His listless length at noontide would he stretch,
And pore upon the brook that babbles by.

    'Hard by yon wood, now frowning as in scorn,
Muttering his wayward fancies he would rove,
Now drooping, woeful wan, like one forlorn,
Or crazed with care, or crossed in hopeless love.

    'One morn I missed him on the customed hill,
Along the heath, and near his favourite tree;
Another came; nor yet beside the rill,

Nor up the lawn, nor at the wood was he.
'The next with dirges due in sad array
Slow through the church-way path we saw him borne.
Approach and read (for thou canst read) the lay,
Graved on the stone beneath yon aged thorn.'

THE EPITAPH

Here rests his head upon the lap of earth
A youth to fortune and to fame unknown:
Fair science frowned not on his humble birth,
And melancholy marked him for her own.
    Large was his bounty, and his soul sincere,
Heaven did a recompense as largely send:
He gave to misery all he had, a tear:
He gained from heaven ('twas all he wished) a friend.
    No farther seek his merits to disclose,
Or draw his frailties from their dread abode,
(There they alike in trembling hope repose)
The bosom of his father and his God.

THOMAS GRAY

Ode
On the Death of a Favourite Cat
Drowned in a Tub of Gold Fishes

'Twas on a lofty vase's side,
Where China's gayest art had dyed
    The azure flowers, that blow;
Demurest of the tabby kind,
The pensive Selima reclined,
    Gazed on the lake below.

Her conscious tail her joy declared;
The fair round face, the snowy beard,
    The velvet of her paws,

Her coat, that with the tortoise vies,
Her ears of jet, and emerald eyes,
   She saw; and purred applause.

Still had she gazed; but 'midst the tide
Two angel forms were seen to glide,
   The genii of the stream:
Their scaly armour's Tyrian hue
Through richest purple to the view
   Betrayed a golden gleam.

The hapless nymph with wonder saw:
A whisker first and then a claw,
   With many an ardent wish,
She stretched in vain to reach the prize.
What female heart can gold despise?
   What cat's averse to fish?

Presumptuous maid! with looks intent
Again she stretched, again she bent,
   Nor knew the gulf between.
(Malignant Fate sat by, and smiled)
The slippery verge her feet beguiled,
   She tumbled headlong in.

Eight times emerging from the flood
She mewed to every watery god,
   Some speedy aid to send.
No dolphin came, no nereid stirred:
Nor cruel Tom, nor Susan heard.
   A favourite has no friend!

From hence, ye beauties, undeceived,
Know, one false step is ne'er retrieved,
   And be with caution bold.
Not all that tempts your wandering eyes
And heedless hearts, is lawful prize;
   Nor all, that glisters, gold.

THOMAS GRAY

From *Solitude:*

AN ODE

Let those toil for gold who please,
Or for fame renounce their ease.
What is fame? an empty bubble;
Gold? a transient, shining trouble.
Let them for their country bleed,
What was Sidney's, Raleigh's meed?
Man's not worth a moment's pain,
Base, ungrateful, fickle, vain.
Then let me, sequestered fair,
To your sibyl grot repair,
On yon hanging cliff it stands
Scooped by Nature's savage hands,
Bosomed in the gloomy shade
Of cypress, not with age decayed.
Where the owl still-hooting sits,
Where the bat incessant flits,
There in loftier strains I'll sing,
Whence the changing seasons spring,
Tell how storms deform the skies,
Whence the waves subside and rise,
Trace the comet's blazing tail,
Weigh the planets in a scale;
Bend, great God, before thy shrine,
The bournless microcosm's thine.

JAMES GRAINGER

The Happy Life

A book, a friend, a song, a glass,
A chaste, yet laughter-loving lass,
To mortals various joys impart,
Inform the sense, and warm the heart.

Thrice happy they, who, careless, laid,
Beneath a kind-embowering shade,
With rosy wreaths their temples crown,
In rosy wine their sorrows drown.

Meanwhile the Muses wake the lyre,
The Graces modest mirth inspire,
Good-natured humour, harmless wit;
Well-tempered joys, nor grave, nor light.

Let sacred Venus with her heir,
And dear Ianthe too be there.
Music and wine in concert move
With beauty, and refining love.

There Peace shall spread her dove-like wing,
And bid her olives round us spring,
There Truth shall reign, a sacred guest!
And Innocence, to crown the rest.

Begone, ambition, riches, toys,
And splendid cares, and guilty joys. –
Give me a book, a friend, a glass,
And a chaste, laughter-loving lass.

WILLIAM THOMPSON

From *The Pleasures of Melancholy*

The tapered choir, at the late hour of prayer,
Oft let me tread, while to th'according voice
The many-sounding organ peals on high,
The clear slow-dittied chant, or varied hymn,
Till all my soul is bathed in ecstasies,
And lapped in paradise. Or let me sit
Far in sequestered aisles of the deep dome,
There lonesome listen to the sacred sounds,

Which, as they lengthen through the Gothic vaults,
In hollow murmurs reach my ravished ear.
Nor when the lamps expiring yield to night,
And solitude returns, would I forsake
The solemn mansion, but attentive mark
The due clock swinging slow with sweepy sway,
Measuring time's flight with momentary sound.

THOMAS WARTON

From *The Spleen*

AN EPISTLE TO MR CUTHBERT JACKSON

First know, my friend, I do not mean
To write a treatise on the spleen;
Nor to prescribe when nerves convulse;
Nor mend th'alarum watch, your pulse.
If I am right, your question lay,
What course I take to drive away
The day-mare Spleen, by whose false pleas
Men prove mere suicides in ease;
And how I do myself demean
In stormy world to live serene.
    When by its magic lantern Spleen
With frightful figures spreads life's scene,
And threatening prospects urged my fears,
A stranger to the luck of heirs;
Reason, some quiet to restore,
Showed part was substance, shadow more;
With Spleen's dead weight though heavy grown,
In life's rough tide I sunk not down,
But swam, 'till Fortune threw a rope,
Buoyant on bladders filled with hope.
    I always choose the plainest food
To mend viscidity of blood.
Hail! water-gruel, healing power,

Of easy access to the poor;
Thy help love's confessors implore,
And doctors secretly adore;
To thee, I fly, by thee dilute –
Through veins my blood doth quicker shoot,
And by swift current throws off clean
Prolific particles of Spleen.

*

    To cure the mind's wrong bias, Spleen,
Some recommend the bowling-green;
Some, hilly walks; all, exercise;
Fling but a stone, the giant dies;
Laugh and be well. Monkeys have been
Extreme good doctors for the Spleen;
And kitten, if the humour hit,
Has harlequined away the fit.
    Since mirth is good in this behalf;
At some partic'lars let us laugh.
Witlings, brisk fools, cursed with half sense,
That stimulates their impotence;
Who buzz in rhyme, and, like blind flies,
Err with their wings for want of eyes.
Poor authors worshipping a calf,
Deep tragedies that make us laugh,
A strict dissenter saying grace,
A lecturer preaching for a place,
Folks, things prophetic to dispense,
Making the past the future tense,
The popish dubbing of a priest,
Fine epitaphs on knaves deceased,
Green-aproned Pythonissa's rage,
Great Æsculapius on his stage,
A miser starving to be rich,
The prior of Newgate's dying speech,
A jointured widow's ritual state,
Two Jews disrupting tête-à-tête,
New almanacs composed by seers,

Experiments on felons' ears,
Disdainful prudes, who ceaseless ply
The superb muscle of the eye,
A coquette's April-weather face,
A Queenborough mayor behind his mace,
And fops in military show,
Are sovereign for the case in view.

*

Sometimes I dress, with women sit,
And chat away the gloomy fit;
Quit the stiff garb of serious sense,
And wear a gay impertinence,
Nor think nor speak with any pains,
But lay on fancy's neck the reins;
Talk of unusual swell of waist
In maid of honour loosely laced,
And beauty borrowing Spanish red,
And loving pair with separate bed,
And jewels pawned for loss of game,
And then redeemed by loss of fame;
Of Kitty (aunt left in the lurch
By grave pretence to go to church)
Perceived in hack with lover fine,
Like Will and Mary on the coin:
And thus in modish manner we,
In aid of sugar, sweeten tea.

*

Forced by soft violence of prayer,
The blithesome goddess soothes my care,
I feel the deity inspire,
And thus she models my desire.
Two hundred pounds half-yearly paid,
Annuity securely made,
A farm some twenty miles from town,
Small, tight, salubrious, and my own;
Two maids, that never saw the town,

A serving-man, not quite a clown,
A boy to help to tread the mow,
And drive, while t'other holds the plough;
A chief, of temper formed to please,
Fit to converse, and keep the keys;
And better to preserve the peace,
Commissioned by the name of niece;
With understandings of a size
To think their master very wise.
May Heav'n (it's all I wish for) send
One genial room to treat a friend,
Where decent cupboard, little plate,
Display benevolence, not state.
And may my humble dwelling stand
Upon some chosen spot of land:
A pond before full to the brim,
Where cows may cool, and geese may swim;
Behind, a green like velvet neat,
Soft to the eye, and to the feet;
Where odorous plants in evening fair
Breathe all around ambrosial air;
From Eurus, foe to kitchen ground,
Fenced by a slope with bushes crowned,
Fit dwelling for the feathered throng,
Who pay their quit-rents with a song;
With opening views of hill and dale,
Which sense and fancy too regale,
Where the half-cirque, which vision bounds,
Like amphitheatre surrounds;
And woods impervious to the breeze,
Thick phalanx of embodied trees,
From hills through plains in dusk array
Extended far, repel the day.
Here stillness, height, and solemn shade
Invite, and contemplation aid:
Here nymphs from hollow oaks relate
The dark decrees and will of Fate,
And dreams beneath the spreading beech

Inspire, and docile fancy teach,
While soft as breezy breath of wind,
Impulses rustle through the mind,
Here dryads, scorning Phoebus' ray,
While Pan melodious pipes away,
In measured motions frisk about,
'Till old Silenus puts them out.
There see the clover, pea, and bean,
Vie in variety of green;
Fresh pastures speckled o'er with sheep,
Brown fields their fallow sabbaths keep,
Plump Ceres golden tresses wear,
And poppy topknots deck her hair,
And silver streams through meadows stray,
And naiads on the margin play,
And lesser nymphs on side of hills
From plaything urns pour down the rills.
　　Thus sheltered, free from care and strife,
May I enjoy a calm through life.

MATTHEW GREEN

From *The Grave*

The sickly taper
By glimmering through thy low-browed misty vaults,
(Furred round with mouldy damps, and ropy slime,)
Lets fall a supernumerary horror,
And only serves to make thy night more irksome.
Well do I know thee by thy trusty yew,
Cheerless, unsocial plant! that loves to dwell
'Midst skulls and coffins, epitaphs and worms:
Where light-heeled ghosts, and visionary shades,
Beneath the wan cold moon (as fame reports)
Embodied, thick, perform their mystic rounds.
No other merriment, dull tree! is thine.

And buried 'midst the wreck of things which were:
There lie interred the more illustrious dead.
The wind is up: hark! how it howls! Methinks
Till now, I never heard a sound so dreary:
Doors creak, and windows clap, and night's foul bird
Rooked in the spire screams loud: the gloomy aisles
Black-plastered, and hung round with shreds of 'scutcheons
And tattered coats of arms, send back the sound
Laden with heavier airs, from the low vaults
The mansions of the dead. Roused from their slumbers
In grim array the grizzly spectres rise,
Grin horrible, and obstinately sullen
Pass and repass, hushed as the foot of night.
Again! the screech-owl shrieks: ungracious sound!
I'll hear no more, it makes one's blood run chill.

ROBERT BLAIR

From *The Complaint:* or, *Night-Thoughts on Life, Death and Immortality*

The bell strikes *one:* we take no note of time,
But from its loss. To give it then a tongue,
Is wise in man. As if an angel spoke,
I feel the solemn sound. If heard aright,
It is the knell of my departed hours;
Where are they? With the years beyond the flood:
It is the signal that demands dispatch;
How much is to be done? My hopes and fears
Start up alarmed, and o'er life's narrow verge
Look down – on what? a fathomless abyss;
A dread eternity! how surely mine!
And can eternity belong to me,
Poor pensioner on the mercies of an hour?
How poor? how rich? how abject? how august?
How complicate? how wonderful is man?

How passing wonder He, who made him such?
Who centered in our make such strange extremes?
From different natures, marvelously mixed,
Connection exquisite of distant worlds!
Distinguished link in being's endless chain!
Midway from nothing to the Deity!
A beam ethereal sullied, and absorbed!
Though sullied, and dishonoured, still divine!
Dim miniature of greatness absolute!
An heir of glory! a frail child of dust!
Helpless immortal! Insect infinite!
A worm! a god! I tremble at myself,
And in myself am lost! at home a stranger,
Thought wanders up and down, surprised, amazed,
And wondering at her own: how reason reels?
O what a miracle to man is man,
Triumphantly distressed? what joy, what dread?
Alternately transported, and alarmed!
What can preserve my life? or what destroy?
An angel's arm can't snatch me from the grave;
Legions of angels can't confine me there.

EDWARD YOUNG

The Day of Judgment

AN ODE

ATTEMPTED IN ENGLISH SAPPHIC

When the fierce north wind with his airy forces
Rears up the Baltic to a foaming fury;
And the red lightning with a storm of hail comes
    Rushing amain down,

How the poor sailors stand amazed and tremble!
While the hoarse thunder like a bloody trumpet
Roars a loud onset to the gaping waters
    Quick to devour them.

Such shall the noise be, and the wild disorder,
(If things eternal may be like these earthly)
Such the dire terror when the great archangel
                       Shakes the creation;

Tears the strong pillars of the vault of heaven,
Breaks up old marble, the repose of princes;
See the graves open, and the bones arising,
                       Flames all around 'em.

Hark the shrill outcries of the guilty wretches!
Lively bright horror and amazing anguish
Stare through their eye-lids, while the living worm lies
                       Gnawing within them.

Thoughts like old vultures prey upon their heartstrings,
And the smart twinges, when their eye beholds the
Lofty judge frowning, and the flood of vengeance
                       Rolling afore him.

Hopeless immortals! how they scream and shiver
While devils push them to the pit wide yawning
Hideous and gloomy, to receive them headlong
                       Down to the centre.

Stop here my fancy: (all away ye horrid
Doleful ideas) come arise to Jesus,
How he sits god-like! and the saints around him
                       Throned, yet adoring!

O may I sit there when he comes triumphant
Dooming the nations: then ascend to glory,
While our Hosannahs all along the passage
                       Shout the Redeemer.

ISAAC WATTS

From *Jubilate Agno*

For I prophesy that they will understand the blessing and
virtue of the rain.

For rain is exceedingly good for the human body.

For it is good therefore to have flat roofs to the houses, as of
old.

For it is good to let the rain come upon the naked body unto
purity and refreshment.

For I prophesy that they will respect decency in all points.

For they will do it in conceit, word, and motion.

For they will go forth afield.

For the Devil can work upon stagnating filth to a very great
degree.

For I prophesy that we shall have our horns again.

For in the day of David Man as yet had a glorious horn upon
his forehead.

For this horn was a bright substance in colour and consistence
as the nail of the hand.

For it was broad, thick and strong so as to serve for defence
as well as ornament.

For it brightened to the Glory of God, which came upon the
human face at morning prayer.

For it was largest and brightest in the best men.

For it was taken away all at once from all of them.

For this was done in the divine contempt of a general
pusillanimity.

For this happened in a season after their return from the
Babylonish captivity.

For their spirits were broke and their manhood impaired by
foreign vices for exaction.

For I prophesy that the English will recover their horns the
first.

For I prophesy that all the nations in the world will do the
like in turn.

For I prophesy that all Englishmen will wear their beards
again.

For a beard is a good step to a horn.

For when men get their horns again, they will delight to go uncovered.

For it is not good to wear any thing upon the head.

For a man should put no obstacle between his head and the blessing of Almighty God.

For a hat was an abomination of the heathen. Lord have mercy upon the Quakers.

For the ceiling of the house is an obstacle and therefore we pray on the house-top.

For the head will be liable to less disorders on the recovery of its horn.

For the horn on the forehead is a tower upon an arch.

For it is a strong munition against the adversary, who is sickness and Death.

For it is instrumental in subjecting the woman.

For the insolence of the woman has increased ever since Man has been crestfallen.

For they have turned the horn into scoff and derision without ceasing.

For we are amerced of God, who has his horn.

For we are amerced of the blessed angels, who have their horns.

For when they get their horns again they will put them upon the altar.

For they give great occasion for mirth and music.

For our Blessed Saviour had not his horn upon the face of the earth.

For this was in meekness and condescension to the infirmities of human nature at that time.

For at his second coming his horn will be exalted in glory.

For his horn is the horn of Salvation.

CHRISTOPHER SMART

The Fakir

A fakir (a religious well known in the East,
Not much like a parson, still less like a priest)
With no canting, no sly Jesuitical arts,
Field-preaching, hypocrisy, learning or parts;
By a happy refinement in mortification,
Grew the oracle, saint, and the pope of his nation.
But what did he do this esteem to acquire?
Did he torture his head or his bosom with fire?
Was his neck in a portable pillory cased?
Did he fasten a chain to his leg or his waist?
No. His holiness rose to this sovereign pitch
By the merit of running long nails in his breech.
  A wealthy young Indian, approaching the shrine,
Thus in banter accosts the prophetic divine:
'This tribute accept for your interest with Fo,
Whom with torture you serve, and whose will you must
    know;
To your suppliant disclose his immortal decree;
Tell me which of the Heavens is allotted for me.'

FAKIR

Let me first know your merits.

INDIAN

                    I strive to be just:
To be true to my friend, to my wife, to my trust:
In religion I duly observe every form:
With a heart to my country devoted and warm:
I give to the poor, and I lend to the rich ...

FAKIR

But how many nails do you run in your breech?

INDIAN

With submission I speak to your reverence's tail;
But mine has no taste for a tenpenny nail.

FAKIR

Well! I'll pray to our prophet and get you preferred;
Though no farther expect than to Heaven the third.
With me in the thirtieth your seat to obtain,
You must qualify duly with hunger and pain.

INDIAN

With you in the thirtieth! You impudent rogue!
Can such wretches as you give to madness a vogue!
Though the priesthood of Fo on the vulgar impose,
By squinting whole years at the end of their nose;
Though with cruel devices of mortification
They adore a vain idol of modern creation;
Does the God of the Heavens such a service direct?
Can his mercy approve a self-punishing sect?
Will his wisdom be worshipped with chains and with nails?
Or e'er look for his rites in your noses and tails?
Come along to my house and these penances leave,
Give your belly a feast, and your breech a reprieve.

This reasoning unhinged each fanatical notion;
And staggered our saint, in his chair of promotion.
At length with reluctance he rose from his seat:
And resigning his nails and his fame for retreat;
Two weeks his new life he admired and enjoyed:
The third he with plenty and quiet was cloyed.
To live undistinguished to him was the pain,
An existence unnoticed he could not sustain.
In retirement he sighed for the fame-giving chair;
For the crowd to admire him, to reverence and stare:
No endearments of pleasure and ease could prevail:
He the saintship resumed, and new larded his tail.

Our Fakir represents all the votaries of fame:
Their ideas, their means, and their end is the same;
The sportsman, the buck; all the heroes of vice,
With their gallantry, lewdness, the bottle and dice;
The poets, the critics, the metaphysicians,
The courtier, the patriot, all politicians;

The statesman begirt with th'importunate ring,
(I had almost completed my list with the king)
All labour alike to illustrate my tale;
All tortured by choice with th'invisible nail.

RICHARD OWEN CAMBRIDGE

The Seeker

When I first came to London, I rambled about
From sermon to sermon, took a slice and went out.
Then on me, in divinity bachelor, tried
Many priests to obtrude a Levitical bride;
And urging their various opinions, intended
To make me wed systems, which they recommended.

Said a lecherous old friar skulking near Lincoln's Inn,
(Whose trade's to absolve, but whose pastime's to sin;
Who, spider-like, seizes weak protestant flies,
Which hung in his sophistry cobweb he spies;)
'Ah! pity your soul; for without our church pale,
If you happen to die, to be damned you can't fail;
The Bible, you boast, is a wild revelation:
Hear a church that can't err if you hope for salvation.'

Said a formal non-con, (whose rich stock of grace
Lies forward exposed in shop-window of face,)
'Ah! pity your soul: come, be of our sect:
For then you are safe, and may plead you're elect.
As it stands in the Acts, we can prove ourselves saints,
Being Christ's little flock every where spoke against.'

Said a jolly church parson, (devoted to ease,
While penal law dragons guard his golden fleece,)
'If you pity your soul, I pray listen to neither;
The first is in error, the last a deceiver:
That ours is the true church, the sense of our tribe is,
And surely *in medio tutissimus ibis*.'

Said a yea and nay friend with a stiff hat and band,

(Who while he talked gravely would hold forth his hand,)
'Dominion and wealth are the aim of all three,
Though about ways and means they may all disagree;
Then prithee be wise, go the Quakers by-way'
'Tis plain, without turnpikes, so nothing to pay.'

MATTHEW GREEN

The Methodist

MAY 1770

Says Tom to Jack, ''Tis very odd,
These representatives of God,
In colour, way of life and evil,
Should be so very like the Devil.'
Jack, understand, was one of those,
Who mould religion in the nose,
A red hot Methodist; his face
Was full of puritanic grace,
His loose lank hair, his low gradation,
Declared a late regeneration;
Among the daughters long renowned,
For standing upon holy ground;
Never in carnal battle beat,
Though sometimes forced to a retreat.
But C—t, hero as he is,
Knight of incomparable phiz,
When pliant doxy seems to yield,
Courageously forsakes the field.
Jack, or to write more gravely, John,
Through hills of Wesley's works had gone;
Could sing one hundred hymns by rote;
Hymns which will sanctify the throat:
But some indeed composed so oddly,
You'd swear 'twas bawdy songs made godly.

THOMAS CHATTERTON

On Bishop Burnet's Being Set on Fire
in His Closet

From that dire era, bane to Sarum's pride,
Which broke his schemes, and laid his friends aside,
He talks and writes that Popery will return,
And we, and he, and all his works will burn.
What touched himself was almost fairly proved:
(Oh, far from Britain be the rest removed!)
For, as of late he meant to bless the age,
With flagrant prefaces of party-rage,
O'er-wrought with passion, and the subject's weight,
Lolling, he nodded in his elbow-seat;
Down fell the candle; grease and zeal conspire,
Heat meets with heat, and pamphlets burn their sire.
Here crawls a Preface on its half-burned maggots,
And there an Introduction brings its faggots:
Then roars the Prophet of the Northern Nation,
Scorched by a flaming speech on moderation.

Unwarned by this, go on, the realm to fright,
Thou Briton vaunting in thy second-sight!
In such a ministry you safely tell,
How much you'd suffer, if religion fell.

THOMAS PARNELL

From *Britannia*

Patriotism

And what, my thoughtless sons, should fire you more,
Than when your well-earned empire of the deep
The least beginning injury receives?
What better cause can call your lightning forth?
Your thunder wake? Your dearest life demand?

What better cause, than when your country sees
The sly destruction at her vitals aimed?
For oh it much imports you, 'tis your all,
To keep your trade entire, entire the force
And honour of your fleets; o'er that to watch,
Even with a hand severe, and jealous eye.
In intercourse be gentle, generous, just,
By wisdom polished, and of manners fair;
But on the sea be terrible, untamed,
Unconquerable still: let none escape,
Who shall but aim to touch your glory there.
Is there the man, into the lion's den
Who dares intrude, to snatch his young away?
And is a Briton seized? and seized beneath
The slumbering terrors of a British fleet?
Then ardent rise! Oh great in vengeance rise!
O'erturn the proud, teach rapine to restore:
And as you ride sublimely round the world,
Make every vessel stoop, make every state
At once their welfare and their duty know.

JAMES THOMSON

Ode XIII

Against War

I hate that drum's discordant sound,
Parading round, and round, and round:
To thoughtless youth it pleasure yields,
And lures from cities and from fields,
To sell their liberty for charms
Of tawdry lace and glittering arms;
And when Ambition's voice commands,
To march, and fight, and fall, in foreign lands.

I hate that drum's discordant sound,
Parading round, and round, and round:

To me it talks of ravaged plains,
And burning towns, and ruined swains,
And mangled limbs, and dying groans,
And widows' tears, and orphans' moans;
And all that Misery's hand bestows,
To fill the catalogue of human woes.

JOHN SCOTT

From *On the Prospect of Peace*

Ah! curst Ambition, to thy lures we owe
All the great ills, that mortals bear below.
Cursed by the hind, when to the spoil he yields
His year's whole sweat, and vainly ripened fields;
Cursed by the maid, torn from her lover's side,
When left a widow, though not yet a bride;
By mothers cursed, when floods of tears they shed,
And scatter useless roses on the dead.
Oh, sacred Bristol! then, what dangers prove
The arts, thou smil'st on with paternal love?
Then, mixed with rubbish by the brutal foes,
In vain the marble breathes, the canvas glows;
To shades obscure the glittering sword pursues
The gentle poet, and defenceless Muse.
A voice like thine, alone, might then assuage
The warrior's fury, and control his rage;
To hear thee speak, might the fierce Vandal stand,
And fling the brandished sabre from his hand.

Far hence be driven to Scythia's stormy shore
The drum's harsh music, and the cannon's roar;
Let grim Bellona haunt the lawless plain,
Where Tartar clans and grizzly Cossacks reign;
Let the steeled Turk be deaf to matrons' cries,
See virgins ravished with relentless eyes,
To death grey heads and smiling infants doom,

Nor spare the promise of the pregnant womb,
O'er wasted kingdoms spread his wide command,
The savage lord of an unpeopled land.
  Her guiltless glory just Britannia draws
From pure religion, and impartial laws,
To Europe's wounds a mother's aid she brings,
And holds in equal scales the rival kings:
Her generous sons in choicest gifts abound,
Alike in arms, alike in arts renowned.

THOMAS TICKELL

Verses Written at Montauban in France, 1750

Papal Tyranny

Tarn, how delightful wind thy willowed waves,
But ah! they fructify a land of slaves!
In vain thy barefoot, sunburnt peasants hide
With luscious grapes yon hill's romantic side;
No cups nectareous shall their toil repay,
The priest's, the soldier's, and the fermier's prey;
Vain glows this sun, in cloudless glory dressed,
That strikes fresh vigour through the pining breast;
Give me, beneath a colder, changeful sky,
My soul's best, only pleasure, Liberty!
What millions perished near thy mournful flood
When the red papal tyrant cried out – 'Blood!'
Less fierce the Saracen, and quivered Moor,
That dashed thy infants 'gainst the stones of yore.
Be warned, ye nations round; and trembling see
Dire superstition quench humanity!
By all the chiefs in freedom's battles lost,
By wise and virtuous Alfred's awful ghost;
By old Galgacus' scythed, iron car,
That, swiftly whirling through the walks of war,
Dashed Roman blood, and crushed the foreign throngs;

By holy Druids' courage-breathing songs;
By fierce Bonduca's shield and foaming steeds;
By the bold Peers that met on Thames's meads;
By the fifth Henry's helm and lightning spear;
O Liberty, my warm petition hear;
Be Albion still thy joy! with her remain,
Long as the surge shall lash her oak-crowned plain!

JOSEPH WARTON

Revenge of America

When fierce Pizarro's legions flew
O'er ravaged fields of rich Peru,
Struck with his bleeding people's woes,
Old India's awful Genius rose.
He sat on Andes' topmost stone,
And heard a thousand nations groan;
For grief his feathery crown he tore,
To see huge Plata foam with gore;
He broke his arrows, stamped the ground,
To view his cities smoking round.
    'What woes,' he cried, 'hath lust of gold
O'er my poor country widely rolled;
Plunderers proceed! my bowels tear,
But ye shall meet destruction there;
From the deep-vaulted mine shall rise
Th'insatiate fiend, pale Avarice!
Whose steps shall trembling Justice fly,
Peace, Order, Law, and Amity!
I see all Europe's children cursed
With lucre's universal thirst:
The rage that sweeps my sons away,
My baneful gold shall well repay.'

JOSEPH WARTON

On the Tack

The globe of th'earth on which we dwell
    Is tacked unto the poles:
The little worlds our carcases
    Are tacked unto our souls:
The parson's chiefest business is
    To tack the soul to heaven:
The doctor's is to keep the tack
    'Tween soul and body even.
The priest besides by office tacks,
    The husband to the wife;
And that's a tack (God help them both)
    That always holds for life.
The lawyer studies how to tack
    His client to the laws:
Th'attorney tacks whole quires and reams
    To lengthen out the cause.
The Commons, Lords and English Crown
    Are all three tacked together,
And if they e'er chance to untack
    No good can come to either.
The Crown is tacked unto the Church,
    The Church unto the Crown,
The Whigs are slightly tacked to both,
    And so may soon come down.
Since all the world's a general tack
    Of one thing to another,
Why then about one honest tack
    Do fools make such a pother?

THOMAS HEARNE

Written for My Son, and Spoken by Him at His
First Putting on Breeches

What is it our mammas bewitches,
To plague us little boys with breeches?
To tyrant Custom we must yield
Whilst vanquished Reason flies the field.
Our legs must suffer by ligation,
To keep the blood from circulation;
And then our feet, though young and tender,
We to the shoemaker surrender;
Who often makes our shoes so strait
Our growing feet they cramp and fret;
Whilst, with contrivance most profound,
Across our insteps we are bound;
Which is the cause, I make no doubt,
Why thousands suffer in the gout.
Our wiser ancestors wore brogues,
Before the surgeons bribed these rogues,
With narrow toes, and heels like pegs,
To help to make us break our legs.

Then, ere we know to use our fists,
Our mothers closely bind our wrists;
And never think our clothes are neat,
Till they're so tight we cannot eat.
And, to increase our other pains,
The hat-band helps to cramp our brains.
The cravat finishes the work,
Like bowstring sent from the Grand Turk.

Thus dress, that should prolong our date,
Is made to hasten on our fate.
Fair privilege of nobler natures,
To be more plagued than other creatures!
The wild inhabitants of air

Are clothed by Heaven with wondrous care:
Their beauteous, well-compacted feathers
Are coats of mail against all weathers;
Enamelled, to delight the eye;
Gay, as the bow that decks the sky.
The beasts are clothed with beauteous skins:
The fishes armed with scales and fins;
Whose lustre lends the sailor light,
When all the stars are hid in night.

O were our dress contrived like these,
For use, for ornament, and ease!
Man only seems to sorrow born,
Naked, defenceless, and forlorn.

Yet we have Reason, to supply
What Nature did to man deny:
Weak viceroy! Who thy power will own,
When Custom has usurped thy throne?
In vain did I appeal to thee,
Ere I would wear his livery;
Who, in defiance to thy rules,
Delights to make us act like fools.
O'er human race the tyrant reigns,
And binds them in eternal chains.
We yield to his despotic sway,
The only monarch all obey.

MARY BARBER

7

'In all, let Nature never be forgot.'

From *The Enthusiast:* or *the Lover of Nature*

Ye green-robed dryads, oft at dusky eve
By wondering shepherds seen, to forests brown,
To unfrequented meads, and pathless wilds,
Lead me from gardens decked with art's vain pomps.
Can gilt alcoves, can marble-mimic gods,
Parterres embroidered, obelisk, and urns,
Of high relief; can the long, spreading lake,
Or vista lessening to the sight; can Stow,
With all her Attic fanes, such raptures raise,
As the thrush-haunted copse, where lightly leaps
The fearful fawn the rustling leaves along,
And the brisk squirrel sports from bough to bough,
While from an hollow oak, whose naked roots
O'erhang a pensive rill, the busy bees
Hum drowsy lullabies?

JOSEPH WARTON

A Thought in a Garden

WRITTEN IN THE YEAR 1704

Delightful mansion! blest retreat!
Where all is silent, all is sweet!
Here Contemplation prunes her wings,
The raptured Muse more tuneful sings,
While May leads on the cheerful hours,
And opens a new world of flowers.
Gay Pleasure here all dresses wears,
And in a thousand shapes appears.
Pursued by Fancy, how she roves
Through airy walks, and museful groves;
Springs in each plant and blossomed tree,

And charms in all I hear and see!
In this elysium while I stray,
And Nature's fairest face survey,
Earth seems new-born, and life more bright;
Time steals away, and smooths his flight;
And Thought's bewildered in delight.
Where are the crowds I saw of late?
What are those tales of Europe's fate?
Of Anjou, and the Spanish crown;
And leagues to pull usurpers down?
Of marching armies, distant wars;
Of factions, and domestic jars?
Sure these are last night's dreams, no more;
Or some romance, read lately o'er;
Like Homer's antique tale of Troy,
And powers confederate to destroy
Priam's proud house, the Dardan name,
With him that stole the ravished dame,
And, to possess another's right,
Durst the whole world to arms excite.
Come, gentle Sleep, my eyelids close,
These dull impressions help me lose:
Let Fancy take her wing, and find
Some better dreams to soothe my mind;
Or waking let me learn to live;
The prospect will instruction give.
For see, where beauteous Thames does glide
Serene, but with a fruitful tide;
Free from extremes of ebb and flow,
Not swelled too high, nor sunk too low:
Such let my life's smooth current be,
Till from Time's narrow shore set free,
It mingle with th'eternal sea;
And, there enlarged, shall be no more
That trifling thing it was before.

JOHN HUGHES

A Nocturnal Rêverie

In such a night, when every louder wind
Is to its distant cavern safe confined;
And only gentle zephyr fans his wings,
And lonely Philomel, still waking, sings;
Or from some tree, famed for the owl's delight,
She, hollowing clear, directs the wanderer right:
In such a night, when passing clouds give place,
Or thinly veil the heaven's mysterious face;
When in some river, overhung with green,
The waving moon and trembling leaves are seen;
When freshened grass now bears itself upright,
And makes cool banks to pleasing rest invite,
Whence springs the woodbind, and the bramble-rose,
And where the sleepy cowslip sheltered grows;
Whilst now a paler hue the foxglove takes,
Yet chequers still with red the dusky brakes:
When scattered glow-worms, but in twilight fine,
Show trivial beauties watch their hour to shine;
Whilst Salisbury stands the test of every light,
In perfect charms, and perfect virtue bright:
When odours, which declined repelling day,
Through temperate air uninterrupted stray;
When darkened groves their softest shadows wear,
And falling waters we distinctly hear;
When through the gloom more venerable shows
Some ancient fabric, awful in repose,
While sunburnt hills their swarthy looks conceal,
And swelling haycocks thicken up the vale:
When the loosed horse now, as his pasture leads,
Comes slowly grazing through the adjoining meads,
Whose stealing pace, and lengthened shade we fear,
Till torn up forage in his teeth we hear:
When nibbling sheep at large pursue their food,
And unmolested kine rechew the cud;
When curlews cry beneath the village-walls,

And to her straggling brood the partridge calls;
Their short-lived jubilee the creatures keep,
Which but endures, whilst tyrant-man does sleep:
When a sedate content the spirit feels,
And no fierce light disturbs, whilst it reveals;
But silent musings urge the mind to seek
Something, too high for syllables to speak;
Till the free soul to a composedness charmed,
Finding the elements of rage disarmed,
Over all below a solemn quiet grown,
Joys in the inferior world and thinks it like her own:
In such a night let me abroad remain,
Till morning breaks, and all's confused again;
Our cares, our toils, our clamours are renewed,
Or pleasures, seldom reached, again pursued.

ANNE, COUNTESS OF WINCHILSEA

From *Windsor Forest*

Here hills and vales, the woodland and the plain,
Here earth and water seem to strive again,
Not chaos-like together crushed and bruised,
But, as the world, harmoniously confused:
Where order in variety we see,
And where, though all things differ, all agree.
Here waving groves a chequered scene display,
And part admit, and part exclude the day;
As some coy nymph her lover's warm address
Not quite indulges, nor can quite repress.
There, interspersed in lawns and opening glades,
Thin trees arise that shun each other's shades.
Here in full light the russet plains extend:
There, wrapped in clouds the bluish hills ascend.
Even the wild heath displays her purple dyes,
And 'midst the desert fruitful fields arise,
That crowned with tufted trees and springing corn,

Like verdant isles the sable waste adorn.
Let India boast her plants, nor envy we
The weeping amber or the balmy tree,
While by our oaks the precious loads are borne,
And realms commanded which those trees adorn.
Not proud Olympus yields a nobler sight,
Though gods assembled grace his towering height,
Than what more humble mountains offer here,
Where, in their blessings, all those gods appear.
See Pan with flocks, with fruits Pomona crowned,
Here blushing Flora paints th'enamelled ground,
Here Ceres' gifts in waving prospect stand,
And nodding tempt the joyful reaper's hand;
Rich Industry sits smiling on the plains,
And peace and plenty tell, a STUART reigns.

*

Hunting and Fishing

See! from the brake the whirring pheasant springs,
And mounts exulting on triumphant wings:
Short is his joy; he feels the fiery wound,
Flutters in blood, and panting beats the ground,
Ah! what avail his glossy, varying dyes,
His purple crest, and scarlet-circled eyes,
The vivid green his shining plumes unfold,
His painted wings, and breast that flames with gold?
  Nor yet, when moist Arcturus clouds the sky,
The woods and fields their pleasing toils deny.
To plains with well-breathed beagles we repair,
And trace the mazes of the circling hare:
(Beasts, urged by us, their fellow-beasts pursue,
And learn of man each other to undo).
With slaughtering guns th'unwearied fowler roves,
When frosts have whitened all the naked groves;
Where doves in flocks the leafless trees o'ershade,
And lonely woodcocks haunt the watery glade.
He lifts the tube, and levels with his eye;

Straight a short thunder breaks the frozen sky.
Oft, as in airy rings they skim the heath,
The clamorous lapwings feel the leaden death:
Oft, as the mounting larks their notes prepare,
They fall, and leave their little lives in air.

In genial spring, beneath the quivering shade,
Where cooling vapours breathe along the mead,
The patient fisher takes his silent stand,
Intent, his angle trembling in his hand;
With looks unmoved, he hopes the scaly breed,
And eyes the dancing cork, and bending reed.
Our plenteous streams a various race supply,
The bright-eyed perch with fins of Tyrian dye,
The silver eel, in shining volumes rolled,
The yellow carp, in scales bedropped with gold,
Swift trouts, diversified with crimson stains,
And pikes, the tyrants of the watery plains.

*

Progress

The time shall come, when free as seas or wind
Unbounded Thames shall flow for all mankind,
Whole nations enter with each swelling tide,
And seas but join the regions they divide;
Earth's distant ends our glory shall behold,
And the new world launch forth to seek the old.
Then ships of uncouth form shall stem the tide,
And feathered people crowd my wealthy side,
And naked youths and painted chiefs admire
Our speech, our colour, and our strange attire!
O stretch thy reign, fair Peace! from shore to shore,
Till conquest cease, and slavery be no more;
Till the freed Indians in their native groves
Reap their own fruits, and woo their sable loves,
Peru once more a race of kings behold,
And other Mexicos be roofed with gold.

ALEXANDER POPE

From *Universal Beauty*

While ocean thus the latent store bequeaths,
Above its humid exhalation breathes;
Its bosom pants beneath the vigorous heat,
And eager beams th'expanding surface beat;
Insinuating, form the lucid cell;
To bladders the circumfluous moisture swell;
Th'inflated vapours spurn the nether tide,
And mounted on the weightier ether ride:
As though in scorn of gravitating power,
Sublime the cloudy congregations tower;
O'er torrid climes collect their sable train,
And form umbrellas for the panting swain;
Or figured wanton in romantic mould,
Careering knights and airy ramparts hold,
(Emblazoning beams the flitting champions gild,
And various paint the visionary field);
Sudden the loose enchanged squadrons fly,
And sweep delusion from the wondering eye;
Thence on the floating atmosphere they sail,
And steer precarious with the varying gale;
Or hovering, with suspended wing delay,
And in disdain the kindred flood survey:
When lo! the afflicting ether checks their pride,
Compressing chills the vain dilated tide;
Their shivering essence to its centre shrinks,
And a cold nuptual their coherence links;
With artful touch the curious meteor forms,
Parent prolific of salubrious storms;
When from on high the rapid tempest's hurled,
Enlivening as a sneeze to man's inferior world.

HENRY BROOKE

Ode to Evening

If ought of oaten stop, or pastoral song,
May hope, chaste Eve, to soothe thy modest ear,
   Like thy own solemn springs,
   Thy springs, and dying gales,
O nymph reserved, while now the bright-haired sun
Sits in yon western tent, whose cloudy skirts,
   With brede ethereal wove,
   O'erhang his wavy bed:
Now air is hushed, save where the weak-eyed bat,
With short shrill shriek flits by on leathern wing,
   Or where the beetle winds
   His small but sullen horn,
As oft he rises 'midst the twilight path,
Against the pilgrim borne in heedless hum:
   Now teach me, maid composed,
   To breathe some softened strain,
Whose numbers stealing through thy darkening vale,
May not unseemly with its stillness suit,
   As musing slow, I hail
   Thy genial loved return!
For when thy folding star arising shows
His paly circlet, at his warning lamp
   The fragrant hours, and elves
   Who slept in flowers the day,
And many a nymph who wreaths her brows with sedge,
And sheds the freshening dew, and lovelier still,
   The pensive pleasures sweet
   Prepare thy shadowy car.
Then lead, calm votaress, where some sheety lake
Cheers the lone heath, or some time-hallowed pile,
   Or upland fallows grey
   Reflect its last cool gleam.
But when chill blustering winds, or driving rain,
Forbid my willing feet, be mine the hut,
   That from the mountain's side,

Views wilds, and swelling floods,
And hamlets brown, and dim-discovered spires,
And hears their simple bell, and marks o'er all
    Thy dewy fingers draw
    The gradual dusky veil.
While spring shall pour his showers, as oft he wont,
And bathe thy breathing tresses, meekest Eve!
    While summer loves to sport
    Beneath thy lingering light;
While sallow autumn fills thy lap with leaves;
Or winter yelling through the troublous air,
    Affrights thy shrinking train,
    And rudely rends thy robes;
So long, sure-found beneath the sylvan shed,
Shall fancy, friendship, science, rose-lipped health,
    Thy gentlest influence own,
    And hymn thy favourite name!

WILLIAM COLLINS

From *An Invocation to Melancholy*

    Child of the potent spell and nimble eye,
Young Fancy, oft in rainbow vest arrayed,
Points to new scenes that in succession pass
Across the wondrous mirror that she bears,
And bids thy unsated soul and wandering eye
A wider range over all her prospects take:
Lo, at her call, New Zealand's wastes arise!
Casting their shadows far along the main,
Whose brows cloud-capped in joyless majesty,
No human foot hath trod since time began;
Here death-like silence ever-brooding dwells,
Save when the watching sailor startled hears,
Far from his native land at darksome night,
The shrill-toned petrel, or the penguin's voice,

That skim their trackless flight on lonely wing,
Through the bleak regions of a nameless main:
Here danger stalks and drinks with glutted ear
The wearied sailor's moan, and fruitless sigh,
Who, as he slowly cuts his daring way,
Affrighted drops his axe, and stops awhile,
To hear the jarring echoes' lengthened din,
That fling from pathless cliffs their sullen sound;
Oft here the fiend his grisly visage shows,
His limbs of giant form in vesture clad
Of drear collected ice and stiffened snow,
The same he wore a thousand years ago,
That thwarts the sun-beam and endures the day.

'Tis thus, by Fancy shown, thou kenn'st entranced
Lone tangled woods, and ever stagnant lakes,
That know no zephyr pure or temperate gale,
By baleful Tigris' banks, where, oft they say,
As late in sullen march for prey he prowls,
The tawny lion sees his shadowed form,
At silent midnight by the moon's pale gleam,
On the broad surface of the dark deep wave;
Here parched at mid-day oft the passenger
Invokes with lingering hope the tardy breeze,
And oft with silent anguish thinks in vain
On Europe's milder air and silver springs.

HENRY HEADLEY

From *The Seasons*

A Winter Tragedy

As thus the snows arise; and foul, and fierce,
All winter drives along the darkened air;
In his own loose-revolving fields, the swain
Disastered stands; sees other hills ascend,

Of unknown joyless brow; and other scenes,
Of horrid prospect, shag the trackless plain:
Nor finds the river, nor the forest, hid
Beneath the formless wild; but wanders on
From hill to dale, still more and more astray;
Impatient flouncing through the drifted heaps,
Stung with the thoughts of home; the thoughts of home
Rush on his nerves, and call their vigour forth
In many a vain attempt. How sinks his soul!
What black despair, what horror fills his heart!
When for the dusky spot, which fancy feigned
His tufted cottage rising through the snow,
He meets the roughness of the middle waste,
Far from the track, and blest abode of man;
While round him night resistless closes fast,
And every tempest, howling o'er his head,
Renders the savage wilderness more wild.
Then throng the busy shapes into his mind,
Of covered pits, unfathomably deep,
A dire descent! beyond the power of frost,
Of faithless bogs; of precipices huge,
Smoothed up with snow; and, what is land unknown,
What water, of the still unfrozen spring,
In the loose marsh or solitary lake,
Where the fresh fountain from the bottom boils.
These check his fearful steps; and down he sinks
Beneath the shelter of the shapeless drift,
Thinking o'er all the bitterness of death,
Mixed with the tender anguish nature shoots
Through the wrung bosom of the dying man,
His wife, his children, and his friends unseen.
In vain for him the officious wife prepares
The fire fair-blazing, and the vestment warm;
In vain his little children, peeping out
Into the mingling storm, demand their sire,
With tears of artless innocence. Alas!
Nor wife, nor children, more shall he behold,
Nor friends, nor sacred home. On every nerve

The deadly winter seizes; shuts up sense;
And, o'er his inmost vitals creeping cold,
Lays him along the snows, a stiffened corpse,
Stretched out, and bleaching in the northern blast.

JAMES THOMSON

From *The Call of Aristippus*

Elves and Fairies

Once when by Trent's pellucid streams,
In days of prattling infancy,
Led by young wondering ecstasy,
To view the sun's refulgent beams
As on the sportive waves they played
Too far I negligently strayed,
The god of day his lamp withdrew,
Evening her dusky mantle spread,
And from her moistened tresses shed
Refreshing drops of pearly dew.
Close by the borders of a wood,
Where an old ruined abbey stood,
Far from a fondling mother's sight,
With toil of childish sport oppressed
My tender limbs sunk down to rest
'Midst the dark horrors of the night.
As Horace erst by fabled doves
With spring's first leaves was mantled o'er
A wanderer from his native groves,
A like regard the British loves
To me their future poet bore,
Nor left me guardianless alone,
For though no nymph or faun appeared,
Nor piping satyr was there heard,
And here the dryads are unknown;
Yet, natives true of English ground,

Sweet elves and fays in mantles green,
By shepherds oft in moonlight seen,
And dapper fairies danced around.
The nightingale, her love-lorn lay
Neglecting on the neighbouring spray,
Strewed with fresh flowers my turfy bed,
And, at the first approach of morn,
The red-breast stripped the fragrant thorn
On roses wild to lay my head.
Thus, as the wondering rustics say,
In smiling sleep they found me laid
Beneath a blossomed hawthorn's shade,
Whilst sportive bees, in mystic play,
With honey filled my little lips
Blent with each sweet that zephyr sips
From flowery cups in balmy May.

JOHN GILBERT COOPER

From *Oppian's Halieutics*

The Sex-life of Fish

Strange the formation of the eely race,
That know no sex, yet love the close embrace.
Their folded lengths they round each other twine,
Twist amorous knots, and slimy bodies join;
Till the close strife brings off a frothy juice,
The seed that must the wriggling kind produce.
Regardless they their future offspring leave,
But porous sands the spumy drops receive.
That genial bed impregnates all the heap,
And little eelets soon begin to creep.
Half-fish, half-slime they try their doubtful strength,
And slowly trail along their wormy length.

*

Justly might female tortoises complain,
To whom enjoyment is the greatest pain,
They dread the trial, and foreboding hate
The growing passion of the cruel mate.
He amorous pursues, they conscious fly
Joyless caresses, and resolved deny.
Since partial Heaven has thus restrained the bliss,
The males they welcome with a closer kiss,
Bite angry, and reluctant hate declare.
The tortoise-courtship is a state of war.
Eager they fight, but with unlike design,
Males to obtain, and females to decline.
The conflict lasts, till these by strength o'ercome
All sorrowing yield to the resistless doom.
Not like a bride, but pensive captive, led
To the loathed duties of an hated bed.
The seal, and tortoise copulate behind
Like earth-bred dogs, and are not soon disjoined;
But secret ties the passive couple bind.

*

The lamprey, glowing with uncommon fires,
The earth-bred serpent's purfled curls admires.
He no less kind makes amorous returns,
With equal love the grateful serpent burns.
Fixed on the joy he bounding shoots along,
Erects his azure crest, and darts his forky tongue.
Now his red eyeballs glow with doubled fires;
Proudly he mounts upon his folded spires,
Displays his glossy coat, and speckled side,
And meets in all his charms the watery bride.
But lest he cautless might his consort harm,
The gentle lover will himself disarm,
Spit out the venomed mass, and careful hide
In crannied rocks, far from the washing tide;
There leaves the furies of his noxious teeth,
And putrid bags, the poisonous fund of death.
His mate he calls with softly hissing sounds;

She joyful hears, and from the ocean bounds.
Swift as the bearded arrow's haste she flies,
To her own love, and meet the serpent's joys.
At her approach, no more the lover bears
Odious delay, nor sounding waters fears.
Onward he moves on shining volumes rolled,
The foam all burning seems with wavy gold.
At length with equal haste the lovers meet,
And strange enjoyments slake their mutual heat.
She with wide-gaping mouth the spouse invites,
Sucks in his head, and feels unknown delights.
When full fruition has assuaged desire,
Well-pleased the bride will to her home retire.

WILLIAM DIAPER

From *The Botanic Garden*

Descend, ye hovering sylphs! aerial choirs,
And sweep with little hands your silver lyres;
With fairy footsteps print your grassy rings,
Ye gnomes! accordant to the tinkling strings:
While in soft notes I tune to oaten reed
Gay hopes, and amorous sorrows of the mead.
From giant oaks, that wave their branches dark,
To the dwarf moss that clings upon their bark,
What beaux and beauties crowd the gaudy groves,
And woo and win their vegetable loves.
How snowdrops cold, and blue-eyed harebells blend
Their tender tears, as o'er the stream they bend;
The lovesick violet, and the primrose pale,
Bow their sweet heads, and whisper to the gale;
With secret sighs the virgin lily droops,
And jealous cowslips hang their tawny cups.
How the young rose in beauty's damask pride
Drinks the warm blushes of his bashful bride;

With honied lips enamoured woodbines meet,
Clasp with fond arms, and mix their kisses sweet.

Stay thy soft-murmuring waters, gentle rill;
Hush, whispering winds; ye rustling leaves be still;
Rest, silver butterflies, your quivering wings;
Alight, ye beetles, from your airy rings;
Ye painted moths, your gold-eyed plumage furl,
Bow your wide horns, your spiral trunks uncurl;
Glitter, ye glow-worms, on your mossy beds;
Descend, ye spiders, on your lengthened threads;
Slide here, ye horned snails, with varnished shells;
Ye bee-nymphs, listen in your waxen cells!

Botanic Muse! who in this latter age
Led by your airy hand the Swedish sage,
Bade his keen eye your secret haunts explore
On dewy dell, high wood, and winding shore;
Say on each leaf how tiny Graces dwell;
How laugh the Pleasures in a blossom's bell;
How insect Loves arise on cobweb wings,
Aim their light shafts, and point their little stings.

ERASMUS DARWIN

8

*'Go wondrous creature! mount
where Science guides'.*

From *Hymn to Science*

Science! thou fair effusive ray
From the great source of mental day,
   Free, generous, and refined!
Descend with all thy treasures fraught,
Illumine each bewildered thought,
   And bless my labouring mind.

But first with thy resistless light,
Disperse those phantoms from my sight,
   Those mimic shades of thee;
The scholiast's learning, sophist's cant,
The visionary bigot's rant,
   The monk's philosophy.

MARK AKENSIDE

From *Creation*

The Digestive System

See, how the human animal is fed,
How nourishment is wrought, and how conveyed:
The mouth, with proper faculties endued,
First entertains, and then divides, the food;
Two adverse rows of teeth the meat prepare,
On which the glands fermenting juice confer;
Nature has various tender muscles placed,
By which the artful gullet is embraced;
Some the long funnel's curious mouth extend,
Through which ingested meats with ease descend;
Other confederate pairs for Nature's use
Contract the fibres, and the twitch produce,
Which gently pushes on the grateful food
To the wide stomach, by its hollow road;

That this long road may unobstructed go,
As it descends, it bores the midriff through;
The large receiver for concoction made
Behold amidst the warmest bowels laid;
The spleen to this, and to the adverse side
The glowing liver's comfort is applied;
Beneath, the pancreas has its proper seat,
To cheer its neighbour, and augment its heat;
More to assist it for its destined use,
This ample bag is stored with active juice,
Which can with ease subdue, with ease unbind,
Admitted meats of every different kind;
This powerful ferment, mingling with the parts,
The leavened mass to milky chyle converts;
The stomach's fibres this concocted food,
By their contraction's gentle force, exclude,
Which by the mouth on the right side descends
Through the wide pass, which from that mouth depends;
In its progression soon the laboured chyle
Receives the confluent rills of bitter bile,
Which by the liver severed from the blood,
And striving through the gall-pipe, here unload
Their yellow streams, more to refine the flood;
The complicated glands, in various ranks
Disposed along the neighbouring channel's banks,
By constant weeping mix their watery store
With the chyle's current, and dilute it more;
Th'intestine roads, inflected and inclined,
In various convolutions turn and wind,
That these meanders may the progress stay,
And the descending chyle, by this delay,
May through the milky vessels find its way,
Whose little mouths in the large channel's side
Suck in the flood, and drink the cheering tide.
These numerous veins (such is the curious frame!)
Receive the pure insinuating stream;
But no corrupt or dreggy parts admit,
To form the blood, or feed the limbs unfit;

Th'intestine spiral fibres these protrude,
And from the winding tubes at length exclude.

SIR RICHARD BLACKMORE

From *The Art of Preserving Health*
Causes of Old Age

What dexterous thousands just within the goal
Of wild debauch direct their nightly course!
Perhaps no sickly qualms bedim their days,
No morning admonitions shock the head.
But, ah! what woes remain! life rolls apace
And that incurable disease, old age,
In youthful bodies more severely felt,
More sternly active, shakes their blasted prime;
Except kind Nature by some hasty blow
Prevent the lingering fates. For know, whate'er
Beyond its natural fervour hurries on
The sanguine tide; whether the frequent bowl,
High-seasoned fare, or exercise to toil
Protracted; spurs to its last stage tired life,
And sows the temples with untimely snow.
When life is new the ductile fibres feel
The heart's increasing force; and, day by day,
The growth advances: 'till the larger tubes
Acquiring (from their elemental veins,
Condensed to solid cords) a firmer tone,
Sustain, and just sustain, th'impetuous blood.
Here stops the growth. With overbearing pulse
And pressure, still the great destroy the small;
Still with the ruins of the small grow strong.
Life glows meantime, amid the grinding force
Of viscous fluids and elastic tubes;
Its various functions vigorously are plied
By strong machinery; and in solid health

The man confirmed long triumphs o'er disease.
But the full ocean ebbs: there is a point,
By Nature fixed, when life must downward tend.
For still the beating tide consolidates
The stubborn vessels, more reluctant still
To the weak throbs of th'ill supported heart.
This languishing, these strengthening by degrees
To hard unyielding unelastic bone,
Through tedious channels the congealing flood
Crawls lazily, and hardly wanders on;
It loiters still; and now it stirs no more.
This is the period few attain; the death
Of Nature; thus (so Heaven ordained it) life
Destroys itself; and could these laws have changed
Nestor might now the fates of Troy relate;
And Homer live immortal as his song.

JOHN ARMSTRONG

From *The Dispensary*

As bold Mirmillo the grey dawn descries,
Armed cap-à-pie, where honour calls, he flies,
And finds the legions planted at their post;
Where mighty Querpo filled the eye the most.
His arms were made, if we may credit fame,
By Mulciber, the mayor of Birmingham.
Of tempered stibium the bright shield was cast,
And yet the work the metal far surpassed.
A foliage of the vulnerary leaves,
Graved round the brim, the wondering sight deceives.
Around the centre Fate's bright trophies lay,
Probes, saws, incision-knives, and tools to slay.
Embossed upon the field, a battle stood
Of leeches spouting haemorrhoidal blood.
The artist too expressed the solemn state

Of grave physicians at a consult met;
About each symptom how they disagree,
But how unanimous in case of fee.
Whilst each assassin his learn'd colleague tires
With learn'd impertinence, the sick expires.
Beneath this blazing orb bright Querpo shone,
Himself an Atlas, and his shield a moon.
A pestle for his truncheon led the van,
And his high helmet was a close-stool pan.

SIR SAMUEL GARTH

From *Sickness*

Next, in a low-browed cave, a little hell,
A pensive hag, moping in darkness, sits
Dolefully-sad: her eyes (so deadly-dull!)
Stare from their stonied sockets, widely wild;
For ever bent on rusty knives, and ropes;
On poignards, bows of poison, daggers red
With clotted gore. A raven by her side
Eternal croaks; her only mate Despair;
Who, scowling in a night of clouds, presents
A thousand burning hells, and damned souls,
And lakes of stormy fire, to mad the brain
Moon-strucken. Melancholy is her name;
Britannia's bitter bane. Thou gracious Power,
(Whose judgments and whose mercies who can tell!)
With bars of steel, with hills of adamant
Crush down the sooty fiend; nor let her blast
The sacred light of Heaven's all-cheering face,
Nor fright, from Albion's isle, the angel Hope.

WILLIAM THOMPSON

From *The Triumphs of the Gout*

TRANSLATED FROM THE GREEK OF LUCIAN

GODDESS

Lives there on Earth to whom I am unknown,
Unconquerable queen of mighty woes?
Whom nor the fuming censer can appease,
Nor victim's blood on blazing altars poured.
Me not Apollo's self with all his drugs,
High Heaven's divine physician, can subdue;
Nor his learned son, wise Æsculapius.
Yet, ever since the race of man began,
All have essayed my fury to repel,
Racking th'invention of still-baffled physic.
Some this receipt 'gainst me, some that explore.
Plantain they bruise, the parsley's odorous herb,
The lenient lettuce, and the purslane wild;
These bitter horehound, and the watery plant
That on the verdant banks of rivers grows;
Those nettles crush, and comfrey's viscid root,
And pluck the lentils in the standing pools;
Some parsnips, some the glossy leaf apply
That shades the downy peach, benumbing henbane,
The poppies' soothing gum, th'emollient bulb,
Rind of the Punic apple, fleawort hot,
The costly frankincense, and searching root
Of potent hellebore, soft fenugreek
Tempered with rosy wine, collamphacum,
Nitre and spawn of frogs, the cypress-cone,
And meal of bearded barley, and the leaf
Of coleworts unprepared, and ointments made
Of pickled garus, and (O vain conceit!)
The dung of mountain-goats and human ordure,
The flower of beans, and hot sarcophagus.
The poisonous ruddock some, and shrew-mouse boil.
The weasel some, the frog, the lizard green,

The fell hyena, and the wily fox,
And branching stone-buck bearded like a goat.
What kind of metals have ye left untried?
What juice? what weeping tree's medicinal tear?
What beasts, what animals, have not bestowed
Their bones, or nerves, or hides, or blood, or marrow,
Or milk, or fat, or excrement, or urine?
The draught of four ingredients some compose,
Some eight, but more from seven expect relief;
Some from the purging hiera seek their cure;
On mystic verses vainly some depend;
The tricking Jew gulls other fools with charms;
While to the cooling fountain others fly,
And in the crystal current seek for health.
But to all these fell anguish I denounce,
To all who tempt me ever more severe.
But they who patiently my visit take,
Nor seek to combat me with anodynes,
Still find me gentle and benevolent.
For in my rites whoe'er participates,
His tongue with eloquence I straight endow,
And teach him with facetious wit to please,
A merry, gay, jocose companion boon,
Round whom the noisy crowd incessant laugh,
As to the baths the crippled wretch is borne.
For that dire Até, of whom Homer sings,
That dreaded powerful deity am I:
Who on the heads of men insulting tread,
And silent, soft, and unobserved, approach.
But as from me the acid drop descends,
The drop of anguish, I the Gout am called,
Now then, my votaries all, my orgies sing,
And praise with hymns th'unconquerable goddess.

GILBERT WEST

WILLIAM SHENSTONE

To the Virtuosos

Hail, curious wights! to whom so fair
    The form of mortal flies is!
Who deem those grubs beyond compare,
    Which common sense despises.

Whether o'er hill, morass, or mound,
    You make your sportsman sallies;
Or that your prey in gardens found
    Is urged through walks and alleys:

Yet, in the fury of the chase,
    No slope could e'er retard you;
Blessed if one fly repay the race,
    Or painted wings reward you.

Fierce as Camilla o'er the plain
    Pursued the glittering stranger;
Still eyed the purple's pleasing stain,
    And knew not fear nor danger.

'Tis you dispense the favourite meat
    To Nature's filmy people;
Know what conserves they choose to eat,
    And what liqueurs to tipple.

And if her brood of insects dies,
    You sage assistance lend her;
Can stoop to pimp for amorous flies,
    And help them to engender.

'Tis you protect their pregnant hour;
    And when the birth's at hand,
Exerting your obstetric power,
    Prevent a mothless land.

Yet oh! howe'er your towering view
  Above gross objects rises,
Whate'er refinements you pursue,
  Hear what a friend advises:

A friend, who, weighed with yours, must prize
  Domitian's idle passion;
That wrought the death of teasing flies,
  But ne'er their propagation.

Let Flavia's eyes more deeply warm,
  Nor thus your hearts determine,
To slight dame Nature's fairest form,
  And sigh for Nature's vermin.

And speak with some respect of beaux,
  Nor more as triflers treat 'em:
'Tis better learn to save one's clothes,
  Than cherish moths, that eat 'em.

WILLIAM SHENSTONE

From *The Dunciad*

A Certain Type of Scientist Speaks

'Let others creep by timid steps, and slow,
On plain experience lay foundations low,
By common sense to common knowledge bred,
And last, to Nature's cause through Nature led.
All-seeing in thy mists, we want no guide,
Mother of arrogance, and source of pride!
We nobly take the high Priori Road,
And reason downward, till we doubt of God;
Make Nature still encroach upon His plan;
And shove Him off as far as e'er we can:
Thrust some mechanic cause into His place;

Or bind in matter, or diffuse in space.
Or, at one bound o'erleaping all His laws,
Make God man's image, man the final cause,
Find virtue local, all relation scorn,
See all in self, and but for self be born:
Of nought so certain as our reason still,
Of nought so doubtful as of soul and will.'

*

Idle Pursuits

Next, bidding all draw near on bended knees,
The Queen confers her titles and degrees.
Her children first of more distinguished sort,
Who study Shakespeare at the Inns of Court,
Impale a glow-worm, or vertú profess,
Shine in the dignity of F.R.S.
Some, deep Freemasons, join the silent race
Worthy to fill Pythagoras's place:
Some botanists, or florists at the least,
Or issue members of an annual feast.
Nor past the meanest unregarded, one
Rose a Gregorian, one a Gormogon.
The last, not least in honour or applause,
Isis and Cam made doctors of her laws.
    Then, blessing all, 'Go, children of my care!
To practice now from theory repair.
All my commands are easy, short, and full:
My sons! be proud, be selfish, and be dull.
Guard my prerogative, assert my throne:
This nod confirms each privilege your own.
The cap and switch be sacred to his Grace;
With staff and pumps the marquis lead the race;
From stage to stage the licensed earl may run,
Paired with his fellow-charioteer, the sun;
The learned baron butterflies design,
Or draw to silk Arachne's subtle line;
The judge to dance his brother sergeant call;

The senator at cricket urge the ball;
The bishop stow (pontific luxury!)
An hundred souls of turkeys in a pie;
The sturdy squire to Gallic masters stoop,
And drown his lands and manors in a soup.
Others import yet nobler arts from France,
Teach kings to fiddle, and make senates dance.
Perhaps more high some daring son may soar,
Proud to my list to add one monarch more;
And nobly conscious, princes are but things
Born for first ministers, as slaves for kings.
Tyrant supreme! shall three estates command,
And make one mighty Dunciad of the land!'

*

The Death of Culture

She somes! she comes! the sable throne behold
Of Night primeval and of Chaos old!
Before her, Fancy's gilded clouds decay,
And all its varying rainbows die away.
Wit shoots in momentary fires,
The meteor drops, and in a flash expires.
As one by one, at dread Medea's strain,
The sickening stars fade off th'ethereal plain;
As Argus' eyes by Hermes' wand oppressed,
Closed one by one to everlasting rest;
Thus at her felt approach, and secret might,
Art after art goes out, and all is night.
See skulking Truth to her old cavern fled,
Mountains of Casuistry heaped o'er her head!
Philosophy, that leaned on Heaven before,
Shrinks to her second cause, and is no more.
Physic of Metaphysic begs defence,
And Metaphysic calls for aid on Sense!
See Mystery to Mathematics fly!
In vain! they gaze, turn giddy, rave, and die.
Religion blushing veils her sacred fires,

And unawares Morality expires.
Nor public flame, nor private, dares to shine,
Nor human spark is left, nor glimpse divine!
Lo! thy dread empire, Chaos! is restored;
Light dies before thy uncreating word:
Thy hand, great Anarch! lets the curtain fall,
And universal darkness buries all.

ALEXANDER POPE

Intended for Sir Isaac Newton

Nature and Nature's laws lay hid in night.
God said, *Let Newton be!* and all was light.

ALEXANDER POPE

9

'Go, work, hunt, exercise!'

From *To Sir Humphry Mackworth*

Coal-mining

The miner thus through perils digs his way,
Equal to theirs, and deeper than the sea!
Drawing, in pestilential steams, his breath,
Resolved to conquer, though he combats Death.
Night's gloomy realms his pointed steel invades,
The courts of Pluto, and infernal shades:
He cuts through mountains, subterraneous lakes,
Plying his work, each nervous stroke he takes
Loosens the earth, and the whole cavern shakes.
Thus, with his brawny arms, the Cyclops stands,
To form Jove's lightning, with uplifted hands,
The ponderous hammer with a force descends,
Loud as the thunder which his art intends;
And as he strikes, with each resistless blow
The anvil yields, and Etna groans below.

THOMAS YALDEN

The Highwayman

I went to London both blithe and gay,
My time I wasted in bowls and play
Until my cash it did get low
And then on the highway I was forced to go.

O next I took me a pretty wife,
I loved her dear as I loved my life,
But for to maintain her both fine and gay
Resolved I was that the world should pay.

I robbed Lord Edgcumbe I do declare
And Lady Templar of Melbourne Square.

I bade them good night, sat in my chair,
With laughter and song went to my dear.

I robbed them of five hundred pounds so bright
But all of it squandered one jovial night,
Till taken by such as I never knew,
But I was informed they were Fielding's crew.

The judge his mercy he did extend,
He pardoned my crime, bade me amend,
But still I pursued a thriving trade.
I always was reckoned a roving blade.

O now I'm judged and doomed to die
And many a maid for me will cry,
For all their sighs and for all salt tear
Where I shall go the Lord knows where.

My father he sighs and he makes his moan,
My mother she weeps for her darling son,
But sighs and tears will never save
Nor keep me from an untimely grave.

ANONYMOUS

From *Eloisa to Abelard*

Life of a Nun

How happy is the blameless Vestal's lot!
The world forgetting, by the world forgot:
Eternal sunshine of the spotless mind!
Each prayer accepted, and each wish resigned;
Labour and rest, that equal periods keep;
'Obedient slumbers that can wake and weep;'
Desires composed, affections ever even;
Tears that delight, and sighs that waft to Heaven.

Grace shines around her with serenest beams,
And whispering angels prompt her golden dreams.
For her th'unfading rose of Eden blooms,
And wings of seraphs shed divine perfumes;
For her the spouse prepares the bridal ring,
For her white virgins hymeneals sing;
To sounds of heavenly harps she dies away,
And melts in visions of eternal day.

ALEXANDER POPE

On Clergymen Preaching Politics

Indeed, Sir Peter, I could wish, I own,
That parsons would let politics alone;
Plead, if they will, the customary plea,
For such like talk, when o'er a dish of tea:
But when they tease us with it from the pulpit,
I own, Sir Peter, that I cannot gulp it.

If on their rules a justice should intrench,
And preach, suppose a sermon, from the bench,
Would you not think your brother magistrate
Was touched a little in his hinder pate?
Now which is worse, Sir Peter, on the total
The lay vagary, or the sacerdotal?

In ancient times, when preachers preached indeed
Their sermons, ere the learned learnt to read,
Another spirit, and another life,
Shut the church doors against all party strife:
Since then, how often heard, from sacred rostrums,
The lifeless din of Whig and Tory nostrums!

'Tis wrong, Sir Peter, I insist upon't;
To common sense 'tis plainly an affront:

The parson leaves the Christian in the lurch,
Whene'er he brings his politics to church;
His cant, on either side, if he calls preaching,
The man's wrong-headed, and his brains want bleaching.

Recall the time from conquering William's reign,
And guess the fruits of such a preaching vein:
How oft its nonsense must have veered about,
Just as the politics were in, or out:
The pulpit governed by no gospel data,
But new success still mending old errata.

Were I a king (God bless me) I should hate
My chaplains meddling with affairs of state;
Nor would my subjects, I should think, be fond,
Whenever theirs the Bible went beyond.
How well, methinks, we both should live together,
If these good folks would keep within their tether!

JOHN BYROM

From *The Task*

Arrival of the Mail

Hark! 'tis the twanging horn! o'er yonder bridge
That with its wearisome but needful length
Bestrides the wintry flood, in which the moon
Sees her unwrinkled face reflected bright,
He comes, the herald of a noisy world,
With spattered boots, strapped waist, and frozen locks,
News from all nations lumbering at his back.
True to his charge the close-packed load behind,
Yet careless what he brings, his one concern
Is to conduct it to the destined inn,
And having dropped th'expected bag – pass on.
He whistles as he goes, light-hearted wretch,

Cold and yet cheerful: messenger of grief
Perhaps to thousands, and of joy to some,
To him indifferent whether grief or joy.
Houses in ashes, and the fall of stocks,
Births, deaths, and marriages, epistles wet
With tears that trickled down the writer's cheeks
Fast as the periods from his fluent quill,
Or charged with amorous sighs of absent swains
Or nymphs responsive, equally affect
His horse and him, unconscious of them all.
But oh th'important budget! ushered in
With such heart-shaking music, who can say
What are its tidings? have our troops awaked?
Or do they still, as if with opium drugged,
Snore to the murmurs of th'Atlantic wave?
Is India free? and does she wear her plumed
And jewelled turban with a smile of peace,
Or do we grind her still? the grand debate,
The popular harangue, the tart reply,
The logic and the wisdom and the wit
And the loud laugh – I long to know them all;
I burn to set th'imprisoned wranglers free,
And give them voice and utterance once again.

Reading the Newspaper

Now stir the fire, and close the shutters fast,
Let fall the curtains, wheel the sofa round,
And while the bubbling and loud-hissing urn
Throws up a steamy column, and the cups
That cheer but not inebriate, wait on each,
So let us welcome peaceful evening in.
Not such his evening, who with shining face
Sweats in the crowded theatre, and, squeezed
And bored with elbow-points through both his sides,
Out-scolds the ranting actor on the stage.
Nor his, who patient stands 'till his feet throb
And his head thumps, to feed upon the breath

Of patriots bursting with heroic rage,
Or placemen, all tranquillity and smiles.
This folio of four pages, happy work!
Which not ev'n critics criticise, that holds
Inquisitive attention while I read
Fast bound in chains of silence, which the fair,
Though eloquent themselves, yet fear to break,
What is it but a map of busy life,
Its fluctuations and its vast concerns?
Here runs the mountainous and craggy ridge
That tempts ambition. On the summit, see,
The seals of office glitter in his eyes;
He climbs, he pants, he grasps them. At his heels,
Close at his heels a demagogue ascends,
And with a dexterous jerk soon twists him down
And wins them, but to lose them in his turn.
Here rills of oily eloquence in soft
Meanders lubricate the course they take;
The modest speaker is ashamed and grieved
T'engross a moment's notice, and yet begs,
Begs a propitious ear for his poor thoughts,
However trivial all that he conceives.
Sweet bashfulness! it claims, at least, this praise,
The dearth of information and good sense
That it foretells us, always comes to pass.
Cataracts of declamation thunder here,
There forests of no-meaning spread the page
In which all comprehension wanders lost;
While fields of pleasantry amuse us there,
With merry descants of a nation's woes.
The rest appears a wilderness of strange
But gay confusion, roses for the cheeks
And lilies for the brows of faded age,
Teeth for the toothless, ringlets for the bald,
Heaven, earth, and ocean plundered of their sweets,
Nectareous essences, Olympian dews,
Sermons and city feasts and favourite airs,
Ethereal journeys, submarine exploits,

And Katterfelto with his hair on end
At his own wonders, wondering for his bread.

WILLIAM COWPER

From *The Favourite Village*

Peasants at Work

Forth goes the weeding dame; her daily task
To travel the green wheat-field, ankle-deep
In the fresh blade of harvest yet remote.
Now with exerted implement she checks
The growth of noisome weeds, to toil averse,
An animal gregarious, fond of talk.
Lo! where the gossiping banditti stand
Amid field idle all, and all alike
With shrill voice prating, fluent as the pie.
Far off let me the noisy group behold,
Nothing molested by their loud harangue,
And think it well to see the fertile field
By their red tunics peopled, and the frock
Of the white husbandman that ploughs hard by,
Or guides the harrow team, or flings the grain
At every footstep with exerted arm
Over the yawning furrow. Never more
Pleases the rural landscape, than when man,
Drawn by the vernal sunbeam from his cell,
The needful culture of the field renews.

JAMES HURDIS

From *The Fleece*

Treating Sheep Ailments

In cold stiff soils the bleaters oft complain
Of gouty ails, by shepherds termed the halt:
Those let the neighbouring fold or ready crook
Detain; and pour into their cloven feet
Corrosive drugs, deep-searching arsenic,
Dry alum, verdigris, or vitriol keen.
But if the doubtful mischief scarce appears,
'Twill serve to shift them to a drier turf,
And salt again: th'utility of salt
Teach thy slow swains: redundant humours cold
Are the diseases of the bleating kind.
Th'infectious scab, arising from extremes
Of want or surfeit, is by water cured
Of lime, or sodden stave-acre, or oil
Dispersive of Norwegian tar, renowned
By virtuous Berkeley, whose benevolence
Explored its powers, and easy medicine thence
Sought for the poor: ye poor, with grateful voice,
Invoke eternal blessings on his head.

*

In the Wool Mill

By gentle steps
Upraised, from room to room we slowly walk,
And view with wonder, and with silent joy,
The sprightly scene; where many a busy hand,
Where spools, cards, wheels, and looms, with motion quick,
And ever-murmuring sound, th'unwonted sense
Wrap in surprise. To see them all employed,
All blithe, it gives the spreading heart delight,
As neither meats, nor drinks, nor aught of joy
Corporeal, can bestow. Nor less they gain

Virtue than wealth, while, on their useful works
From day to day intent, in their full minds
Evil no place can find. With equal scale
Some deal abroad the well-assorted fleece;
These card the short, those comb the longer flake;
Others the harsh and clotted lock receive,
Yet sever and refine with patient toil,
And bring to proper use. Flax too, and hemp,
Excite their diligence. The younger hands
Ply at the easy work of winding yarn
On swiftly-circling engines, and their notes
Warble together, as a choir of larks;
Such joy arises in the mind employed.
Another scene displays the more robust,
Rasping or grinding tough Brazilian woods,
And what Campeachy's disputable shore
Copious affords to tinge the thirsty web;
And the Caribbee isles, whose dulcet canes
Equal the honeycomb. We next are shown
A circular machine, of new design,
In conic shape: it draws and spins a thread
Without the tedious toil of needless hands,
A wheel, invisible, beneath the floor,
To every member of th'harmonious frame
Gives necessary motion. One, intent
O'erlooks the work: the carded wool, he says,
Is smoothly lapped around those cylinders,
Which, gently turning, yield it to yon cirque
Of upright spindles, which, with rapid whirl,
Spin out, in long extent, an even twine.

JOHN DYER

From *The Sweepers*

I sing of sweepers, frequent in thy streets,
Augusta, as the flowers which grace the spring,
Or branches withering in autumnal shades
To form the brooms they wield. Preserved by them
From dirt, from coach-hire, and th'oppressive rheums
Which clog the springs of life, to them I sing,
And ask no inspiration but their smiles.

Hail, unowned youths, and virgins unendowed!
Whether on bulk begot, while rattled loud
The passing coaches, or th'officious hand
Of sportive link-boy wide around him dashed
The pitchy flame obstructive of the joy;
Or more propitious to the dark retreat
Of round-house owe your birth, where Nature's reign
Revives, and emulous of Spartan fame
The mingling sexes share promiscuous love;
And scarce the pregnant female knows to whom
She owes the precious burthen, scarce the sire
Can claim, confused, the many-featured child.

Nor blush that hence your origin we trace:
'Twas thus immortal heroes sprung of old
Strong from the stol'n embrace: by such as you
Unhoused, unclothed, unlettered, and unfed,
Were kingdoms modelled, cities taught to rise,
Firm laws enacted, freedom's rights maintained,
The gods and patriots of an infant world!

Let others meanly chant in tuneful song
The black-shoe race, whose mercenary tribes
Allured by halfpence take their morning stand
Where streets divide, and to their proffered stools
Solicit wandering feet; vain pensioners,
And placemen of the crowd! Not so you pour
Your blessings on mankind. Nor traffic vile
Be your employment deemed, ye last remains
Of public spirit, whose laborious hands,

Uncertain of reward, bid kennels know
Their wonted bounds, remove the bordering filth,
And give th'obstructed ordure where to glide.

WILLIAM WHITEHEAD

From *Edge Hill*

The Metal Industry

Nor does the barren soil conceal alone
The sable rock inflammable. Oft-times
More ponderous ore beneath its surface lies,
Compact, metallic, but with earthy parts
Encrusted. These the smoky kiln consumes,
And to the furnace's impetuous rage
Consigns the solid ore. In the fierce heat
The pure dissolves, the dross remains behind.
This pushed aside, the trickling metal flows
Through secret valves along the channelled floor,
Where in the mazy moulds of figured sand,
Anon it hardens. Now the busy forge
Reiterates its blows, to form the bar
Large, massy, strong. Another art expands,
Another yet divides the yielding mass
To many a taper length, fit to receive
The artist's will, and take its destined form.
Soon o'er thy furrowed pavement, Bremicham!
Ride the loose bars obstreperous; to the sons
Of languid sense, and frame too delicate
Harsh noise perchance, but harmony to thine.
Instant innumerable hands prepare
To shape, and mould the malleable ore.
Their heavy sides th'inflated bellows heave,
Tugged by the pulleyed line, and, with their blast
Continuous, the sleeping embers rouse,
And kindle into life. Straight the rough mass,

Plunged in the blazing hearth, its heat contracts,
And glows transparent. Now, Cyclopean chief!
Quick on the anvil lay the burning bar,
And with thy lusty fellows, on its sides
Impress the weighty stroke. See, how they strain
The swelling nerve, and lift the sinewy arm
In measured time; while with their clattering blows,
From street to street the propagated sound
Increasing echoes, and, on every side,
The tortured metal spreads a radiant shower.

  'Tis noise, and hurry all! The thronged street,
The close-piled warehouse, and the busy shop!
With nimble stroke the tinkling hammers move;
While slow and weighty the vast sledge descends,
In solemn bass responsive, or apart,
Or socially conjoined in tuneful peal.
The rough file grates; yet useful is its touch,
As sharp corrosives to the schirrhous flesh,
Or, to the stubborn temper, keen rebuke.

  How the coarse metal brightens into flame
Shaped by their plastic hands! what ornament!
What various use! See there the glittering knife
Of tempered edge! The scissors' double shaft,
Useless apart, in social union joined,
Each aiding each! Emblem how beautiful
Of happy nuptial leagues! The button round,
Plain, or embossed, or bright with steely rays!
Or oblong buckle, on the lacquered shoe,
With polished lustre, bending elegant
In shapely rim. But who can count the forms
That hourly from the glowing embers rise,
Or shine attractive through the glittering pane,
And emulate their parent fires? what art
Can, in the scanty bounds of measured verse,
Display the treasure of a thousand mines
To wondrous shapes by stubborn labour wrought?

RICHARD JAGO

From *The Shipwreck*

Amid this fearful trance, a thundering sound
He hears, and thrice the hollow decks rebound;
Upstarting from his couch on deck he sprung,
Thrice with shrill note the boatswain's whistle rung:
All hands unmoor! proclaims a boisterous cry,
All hands unmoor! the caverned rocks reply.
Roused from repose, aloft the sailors swarm,
And with their levers soon the windlass arm:
The order given, up springing with a bound,
They fix the bars, and heave the windlass round,
At every turn the clanging pauls resound:
Up-torn reluctant from its oozy cave
The ponderous anchor rises o'er the wave.
High on the slippery masts the yards ascend,
And far abroad the canvas wings extend.
Along the glassy plain the vessel glides,
While azure radiance trembles on her sides;
The lunar rays in long reflection gleam,
With silver deluging the fluid stream.
Levant and Thracian gales alternate play,
Then in th'Egyptian quarter die away.
A calm ensues; adjacent shores they dread,
The boats, with rowers manned, are sent ahead;
With cordage fastened to the lofty prow,
Aloof to sea the stately ship they tow;
The nervous crew their sweeping oars extend,
And pealing shouts the shore of Candia rend:
Success attends their skill! the danger's o'er!
The port is doubled, and beheld no more.

WILLIAM FALCONER

The Tears of Scotland

WRITTEN IN THE YEAR 1746

Mourn, hapless Caledonia, mourn
Thy banished peace, thy laurels torn!
Thy sons, for valour long renowned,
Lie slaughtered on their native ground;
Thy hospitable roofs no more
Invite the stranger to the door;
In smoky ruins sunk they lie,
The monuments of cruelty.

The wretched owner sees afar
His all become the prey of war;
Bethinks him of his babes and wife,
Then smites his breast, and curses life.
Thy swains are famished on the rocks,
Where once they fed their wanton flocks:
Thy ravished virgins shriek in vain;
Thy infants perish on the plain.

What boots it then, in every clime,
Through the wide-spreading waste of time,
Thy martial glory, crowned with praise,
Still shone with undiminished blaze?
Thy towering spirit now is broke,
Thy neck is bended to the yoke.
What foreign arms could never quell,
By civil rage and rancour fell.

The rural pipe and merry lay
No more shall cheer the happy day:
No social scenes of gay delight
Beguile the dreary winter night:
No strains but those of sorrow flow,
And nought be heard but sounds of woe,

While the pale phantoms of the slain
Glide nightly o'er the silent plain.

O baneful cause, oh, fatal morn,
Accursed to ages yet unborn!
The sons against their fathers stood,
The parent shed his children's blood.
Yet, when the rage of battle ceased,
The victor's soul was not appeased:
The naked and forlorn must feel
Devouring flames, and murdering steel!

The pious mother doomed to death,
Forsaken wanders o'er the heath,
The bleak wind whistles round her head,
Her helpless orphans cry for bread;
Bereft of shelter, food, and friend,
She views the shades of night descend,
And, stretched beneath th'inclement skies,
Weeps o'er her tender babes and dies.

While the warm blood bedews my veins,
And unimpaired remembrance reigns,
Resentment of my country's fate
Within my filial breast shall beat;
And, spite of her insulting foe,
My sympathizing verse shall flow:
'Mourn, hapless Caledonia, mourn
Thy banished peace, thy laurels torn.'

TOBIAS SMOLLETT

Sweet Meat Has Sour Sauce
or, The Slave-Trader in the Dumps

A trader I am to the African shore,
But since that my trading is like to be o'er,

I'll sing you a song that you ne'er heard before,
   Which nobody can deny, deny,
   Which nobody can deny.

When I first heard the news it gave me a shock,
Much like what they call an electrical knock,
And now I am going to sell off my stock,
   Which nobody can deny, deny,
   Which nobody can deny.

'Tis a curious assortment of dainty regales,
To tickle the negroes with when the ship sails,
Fine chains for the neck, and a cat with nine tails,
   Which nobody can deny, deny,
   Which nobody can deny.

Here's supple-jack plenty, and store of rat-tan,
That will wind itself round the sides of a man,
As close as a hoop round a bucket or can,
   Which nobody can deny, deny,
   Which nobody can deny.

Here's padlocks and bolts, and screws for the thumbs,
That squeeze them so lovingly till the blood comes,
They sweeten the temper like comfits or plums,
   Which nobody can deny, deny,
   Which nobody can deny.

When a negro his head from his victuals withdraws,
And clenches his teeth and thrusts out his paws,
Here's a notable engine to open his jaws,
   Which nobody can deny, deny,
   Which nobody can deny.

Thus going to market, we kindly prepare
A pretty black cargo of African ware,
For what they must meet with when they get there,
   Which nobody can deny, deny,
   Which nobody can deny.

'Twould do your heart good to see 'em below
Lie flat on their backs all the way as we go,
Like sprats on a gridiron, scores in a row,
    Which nobody can deny, deny,
    Which nobody can deny.

But ah! if in vain I have studied an art
So gainful to me, all boasting apart,
I think it will break my compassionate heart,
    Which nobody can deny, deny,
    Which nobody can deny.

For oh! how it enters my soul like an awl!
This pity, which some people self-pity call,
Is sure the most heart-piercing pity of all,
    Which nobody can deny, deny,
    Which nobody can deny.

So this is my song, as I told you before;
Come buy off my stock, for I must no more
Carry Caesars and Pompeys to sugar-cane shore,
    Which nobody can deny, deny,
    Which nobody can deny.

WILLIAM COWPER

Farewell to Kingsbridge

Military Life

On the ninth of November by the dawning of the day
Ere we sailed for New York we did lie in the bay.
O'er the fair fields of Kingsbridge the mist it lay grey,
We were bound against the rebels of North America.

O so sad was the parting 'twixt soldiers and wives
For they knew not if all would return with their lives.

O the women they wept and they cursed the day
That we sailed 'gainst the rebels in North America.

The babes held up their arms with the saddest of cries
And the tears trickled down from their innocent eyes
That their red-coated daddies must hasten away
For to fight with the rebels in North America.

Now God save King George, I will finish my strain.
May his subjects all loyal his honour maintain.
God prosper our voyage and arms across the sea
And pull down the proud rebels in North America.

ANONYMOUS

10

'Ye gods! and is there no
relief for love?'

The Progress of Love

Beneath the myrtle's secret shade,
　　When Delia blessed my eyes;
At first I viewed the lovely maid
　　In silent soft surprise.
With trembling voice, and anxious mind,
　　I softly whispered love;
She blushed a smile so sweetly kind,
　　Did all my fears remove.
Her lovely yielding form I pressed,
　　Sweet maddening kisses stole;
And soon her swimming eyes confessed
　　The wishes of her soul:
In wild tumultuous bliss, I cry,
　　'O Delia, now be kind!'
She pressed me close, and with a sigh,
　　To melting joys resigned.

ROBERT DODSLEY

On Platonic Love

Platonic love! – a pretty name
　　For that romantic fire,
When souls confess a mutual flame,
　　Devoid of loose desire.

If this new doctrine once prove true,
　　I own it something odd is,
That lovers should each other view
　　As if they wanted bodies.

If spirits thus can live embraced,
　　The union may be lasting:

But, faith – 'tis hard the mind should feast,
    And keep its partner fasting.

'Nature,' says Horace, 'is in tears,
    When her just claim's denied her;'
And this platonic love appears
    To be a scrimp provider.

Long may it preach, one comfort is,
    For all its vain pretences,
Mankind have other thoughts of bliss,
    Than to exclude their senses.

Not all their logic can perplex
    A principle so common:
While Venus whispers either sex,
    'That man was made for woman.'

Such passion is pedantic work;
    (As sung the bard of yore)
'That thrust out Nature with a fork,
    She but recoils the more.'

SAMUEL BOYSE

Song

Pious Selinda goes to prayers,
    If I but ask the favour;
And yet the tender fool's in tears,
    When she believes I'll leave her.

Would I were free from this restraint,
    Or else had hopes to win her!
Would she could make of me a saint,
    Or I of her a sinner!

WILLIAM CONGREVE

Song III

As Phyllis the gay, at the break of the day,
    Went forth to the meadows a-maying,
A clown lay asleep by a river so deep,
    That round in meanders was straying.

His bosom was bare, and for whiteness so rare,
    Her heart it was gone without warning,
With cheeks of such hue, that the rose wet with dew,
    Ne'er looked half so fresh in a morning.

She culled the new hay, and down by him she lay,
    Her wishes too warm for disguising;
She played with eyes, till he waked in surprise,
    And blushed like the sun at his rising.

She sung him a song, as he leaned on his prong,
    And rested her arm on his shoulder;
She pressed his coy cheek to her bosom so sleek,
    And taught his two arms to enfold her.

The rustic grown kind, by a kiss told his mind,
    And called her his dear and his blessing:
Together they strayed, and sung, frolicked, and played,
    And what they did more there's no guessing.

EDWARD MOORE

Advice to a Lover

For many unsuccessful years,
    At Cynthia's feet I lay;
Battering them often with my tears,
    I sighed, but durst not pray.

No prostrate wretch, before the shrine
    Of some loved saint above,
E'er thought his goddess more divine,
    Or paid more awful love.

Still the disdainful nymph looked down
    With coy insulting pride;
Received my passion with a frown,
    Or turned her head aside.
Then Cupid whispered in my ear,
    'Use more prevailing charms;
You modest whining fool, draw near,
    And clasp her in your arms,

With eager kisses tempt the maid,
    From Cynthia's feet depart;
The lips he briskly must invade,
    That would possess the heart.'
With that I shook off all the slave,
    My better fortunes tried;
When Cynthia in a moment gave
    What she for years denied.

THOMAS YALDEN

The Stolen Kiss

On a mossy bank reclined,
    Beauteous Chloe lay reposing,
O'er her breast each amorous wind
    Wanton played, its sweets disclosing:
Tempted with the swelling charms,
    Colin, happy swain, drew nigh her,
Softly stole into her arms,
    Laid his scrip and sheep-hook by her.

O'er her downy panting breast
    His delighted fingers roving;
To her lips his lips he pressed,
    In the ecstasy of loving:
Chloe, wakened with his kiss,
    Pleased, yet frowning to conceal it,
Cried, 'True lovers share the bliss;
    Why then, Colin, would you steal it?'

ROBERT DODSLEY

A Song

After the fiercest pangs of hot desire,
    Between Panthea's rising breasts
    His bending breast Philander rests;
Though vanquished, yet unknowing to retire:
Close hugs the charmer, and ashamed to yield,
Though he has lost the day, yet keeps the field.

When, with a sigh, the fair Panthea said,
    'What pity 'tis, ye gods, that all
    The noblest warriors soonest fall!'
Then with a kiss she gently reared his head;
Armed him again to fight, for nobly she
More loved the combat than the victory.

But, more enraged for being beat before,
    With all his strength he does prepare
    More fiercely to renew the war;
Nor ceased he till the noble prize he bore:
Ev'n her such wondrous courage did surprise;
She hugs the dart that wounded her, and dies.

RICHARD DUKE

Olivia

Olivia's lewd, but looks devout,
And scripture-proofs she throws about,
   When first you try to win her:
Pull your fob of guineas out;
Fee Jenny first, and never doubt
   To find the saint a sinner.

Baxter by day is her delight:
No chocolate must come in sight
   Before two morning chapters:
But, lest the spleen should spoil her quite,
She takes a civil friend at night,
   To raise her holy raptures.

Thus oft we see a glow-worm gay,
At large her fiery tail display,
   Encouraged by the dark:
And yet the sullen thing all day
Snug in the lonely thicket lay,
   And hid the native spark.

ELIJAH FENTON

To a Young Lady
with some Lampreys

With lovers 'twas of old the fashion
By presents to convey their passion;
No matter what the gift they sent,
The lady saw that love was meant.
Fair Atalanta, as a favour,
Took the boar's head her hero gave her;
Nor could the bristly thing affront her;

'Twas a fit present from a hunter.
When squires send woodcocks to the dame,
It serves to show their absent flame.
Some by a snip of woven hair,
In posied lockets, bribe the fair.
How many mercenary matches
Have sprung from diamond-rings and watches!
But hold – a ring, a watch, a locket,
Would drain at once a poet's pocket;
He should send songs that cost him nought,
Nor ev'n be prodigal of thought.
Why then send lampreys? Fie, for shame!
'Twill set a virgin's blood on flame.
This to fifteen a proper gift!
It might lend sixty-five a lift.
I know your maiden aunt will scold,
And think my present somewhat bold.
I see her lift her hands and eyes:
'What; eat it, niece; eat Spanish flies!
Lamprey's a most immodest diet:
You'll neither wake nor sleep in quiet.
Should I tonight eat sago-cream,
'Twould make me blush to tell my dream:
If I eat lobster, 'tis so warming,
That every man I see looks charming.
Wherefore had not the filthy fellow
Laid Rochester upon your pillow?
I vow and swear, I think the present
Had been as modest and as decent.
Who has her virtue in her power?
Each day has its unguarded hour,
Always in danger of undoing,
A prawn, a shrimp, may prove our ruin!
The shepherdess, who lives on salad,
To cool her youth, controls her palate.
Should Dian's maids turn liquorish livers,
And of huge lampreys rob the rivers,
Then, all beside each glade and visto,

You'd see nymphs lying like Calisto.
The man, who meant to heat your blood,
Needs not himself such vicious food –'
    In this, I own, your aunt is clear,
I sent you what I well might spare:
For, when I see you, (without joking)
Your eyes, lips, breasts, are so provoking,
They set my heart more cock-a-hoop,
Than could whole seas of craw-fish soup.

JOHN GAY

To a Nosegay
in Pancharilla's Breast

WRITTEN IN 1729

Must you alone then, happy flowers,
Ye short-lived sons of vernal showers,
Must you alone be still thus blessed,
And dwell in Pancharilla's breast?
Oh would the gods but hear my prayer,
To change my form and place me there!
I should not sure so quickly die,
I should not so unactive lie;
But ever wandering to and fro,
From this to that fair ball of snow,
Enjoy ten thousand thousand blisses,
And print on each ten thousand kisses.
    Nor would I thus the task give o'er;
Curious new secrets to explore,
I'd never rest till I had found
Which globe was softest, which most round –
Which was most yielding, smooth, and white,
Or the left bosom, or the right;
Which was the warmest, easiest bed,
And which was tipped with purest red.

Nor could I leave the beauteous scene,
Till I had traced the path between,
That milky way so smooth and even,
That promises to lead to Heav'n:
Lower and lower I'd descend,
To find where it at last would end;
Till fully bless'd I'd wandering rove
O'er all the fragrant Cyprian grove.

But ah! those wishes all are vain,
The fair one triumphs in my pain;
To flowers that know not to be blessed
The nymph unveils her snowy breast;
While to her slave's desiring eyes
The heavenly prospect she denies:
Too cruel fate, too cruel fair,
To place a senseless nosegay there,
And yet refuse my lips the bliss
To taste one dear transporting kiss.

SOAME JENYNS

To Miss Kitty Phillips

Your bosom's sweet treasures thus ever disclose!
    For believe my ingenuous confession,
The veil meant to hide them but only bestows
    A softness transcending expression.

'Good Heaven!' cries Kitty, 'what language I hear!
    Have I trespassed on chastity's laws?
Is my tucker's clean muslin indecently clear?
    Is it no satin apron, but gauze?'

Ah no! – not the least swelling charm is descried
    Through the tucker, too bashfully decent;
And your apron hides all that short aprons can hide,
    From the fashion of Eve to the present.

The veil, too transparent to hinder the sight,
    Is what modesty throws on your mind:
That veil only shades, with a tenderer light,
    All the feminine graces behind.

EDWARD LOVIBOND

The Fable of the Young Man and His Cat

A hapless youth, whom fates averse had drove
To a strange passion, and preposterous love,
Longed to possess his puss's spotted charms,
And hug the tabby beauty in his arms.
To what odd whimsies love inveigles men,
Sure if the boy was ever blind, 'twas then.
Racked with his passion, and in deep despair,
The youth to Venus thus addressed his prayer.
    O queen of beauty, since thy Cupid's dart
Has fired my soul, and rankles in my heart;
Since doomed to burn in this unhappy flame,
From thee at least a remedy I claim;
If once, to bless Pygmalion's longing arms,
The marble softened into living charms;
And warm with life the purple current ran
In circling streams through every flinty vein;
If, with his own creating hands displayed,
He hugged the statue, and embraced a maid;
And with the breathing image fired his heart,
The pride of Nature, and the boast of Art:
Hear my request, and crown my wondrous flame,
The same its nature, be thy gift the same;
Give me the like unusual joys to prove,
And though irregular, indulge my love.
    Delighted Venus heard the moving prayer,
And soon resolved to ease the lover's care,
To set Miss Tabby off with every grace,

To dress, and fit her for the youth's embrace.
  Now she by gradual change her form forsook,
First her round face an oval figure took;
The roguish dimples next his heart beguile,
And each grave whisker softened to a smile;
Unusual ogles wantoned in her eye,
Her solemn purring dwindled to a sigh:
Sudden, a huge hoop-petticoat displayed,
A wide circumference! entrenched the maid,
And for the tail in waving circles played.
Her fur, as destined still her charms to deck,
Made for her hands a muff, a tippet for her neck.

  In the fine lady now her shape was lost,
And by such strange degrees she grew a toast;
Was all for ombre now; and who but she,
To talk of modes and scandal o'er her tea.
To settle every fashion of the sex,
And run through all the female politics;
To spend her time at toilet and basset,
To play, to flaunt, to flutter, and coquette:
From a grave thinking mouser, she was grown
The gayest flirt that coached it round the town.

  But see how often some intruding woe,
Nips all our blooming prospects at a blow!
For as the youth his lovely consort led
To the dear pleasures of the nuptial bed,
Just on that instant from an inner house,
Into the chamber popped a heedless mouse.
Miss Tabby saw, and brooking no delay,
Sprung from the sheets, and seized the trembling prey,
Nor did the bride, in that ill-fated hour,
Reflect that all her mousing-days were o'er.
The youth, astonished, felt a new despair,
Ixion-like he grasped, and grasped but air;
He saw his vows and prayers in vain bestowed,
And lost the jilting goddess in a cloud.

CHRISTOPHER PITT

A Riddle

Upon a bed of humble clay,
   In all her garments loose,
A prostitute my mother lay,
   To every comer's use.

Till one gallant, in heat of love,
   His own peculiar made her;
And to a region far above,
   And softer beds, conveyed her.

But, in his absence, to his place
   His rougher rival came;
And, with a cold constrained embrace,
   Begat me on the dame.

I then appeared to public view
   A creature wondrous bright;
But shortly perishable too,
   Inconstant, nice, and light.

On feathers not together fast
   I wildly flew about,
And from my father's country passed
   To find my mother out.

Where her gallant, of her beguiled,
   With me enamoured grew,
And I, that was my mother's child,
   Brought forth my mother too.

THOMAS PARNELL

On a Lady, Preached into the Colic, by One of Her Lovers

Bellona the fierce, who held man in disdain,
And despised her own sex, to whom love could give pain;
Went to church, in defiance, and met with her fate,
From a pulpited Cupid, who there lay in wait:
But her head was so armed, and so hard was her heart,
That his arrows rebounded, in scorn of his art,
Then, with voice of revenge, he exalted his pipes,
Shot in spleen at her belly, and gave her the gripes.
Thus I wound her, cried he, in a whimsical place,
'Cause she covers kind wishes, with haughty grimace.
Let her now twist and screw – 'twill but fasten the dart;
She has love in her bowels, though she hates in her heart.

AARON HILL

The Nun

A CANTATA

RECITATIVE

Of Constance holy legends tell,
The softest sister of the cell;
None sent to Heaven so sweet a cry,
Or rolled at mass so bright an eye.
No wanton taint her bosom knew,
Her hours in heavenly vision flew,
Her knees were worn with midnight prayers,
And thus she breathed divinest airs.

AIR

In hallowed walks, and awful cells,
    Secluded from the light and vain,
The chaste-eyed maid with virtue dwells,

275

And solitude, and silence reign.
The wanton's voice is heard not here,
  To Heaven the sacred pile belongs;
Each wall returns the whispered prayer,
  And echoes but to holy songs.

RECITATIVE

Alas, that pampered monks should dare
Intrude where sainted vestals are!
Ah, Francis! Francis! well I weet
Those holy looks are all deceit.
With shame the Muse prolongs her tale,
The priest was young, the nun was frail,
Devotion faltered on her tongue,
Love tuned her voice, and thus she sung.

AIR

'Alas, how deluded was I,
  To fancy delights as I did!
With maidens at midnight to sigh,
  And love, the sweet passion, forbid!
O, father! my follies forgive,
  And still to absolve me be nigh;
Your lessons have taught me to live,
  Come teach me, O! teach me to die!'

To her arms in a rapture he sprung,
  Her bosom, half-naked, met his;
Transported in silence she hung,
  And melted away at each kiss.
'Ah, father!' expiring she cried,
  'With rapture I yield up my breath!'
'Ah, daughter!' he fondly replied,
  'The righteous find comfort in death.'

EDWARD MOORE

From *The Times*

Against Sodomy

Go where we will, at every time and place,
Sodom confronts, and stares us in the face;
They ply in public at our very doors,
And take the bread from much more honest whores.
Those who are mean high paramours secure,
And the rich guilty screen the guilty poor;
The sin too proud to feel from reason awe,
And those who practise it, too great for law.

Woman, the pride and happiness of man,
Without whose soft endearments Nature's plan
Had been a blank, and life not worth a thought;
Woman, by all the Loves and Graces taught,
With softest arts, and sure, though hidden skill,
To humanize, and mould us to her will;
Woman, with more than common grace formed here,
With the persuasive language of a tear
To melt the rugged temper of our isle,
Or win us to her purpose with a smile;
Woman, by Fate the quickest spur decreed,
The fairest, best reward of every deed
Which bears the stamp of honour; at whose name
Our ancient heroes caught a quicker flame,
And dared beyond belief, whilst o'er the plain,
Spurning the carcases of princes slain,
Confusion proudly strode, whilst Horror blew
The fatal trump, and Death stalked full in view;
Woman is out of date, a thing thrown by,
As having lost its use; no more the eye,
With female beauty caught, in wild amaze,
Gazes entranced, and could for ever gaze;
No more the heart, that seat where Love resides,
Each breath drawn quick and short, in fuller tides
Life posting through the veins, each pulse on fire,

And the whole body tingling with desire,
Pants for those charms, which Virtue might engage,
To break his vow, and thaw the frost of Age,
Bidding each trembling nerve, each muscle strain,
And giving pleasure which is almost pain.
Women are kept for nothing but the breed;
For pleasure we must have a Ganymede,
A fine, fresh Hylas, a delicious boy,
To serve our purposes of beastly joy.

CHARLES CHURCHILL

Elegy to the Memory of an Unfortunate Lady

What beckoning ghost, along the moonlight shade
Invites my step, and points to yonder glade?
'Tis she! – but why that bleeding bosom gored,
Why dimly gleams the visionary sword?
Oh, ever beauteous, ever friendly! tell,
Is it, in heaven, a crime to love too well?
To bear too tender, or too firm a heart,
To act a lover's or a Roman's part?
Is there no bright reversion in the sky
For those who greatly think, or bravely die?

    Why bade ye else, ye powers! her soul aspire
Above the vulgar flight of low desire?
Ambition first sprung from your blest abodes,
The glorious fault of angels and of gods:
Thence to their images on earth it flows,
And in the breasts of kings and heroes glows.
Most souls, 'tis true, but peep out once an age,
Dull sullen prisoners in the body's cage:
Dim lights of life, that burn a length of years,
Useless, unseen, as lamps in sepulchres;
Like Eastern kings a lazy state they keep,
And, close confined in their own palace sleep.

From these perhaps (ere Nature bade her die)
Fate snatched her early to the pitying sky.
As into air the purer spirits flow,
And separate from their kindred dregs below;
So flew the soul to its congenial place,
Nor left one virtue to redeem her race.

But thou, false guardian of a charge too good,
Thou, mean deserter of thy brother's blood!
See on these ruby lips the trembling breath,
These cheeks, now fading at the blast of death;
Cold is that breast which warmed the world before,
And those love-darting eyes must roll no more.
Thus, if eternal justice rules the ball,
Thus shall your wives, and thus your children fall:
On all the line a sudden vengeance waits,
And frequent hearses shall besiege your gates.
There passengers shall stand, and pointing say,
(While the long funerals blacken all the way,)
'Lo! these were they, whose souls the Furies steeled,
And cursed with hearts unknowing how to yield.'
Thus unlamented pass the proud away,
The gaze of fools, and pageant of a day!
So perish all, whose breast ne'er learned to glow
For others' good, or melt at others' woe.

What can atone (oh ever-injured shade!)
Thy fate unpitied, and thy rites unpaid?
No friend's complaint, no kind domestic tear
Pleased thy pale ghost, or graced thy mournful bier;
By foreign hands thy dying eyes were closed,
By foreign hands thy decent limbs composed,
By foreign hands thy humble grave adorned,
By strangers honoured, and by strangers mourned!
What though no friends in sable weeds appear,
Grieve for an hour, perhaps, then mourn a year,
And bear about the mockery of woe
To midnight dances, and the public show?
What though no weeping loves thy ashes grace,
Nor polished marble emulate thy face?

What though no sacred earth allow thee room,
Nor hallowed dirge be muttered o'er thy tomb?
Yet shall thy grave with rising flowers be dressed,
And the green turf lie lightly on thy breast:
There shall the morn her earliest tears bestow,
There the first roses of the year shall blow;
While angels with their silver wings o'ershade
The ground now sacred by thy reliques made.

So peaceful rests, without a stone, a name,
What once had beauty, titles, wealth, and fame.
How loved, how honoured once, avails thee not,
To whom related, or by whom begot;
A heap of dust alone remains of thee;
'Tis all thou art, and all the proud shall be!

Poets themselves must fall, like those they sung;
Deaf the praised ear, and mute the tuneful tongue.
Even he, whose soul now melts in mournful lays,
Shall shortly want the generous tear he pays;
Then from his closing eyes thy form shall part,
And the last pang shall tear thee from his heart,
Life's idle business at one gasp be o'er,
The Muse forgot, and thou beloved no more!

ALEXANDER POPE

Bryan and Pereene

A WEST INDIAN BALLAD
FOUNDED ON A REAL FACT, THAT HAPPENED
IN THE ISLAND OF ST CHRISTOPHER'S ABOUT
TWO YEARS AGO

The north-east wind did briskly blow,
    The ship was safely moored,
Young Bryan thought the boat's crew slow,
    And so leapt overboard.

Pereene, the pride of Indian dames,
   His heart long held in thrall,
And whoso his impatience blames,
   I wot, ne'er loved at all.

A long long year, one month and day,
   He dwelt on English land,
Nor once in thought or deed would stray,
   Though ladies sought his hand.

For Bryan he was tall and strong,
   Right blithesome rolled his een,
Sweet was his voice whene'er he sung,
   He scant had twenty seen.

But who the countless charms can draw,
   That graced his mistress true;
Such charms the old world seldom saw,
   Nor oft I ween the new.

Her raven hair plays round her neck,
   Like tendrils of the vine;
Her cheeks red dewy rose-buds deck,
   Her eyes like diamonds shine.

Soon as his well-known ship she spied,
   She cast her weeds away,
And to the palmy shore she hied,
   All in her best array.

In sea-green silk so neatly clad,
   She there impatient stood;
The crew with wonder saw the lad
   Repel the foaming flood.

Her hands a handkerchief displayed,
   Which he at parting gave;
Well pleased the token he surveyed,
   And manlier beat the wave.

Her fair companions, one and all,
　　Rejoicing crowd the strand;
For now her lover swam in call,
　　And almost touched the land.

Then through the white surf did she haste,
　　To clasp her lovely swain;
When, ah! a shark bit through his waist:
　　His heart's blood dyed the main!

He shrieked! his half sprang from the wave,
　　Streaming with purple gore,
And soon it found a living grave,
　　And ha! was seen no more.

Now haste, now haste, ye maids, I pray,
　　Fetch water from the spring:
She falls, she swoons, she dies away,
　　And soon her knell they ring.

Now each May morning round her tomb,
　　Ye fair, fresh flowerets strew,
So may your lovers 'scape his doom,
　　Her hapless fate 'scape you.

JAMES GRAINGER

From *Visions of the Daughters of Albion*

Desire and Jealousy

But Oothoon is not so; a virgin filled with virgin fancies
Open to joy and to delight where ever beauty appears.
If in the morning sun I find it, there my eyes are fixed
In happy copulation; if in evening mild, wearied with work,
Sit on a bank and draw the pleasures of this free-born joy.

The moment of desire! the moment of desire! the virgin
That pines for man shall awaken her womb to enormous joys
In the secret shadows of her chamber; the youth shut up from
The lustful joy shall forget to generate, and create an
    amorous image
In the shadows of his curtains and in the folds of his silent
    pillow.
Are not these the places of religion? the rewards of
    continence?
The self-enjoyings of self-denial? Why dost thou seek
    religion?
Is it because acts are not lovely that thou seekest solitude,
Where the horrible darkness is impressed with reflections of
    desire?

Father of Jealousy, be thou accursed from the earth!
Why hast thou taught my Theotormon this accursed thing?
Till beauty fades from off my shoulders, darkened and cast
    out,
A solitary shadow wailing on the margin of non-entity.

I cry: Love! Love! Love! happy happy love! free as the
    mountain wind!
Can that be love, that drinks another as a sponge drinks
    water?
That clouds with jealousy his nights, with weepings all the
    day,
To spin a web of age around him, grey and hoary! dark!
Till his eyes sicken at the fruit that hangs before his sight.
Such is self-love that envies all! a creeping skeleton
With lamplike eyes watching around the frozen marriage bed.

But silken nets and traps of adamant will Oothoon spread,
And catch for thee girls of mild silver, or of furious gold.
I'll lie beside thee on a bank and view their wanton play
In lovely copulation, bliss on bliss, with Theotormon.
Red as the rosy morning, lustful as the first-born beam,

Oothoon shall view his dear delight, nor e'er with jealous
    cloud
Come in the heaven of generous love, nor selfish blightings
    bring.

WILLIAM BLAKE

From *Callipædia:* or, *the Art of Getting Beautiful Children*

Beneath those parts, where stretching to its bound,
The low abdomen girds the belly round,
The shop of Nature lies; a vacant space
Of small circumference divides the place,
Pear-like the shape; within a membrane spreads
Her various texture of meandrous threads;
These draw the vessel to a pursy state,
And or contract their substance, or dilate.
Here veins, nerves, arteries in pairs declare,
How nobler parts deserve a double care;
They from the mass the blood and spirits drain,
That irrigate profuse the thirsty plain;
The bottom of the womb 'tis called; the sides are cleft,
By cells distinguished into right and left.
'Tis thought that females in the left prevail,
And that the right contains the sprightly male.
A passage here in form oblong extends,
Where fast compressed the stiffened nerve ascends,
And the warm fluid with concurring fluids blends.
The sages this the womb's neck justly name;
Within the hollow of its inward frame,
Joined to the parts a small protuberance grows,
Whose rising lips the deep recesses close.
For while the tiller all his strength collects,
While Hope anticipates the fair effects,
The lubricated parts their station leave,
And closely to the working engine cleave;

Each vessel stretches, and distending wide,
The greedy womb attracts the glowing tide,
And either sex commixed, the streams united glide.
But now the womb relaxed, with pleasing pain
Gently subsides into itself again;
The seed moves with it, and thus closed within,
The tender drops of entity begin.
What joy the fibres of the stomach feel,
Long pinched with hunger, at a grateful meal,
Such tickling pleasure through the womb is sent,
When the first particles of life ferment.
This easy picture of the parts explains
How frequent motion no effect obtains;
The seed and pleasure lost in eager strife;
A useful lesson to the forward wife.

GEORGE SEWELL
from the Latin of Claudius Quillet

To a Child of Five Years Old

Fairest flower, all flowers excelling,
    Which in Milton's page we see;
Flowers of Eve's embowered dwelling
    Are, my fair one, types of thee.

Mark, my Polly, how the roses
    Emulate thy damask cheek;
How the bud its sweets discloses –
    Buds thy opening bloom bespeak.

Lilies are by plain direction
    Emblems of a double kind;
Emblems of thy fair complexion,
    Emblems of thy fairer mind.

But, dear girl, both flowers and beauty
    Blossom, fade, and die away;
Then pursue good sense and duty,
    Evergreens! which ne'er decay.

NATHANIEL COTTON

Long John Brown and Little Mary Bell

Little Mary Bell had a fairy in a nut,
Long John Brown had the devil in his gut;
Long John Brown loved little Mary Bell,
And the fairy drew the devil into the nutshell.

Her fairy skipped out and her fairy skipped in;
He laughed at the devil, saying 'Love is a sin.'
The devil he raged, and the devil he was wroth,
And the devil entered into the young man's broth.

He was soon in the gut of the loving young swain,
For John ate and drank to drive away love's pain;
But all he could do he grew thinner and thinner,
Though he ate and drank as much as ten men for his dinner.

Some said he had a wolf in his stomach day and night,
Some said he had the devil, and they guessed right;
The fairy skipped about in his glory, joy and pride,
And he laughed at the devil till poor John Brown died.

Then the fairy skipped out of the old nutshell,
And woe and alack for pretty Mary Bell!
For the devil crept in when the fairy skipped out,
And there goes Miss Bell with her fusty old nut.

WILLIAM BLAKE

II

'And only vocal with the Maker's praise.'

Ode

The spacious firmament on high,
With all the blue ethereal sky,
And spangled heavens, a shining frame,
Their great original proclaim:
The unwearied sun, from day to day,
Does his creator's power display,
And publishes to every land
The work of an almighty hand.

Soon as the evening shades prevail,
The moon takes up the wondrous tale,
And nightly to the listening earth
Repeats the story of her birth:
Whilst all the stars that round her burn,
And all the planets, in their turn,
Confirm the tidings as they roll,
And spread the truth from pole to pole.

What though, in solemn silence, all
Move round the dark terrestrial ball?
What though nor real voice nor sound
Amid their radiant orbs be found?
In reason's ear they all rejoice,
And utter forth a glorious voice,
For ever singing, as they shine,
'The hand that made us is divine.'

JOSEPH ADDISON

Crucifixion to the World by the Cross of Christ

When I survey the wondrous cross
On which the Prince of Glory died,
My richest gain I count but loss,
And pour contempt on all my pride.

Forbid it, Lord, that I should boast
Save in the death of Christ my God;
All the vain things that charm me most,
I sacrifice them to his blood.

See from his head, his hands, his feet,
Sorrow and love flow mingled down;
Did e'er such love and sorrow meet?
Or thorns compose so rich a crown?

His dying crimson like a robe
Spreads o'er his body on the tree,
Then am I dead to all the globe,
And all the globe is dead to me.

Were the whole realm of nature mine,
That were a present far too small;
Love so amazing, so divine
Demands my soul, my life, my all.

ISAAC WATTS

Man Frail, and God Eternal

Our God, our help in ages past,
　　Our hope for years to come,
Our shelter from the stormy blast,
　　And our eternal home.

Under the shadow of thy throne
　　Thy saints have dwelt secure;
Sufficient is thine arm alone,
　　And our defence is sure.

Before the hills in order stood,
　　Or earth received her frame,

From everlasting thou art God,
    To endless years the same.

Thy word commands our flesh to dust,
    'Return, ye sons of men:'
All nations rose from earth at first,
    And turn to earth again.

A thousand ages in thy sight
    Are like an evening gone;
Short as the watch that ends the night
    Before the rising sun.

The busy tribes of flesh and blood
    With all their lives and cares
Are carried downwards by thy flood,
    And lost in following years.

Time like an ever-rolling stream
    Bears all its sons away;
They fly forgotten as a dream
    Dies at the opening day.

Like flowery fields the nations stand
    Pleased with the morning-light;
The flowers beneath the mower's hand
    Lie withering ere 'tis night.

Our God, our help in ages past,
    Our hope for years to come,
Be thou our guard while troubles last,
    And our eternal home.

ISAAC WATTS

Hymn for Christmas Day

Christians awake, salute the happy morn,
Whereon the saviour of the world was born;
Rise, to adore the mystery of love,
Which hosts of angels chanted from above:
With them the joyful tidings first begun
Of God incarnate, and the Virgin's son:
Then to the watchful shepherds it was told,
Who heard the angelic herald's voice – 'Behold!
I bring good tidings of a saviour's birth
To you, and all the nations upon earth;
This day hath God fulfilled his promised word;
This day is born a saviour, Christ, the Lord:
In David's city, shepherds, ye shall find
The long foretold redeemer of mankind;
Wrapped up in swaddling clothes, the babe divine
Lies in a manger; this shall be your sign.'
He spoke, and straightway the celestial choir,
In hymns of joy, unknown before, conspire;
The praises of redeeming love they sung,
And heaven's whole orb with hallelujahs rung:
God's highest glory was their anthem still;
Peace upon earth, and mutual good-will.
To Bethlehem straight the enlightened shepherds ran,
To see the wonder God had wrought for man;
And found, with Joseph and the blessed maid,
Her son, the saviour, in a manger laid.
Amazed, the wondrous story they proclaim;
The first apostles of his infant fame:
While Mary keeps, and ponders in her heart,
The heavenly vision, which the swains impart;
They to their flocks, still praising God, return,
And their glad hearts within their bosoms burn.
 Let us, like these good shepherds then, employ
Our grateful voices to proclaim the joy:
Like Mary, let us ponder in our mind

God's wondrous love in saving lost mankind;
Artless, and watchful, as these favoured swains,
While virgin meekness in the heart remains:
Trace we the babe, who has retrieved our loss,
From his poor manger to his bitter cross;
Treading his steps, assisted by his grace,
Till man's first heavenly state again takes place:
Then may we hope, the angelic thrones among,
To sing, redeemed, a glad triumphal song:
He that was born, upon this joyful day,
Around us all, his glory shall display;
Saved by his love, incessant we shall sing
Of angels, and of angel-men, the king.

JOHN BYROM

Hymn

Ye golden lamps of heaven, farewell
    With all your feeble light:
Farewell, thou ever-changing moon,
    Pale empress of the night.

And thou refulgent orb of day
    In brighter flames arrayed,
My soul, that springs beyond thy sphere,
    No more demands thine aid.

Ye stars are but the shining dust
    Of my divine abode,
The pavement of those heavenly courts,
    Where I shall reign with God.

The father of eternal light
    Shall there his beams display;
Nor shall one moment's darkness mix
    With that unvaried day.

No more the drops of piercing grief
   Shall swell into mine eyes;
Nor the meridian sun decline
   Amidst those brighter skies.

There all the millions of his saints
   Shall in one song unite,
And each the bliss of all shall view
   With infinite delight.

PHILIP DODDRIDGE

Hymn

Thou hidden love of God, whose height,
   Whose depth unfathomed no man knows,
I see from far thy beauteous light,
   Inly I sigh for thy repose;
My heart is pained, nor can it be
At rest, till it finds rest in thee.

Thy secret voice invites me still,
   The sweetness of thy yoke to prove:
And fain I would: but though my will
   Seem fixed, yet wide my passions rove;
Yet hindrances strew all the way;
I aim at thee, yet from thee stray.

'Tis mercy all, that thou hast brought
   My mind to seek her peace in thee;
Yet while I seek, but find thee not,
   No peace my wandering soul shall see;
O when shall all my wanderings end,
And all my steps to thee-ward tend!

Is there a thing beneath the sun
   That strives with thee my heart to share?

Ah! tear it thence, and reign alone,
　The Lord of every motion there;
Then shall my heart from earth be free,
When it hath found repose in thee.

O hide this self from me, that I
　No more, but Christ in me may live;
My vile affections crucify,
　Nor let one darling lust survive;
In all things nothing may I see,
Nothing desire or seek but thee.

O love, thy sovereign aid impart,
　To save me from low-thoughted care:
Chase this self-will through all my heart,
　Through all its latent mazes there:
Make me thy duteous child, that I
Ceaseless may Abba, Father, cry!

Ah no! ne'er will I backward turn:
　Thine wholly, thine alone I am!
Thrice happy he who views with scorn
　Earth's toys, for thee his constant flame;
O help that I may never move
From the blest footsteps of thy love!

Each moment draw from earth away
　My heart that lowly waits thy call:
Speak to my inmost soul, and say,
　I am thy love, thy God, thy all!
To feel thy power, to hear thy voice,
To taste thy love, be all my choice.

JOHN WESLEY

A Prayer, Living and Dying

Rock of ages, cleft for me,
Let me hide myself in thee!
Let the water and the blood,
From thy riven side which flowed,
Be of sin the double cure;
Cleanse me from its guilt and power.

Not the labours of my hands
Can fulfil thy law's demands:
Could my zeal no respite know,
Could my tears for ever flow,
All for sin could not atone:
Thou must save, and thou alone.

Nothing in my hand I bring;
Simply to thy cross I cling;
Naked, come to thee for dress;
Helpless, look to thee for grace;
Foul, I to the fountain fly:
Wash me, Saviour, or I die!

While I draw this fleeting breath –
When my eye-strings break in death –
When I soar to worlds unknown –
See thee on thy judgment-throne –
Rock of ages, cleft for me,
Let me hide myself in thee.

AUGUSTUS MONTAGUE TOPLADY

Walking with God

Oh! for a closer walk with God,
    A calm and heavenly frame;
A light to shine upon the road
    That leads me to the lamb!

Where is the blessedness I knew
    When first I saw the Lord?
Where is the soul-refreshing view
    Of Jesus, and his word?

What peaceful hours I once enjoyed!
    How sweet their memory still!
But they have left an aching void,
    The world can never fill.

Return, o holy dove, return,
    Sweet messenger of rest;
I hate the sins that made thee mourn,
    And drove thee from my breast.

The dearest idol I have known,
    Whate'er that idol be;
Help me to tear it from thy throne,
    And worship only thee.

So shall my walk be close with God,
    Calm and serene my frame;
So purer light shall mark the road
    That leads me to the lamb.

WILLIAM COWPER

The Name of Jesus

How sweet the name of Jesus sounds
   In a believer's ear!
It soothes his sorrows, heals his wounds,
   And drives away his fear.

It makes the wounded spirit whole,
   And calms the troubled breast;
'Tis manna to the hungry soul,
   And to the weary rest.

Dear name! the rock on which I build,
   My shield and hiding place;
My never-failing treasury filled
   With boundless stores of grace.

By thee my prayers acceptance gain,
   Although with sin defiled;
Satan accuses me in vain,
   And I am owned a child.

Jesus! my shepherd, husband, friend,
   My prophet, priest, and king;
My lord, my life, my way, my end,
   Accept the praise I bring.

Weak is the effort of my heart,
   And cold my warmest thought,
But when I see thee as thou art,
   I'll praise thee as I ought.

'Till then I would thy love proclaim
   With every fleeting breath;
And may the music of thy name
   Refresh my soul in death.

JOHN NEWTON

Light Shining out of Darkness

God moves in a mysterious way,
　　His wonders to perform;
He plants his footsteps in the sea,
　　And rides upon the storm.

Deep in unfathomable mines
　　Of never failing skill,
He treasures up his bright designs,
　　And works his sovereign will.

Ye fearful saints fresh courage take,
　　The clouds ye so much dread
Are big with mercy, and shall break
　　In blessings on your head.

Judge not the Lord by feeble sense,
　　But trust him for his grace;
Behind a frowning providence,
　　He hides a smiling face.

His purposes will ripen fast,
　　Unfolding every hour;
The bud may have a bitter taste,
　　But sweet will be the flower.

Blind unbelief is sure to err,
　　And scan his work in vain;
God is his own interpreter,
　　And he will make it plain.

WILLIAM COWPER

BIOGRAPHICAL NOTES

JOSEPH ADDISON (1672–1719). He was educated at Charterhouse (with his future collaborator Steele) and became a Fellow of Magdalen College, Oxford. A distinguished classical scholar, he held a variety of state posts and was an M.P. from 1708 to his death. He formed a close friendship with Swift, Steele, Congreve, Garth, Vanbrugh, all members of the Kit-Kat Club, and joined with Steele in the production of the *Spectator* in 1711. He was satirized by Pope in the character of 'Atticus' (in *Epistle to Dr. Arbuthnot*).

MARK AKENSIDE (1721–70). Son of a butcher of Newcastle-upon-Tyne, Akenside was sent to Edinburgh to study theology but abandoned it for medicine. He became physician to the Queen, and is mainly remembered for his poem *The Pleasures of the Imagination* (1744).

CHRISTOPHER ANSTEY (1724–1805). He was educated at Eton and King's College, Cambridge. In conjunction with Dr Roberts he translated Gray's *Elegy* into Latin (1762), but is remembered as the author of the *New Bath Guide* (1766), a series of amusing verse letters (one of which is reprinted in this anthology), satirizing the types who patronized watering-places and mischievously alluding to Methodist ministers and converts.

JOHN ARBUTHNOT (1667–1735). This Physician Extraordinary to Queen Anne was a graduate of St Andrews, and a member of the literary circle connected with Pope and Swift. He wrote various pamphlets and medical works, the poem included here (1734), and contributed to the *Memoirs of Martinus Scriblerus*. The prologue to Pope's *Satires* is addressed to Arbuthnot. The *Life and Works* (Oxford, 1892) contains a portrait of him.

JOHN ARMSTRONG (1709–79). Armstrong was a physician (M.D., Edinburgh) and not surprisingly wrote *The Art of Preserving Health*. He is known also for another poem, *Taste*, a satirical epistle of literary criticism. He was a friend of James Thomson and wrote the Cave of Spleen stanzas for the latter's *The Castle of Indolence*.

MARY BARBER (1690?–1757). She was the wife of a Dublin tailor whose poems came to the attention of Swift: he provided her with introductions in England. Her *Poems on Several Occasions* (London, 1735) has a preface by Swift, and contains an enormous list of distinguished subscribers (including Pope and Southern).

SIR RICHARD BLACKMORE (1652–1729). Educated at Westminster, Oxford (where he was a contemporary of Oldham at St Edmund Hall), and Padua, Blackmore, a physician to Queen Anne, only appeared in print in 1695 with his epic, *Prince Arthur*. His *Satire against Wit* (1700) made him the butt of Tory satirists. *The Creation* (1712) was warmly praised by Dr Johnson.

ROBERT BLAIR (1699–1746). He was educated at Edinburgh and in Holland, and ordained in 1731. *The Grave*, published in 1743, has some 800 lines (and was illustrated by William Blake many years later).

WILLIAM BLAKE (1757–1827). Blake was born in London and did not attend school: he was apprenticed to an engraver. Many of his poems he engraved on plates, and around the text were often hand-coloured illustrations. Blake supported the American and French Revolutions and was a friend of Tom Paine and Henry Fuseli. In 1803 he was tried for sedition, but acquitted. He attacked sharply the authoritarian aspects of Christianity and sexual prudery, as well as a wide variety of social ills. The *Visions of the Daughters of Albion* was published in 1793, and *Long John Brown and Little Mary Bell* comes from the *Pickering Manuscript* (c. 1801–3).

ROBERT BLOOMFIELD (1766–1823). Bloomfield was born in Honington, Suffolk, and worked as an agricultural labourer and shoemaker. His poem, *The Farmer's Boy*, published in 1800, is reported to have sold 26,000 copies in three years. He composed the poem in his head while working at his shoemaker's bench in Coleman St, London, and wrote it down afterwards. The Duke of Grafton patronized him and obtained him a post in the Seal Office: he found the work dull and became a bookseller. When his business failed he earned a living by making and selling Æolian harps. He died in poverty at Shefford, Bedfordshire.

SAMUEL BOYSE (1708–49). He was the son of a Presbyterian minister and educated at a private school in Dublin and then at

Glasgow University, but he took no degree and adopted no profession; during the latter part of his life he suffered great poverty. His writings include *The Deity: a Poem*, 1739, and he modernized parts of the *Canterbury Tales*.

HENRY BROOKE (1703?–83). An Irishman by birth, he lived in Ireland most of his life, and was educated at Trinity College, Dublin. He is mainly remembered for an unusual novel, *The Fool of Quality*, reflecting moods of revolt against oppression: it was highly admired by John Wesley. His poem, *Universal Beauty*, is said to have furnished ideas for Darwin's *Botanic Garden*, and was published in six parts from 1734 to 1736.

WILLIAM BROOME (1689–1745). After an education at Eton and Cambridge, he was at one time employed by Pope to aid in the translation of Homer. He became Rector of Oakley Magna, and Vicar of Eye, Suffolk, and published poems and sermons.

ISAAC HAWKINS BROWNE (1705–60). Educated at Westminster and Cambridge, he studied law at Lincoln's Inn, and became an M.P. for Wenlock (1744–54) and a Fellow of the Royal Society. His wit and conversational talent were praised by Dr Johnson, and many of his poems were humorous. In *A Pipe of Tobacco* he parodied several poets, including Swift, Pope and Thomson. His Latin poem, *De animi immortalitate*, was well translated by Soame Jenyns.

JOHN BYROM (1692–1763). He attended Merchant Taylors' School and was a Fellow of Trinity College, Cambridge: he studied medicine at Montpellier, but he earned his living teaching shorthand, and his system was copyrighted in 1742. He was an admirer of William Law, whose writings sowed the seed of Methodism: he wrote the hymn 'Christians awake! Salute the happy morn'. He published two advanced essays on dreams in the *Spectator*, attended boxing matches, wrote a poem on a fencing-match, was interested in dietary experiments, disliked the theatre, was active in Manchester local politics, and deeply attracted to Christian mystical writing.

RICHARD OWEN CAMBRIDGE (1717–1802). He was educated at Eton and Oxford, and entered Lincoln's Inn in 1737. He published satirical verses between 1752 and 1756.

HENRY CAREY (1687–1743). He wrote farces, burlesques, and songs for the London theatre. He is remembered as the author of the burlesque *Chronohotonthologos*, as inventor of the nickname 'Namby-Pamby' for Ambrose Philips, and for the ballad *Sally in our Alley*. Carey was possibly the son of Henry Savile: he was educated at his mother's school in Yorkshire and made a living by teaching music in boarding-schools.

JAMES CAWTHORN (1719–61). The son of a Sheffield upholsterer, he was usher in several country schools before becoming headmaster of Tonbridge School c. 1743. He published *Abelard and Heloise* in *Poetical Calendar*, 1746.

THOMAS CHATTERTON (1752–70). At one stage bound to an attorney, he tried unsuccessfully to gain the patronage of Walpole and to live by his pen, but he was reduced to poverty and committed suicide at the age of seventeen. He is mainly known for 'medieval' poems he wrote and attributed to an imaginary fifteenth-century poet, Rowley.

CHARLES CHURCHILL (1731–64). Son of a Westminster curate, he was educated at Westminster and Cambridge, where his career was interrupted by his marriage at the age of eighteen. He became famous for his satire on contemporary actors, *The Rosciad*, 1761, and he wrote many political and social satires. He attached himself politically to John Wilkes.

WILLIAM COLLINS (1721–59). Educated at Winchester and Magdalen College, Oxford, Collins produced only a small amount of lyrical poems. His *Odes* were published in 1747. He became insane.

WILLIAM CONGREVE (1670–1729). He was a fellow-student with Swift at Kilkenny School and Trinity College, Dublin, from which he went to the Middle Temple. He became Inspector of Hackney Coaches, and Secretary to the Island of Jamaica. He achieved fame with his comedies of manners, but *The Way of the World*, for which he is now mainly remembered, had a disappointing reception in 1700, causing Congreve to abandon playwriting.

JOHN GILBERT COOPER (1723–69). Educated at Westminster and Cambridge, he contributed verses to Dodsley's *Museum* and published treatises on aesthetics and a life of Socrates.

NATHANIEL COTTON (1705–88). He studied medicine at Leyden and practised as a physician. He was keeper of a private lunatic asylum at St Albans, in which Cowper was an inmate 1763–5. His collected verse was published in 1791.

WILLIAM COWPER (1731–1800). He was the son of the Rector of Great Berkhampstead, Hertfordshire, and educated at Westminster before commencing law studies, being called to the bar in 1754. His friendship with Lady Austen was the source of *The Task, a Poem in six books*, 1785. He became insane in later life, and spent one period in Nathaniel Cotton's private asylum.

GEORGE CRABBE (1754–1832). Crabbe was born at Aldeburgh, a remote town on the Suffolk coast. Mostly self-taught, he was apprenticed to a doctor and subsequently practised medicine. In 1781 he took orders, and from 1782–5 he was chaplain to the Duke of Rutland. He was also befriended by Edmund Burke. *The Village*, 1783, brought him fame. He led the life of a quiet, industrious clergyman, devoted to literature and botany – he once astonished Wordsworth by his knowledge of botany as they walked together on Hampstead Heath. After *The Village* he published nothing of importance for over twenty years: *The Parish Register* appeared in 1807 and *The Borough* in 1810. Despite his poetic revelation of social misery in the provinces he was conservative in religion and politics, abhorring equally Tom Paine, Voltaire and Methodism.

JOHN CUNNINGHAM (1729–73). He was a strolling actor, born in Dublin, the author of tuneful verses and of the successful farce *Love in a Mist* (1747).

ERASMUS DARWIN (1731–1802). Educated at St John's, Cambridge, he spent much of his life as a physician at Lichfield, where he established a botanical garden. His poem, *The Botanic Garden*, published in two parts (in 1789 and 1791), embodies the system of the Swedish naturalist Linnæus. The verses, *Visit of Hope to Sydney Cove, near Botany Bay*, were written to accompany medallions made by Wedgwood from Sydney Cove clay given to him by Sir Joseph Banks. They represented Hope encouraging Art and Labour, under the influence of Peace, to conduct a local pottery industry.

WILLIAM DIAPER (1685–1717). Diaper was at Balliol College, Oxford, and held curacies at East Brent, Somerset, and later at Crick, Northamptonshire. In 1712 he published *Nereides: or Sea-Eclogues* and *Dryades: or, The Nymph's Prophecy*, and collaborated with Rowe, Sewell and Cobb in translating *Callipædia*. His translation of Part I of Oppian's *Halieutics* appeared in 1722. A modern edition of Diaper's works, edited by Dorothy Broughton, was published in the Muses' Library in 1951.

PHILIP DODDRIDGE (1702–51). He was a non-conformist divine, minister of Kibworth, 1732, who opened an academy at Market Harborough in 1729. He removed later to Northampton, where he founded a charity school. He died at Lisbon. He was a celebrated hymn-writer.

ROBERT DODSLEY (1703–64). While a footman he published *Servitude, a poem* (1729). He wrote several plays and became a bookseller, but today is chiefly remembered as the publisher of works by Pope, Johnson, Young, Goldsmith and Gray.

RICHARD DUKE (1658–1711). Educated at Westminster and Cambridge, he became chaplain to Dr Jonathan Trelawney and a friend of Atterbury and Prior. His *Poems on Several Occasions* were published in 1717.

JOHN DYER (1699–1758). A Welshman, and son of a lawyer, Dyer was educated at Westminster and designed for the law, which he abandoned for painting and art studies. He explored his native country as a wandering artist, and published the well-known poem *Grongar Hill* in 1726. After travels in Italy he published *The Ruins of Rome, a Poem* in 1740. In 1741 he took orders and became Vicar of Catthorpe in Leicestershire. *The Fleece: a Poem, in four books* appeared in 1757.

WILLIAM FALCONER (1732–69). He was the second mate on a ship in the Levant trade, which was wrecked between Alexandria and Venice. This is the source of his long poem *The Shipwreck*, the first version of which appeared in 1762 and had a considerable vogue. Falconer was drowned at sea.

ELIJAH FENTON (1683–1730). He graduated from Jesus College, Cambridge, accompanied the Earl of Orrery to Flanders as his private secretary, and finally became Master of the Free Grammar School at Sevenoaks. He edited Milton and Waller, wrote one tragedy *Mariamne* (1727) and translated several books of Pope's *Odyssey* for him, completely catching Pope's manner.

DAVID GARRICK (1717–79). A pupil of Dr Johnson at Edial, he accompanied him when he left Lichfield for London, making his reputation as an actor, and later manager, at Drury Lane, especially in Shakespearean productions. He wrote many lively farces, was a member of Johnson's Literary Club, and was painted by Reynolds, Hogarth and Gainsborough.

SIR SAMUEL GARTH (1661–1719). He came from Bowland Forest in Yorkshire and was educated at Ingleton School, at Peterhouse, Cambridge, and at Leyden where he studied medicine. He was elected a Fellow of the College of Physicians and in 1700 supervised Dryden's funeral. His satire *The Dispensary* (1699) ridiculed those who opposed a plan for a dispensary for the poor. He was a friend of the young Alexander Pope.

JOHN GAY (1685–1732). Orphaned when young, Gay went to Barnstaple School before being apprenticed to a silk-mercer. He was secretary to the Duchess of Monmouth and to the Ambassador at Hanover, but lived mainly by the aid of various patrons. He spent the last few years of his life as a guest of the Duke of Queensberry. *Trivia: or the Art of Walking the Streets of London* appeared in 1716, and *The Beggar's Opera* in 1728. He collaborated with Pope and Arbuthnot on a play, *Three Hours After Marriage*, produced in 1717.

OLIVER GOLDSMITH (1728–74). The son of an Irish clergyman, he graduated B.A. and then travelled in Europe, where he is said to have obtained a degree in medicine. He lived in penury, staving off debts by writing. He was an intimate friend of Samuel Johnson. His best known works are the novel *The Vicar of Wakefield* (1766), the play *She Stoops to Conquer* (1773), and *The Deserted Village* (1769; 1770 on the title page).

JAMES GRAINGER (1721?–66). He took a degree in medicine at Edinburgh, became an army surgeon 1745–8, and practised in St Christopher (West Indies) from 1759–63, where he died. He was a friend of Dr Johnson, Shenstone and Bishop Percy. His poem *The Sugar-Cane* gives an interesting picture of a sugar plantation.

THOMAS GRAY (1716–71). Born in London he was educated at Eton (with Horace Walpole) and Cambridge. He toured the continent with Walpole and began writing poetry in 1742. The *Ode on the Death of a Favourite Cat* (1747) was written about Walpole's cat. His celebrated *Elegy* (1751) brought him fame and the offer of the Laureateship in 1757, which he refused. In 1768 he was appointed Professor of History and Modern Languages at Cambridge.

MATTHEW GREEN (1696–1737). Green came from a dissenting family and had a post in the Customs House. He was a friend of Richard Glover and his gay moralizing in *The Spleen* (1737) was admired by Pope and Gray.

HENRY HEADLEY (1765–88). He was educated at Trinity College, Oxford, and published *Select Beauties of Ancient English Poetry, with Remarks*, in 1787. His poems were printed in 1786.

THOMAS HEARNE (1678–1735). Educated at St Edmund Hall, Oxford, this notable antiquary and editor of early English chronicles became second Keeper of the Bodleian Library in 1712, but was deprived of this post in 1716 as a non-juror, refusing to take the oath of allegiance to George I. His *Reliquiæ Hearnianæ* records the public gossip of the day and details of university politics. He is satirized as 'Wormius' in Pope's *Dunciad*. *On the Tack* appears in Doble's *Remarks and Collections of Thomas Hearne* (Oxford, 1865), where it is seemingly assigned to Hearne, though it is possibly a poem Hearne collected. In Doble's volume on page 107 there is also an amusing Oxford poem called *W. Elstob's verses on Mr Prickett*.

AARON HILL (1685–1750). Barnstaple Grammar School, Westminster, and Constantinople (where he went in 1700) were responsible for Hill's education, and he continued to travel in the East. He proposed several unsuccessful projects, including one for a settlement in Georgia, and became Master of the Stage at Drury Lane in 1709 and of the Haymarket Opera in 1710. He wrote plays, the words to Handel's *Rinaldo*, and was satirized by

Pope. He adapted Voltaire's dramas and edited a periodical with William Bond. His major poems are *The Creation* (1720), an epic, *Gideon the Patriot* (1741) and *The Fanciad* (1743).

JOHN HUGHES (1677–1720). He attended the Dissenting Academy in Little Britain at the same time as Isaac Watts, and obtained posts in the Ordnance Office and as secretary to the commissioners for purchasing lands for the Royal Docks. He wrote many odes (e.g. *The House of Nassau, Princess of Wales, Praise of Music*), an opera, a masque, and a tragedy; collected material for White Kennett's *Complete History of England*; translated Fontenelle's *Dialogues of the Dead*; and edited the works of Spenser.

JAMES HURDIS (1763–1801). He was born at Bishopstone, Sussex, and took orders. In 1793 he was appointed Professor of Poetry at Oxford. His hobby was building church-organs. He wrote a tragedy, *Sir Thomas More*; his poem *The Village Curate* includes interesting comments on poets from Spenser to his own day, and on the education of women – a topic which is touched on in a letter, referring to his sister: 'She once entertained a desire to engage in the pursuit of languages. I told her I did not think it the province of a woman. It could never be useful or ornamental; for the graces of a linguist are masculine. At my request she refrained, but not altogether; for some time after I had become a student of Hebrew, I found she had followed me through all my grammatical memoranda, and was able to read and to construe the original Scriptures as well as myself.'

RICHARD JAGO (1715–81). Jago held three livings in Warwickshire and was a friend of Shenstone and Somerville. *Edge Hill*, in four books, described – with many digressions – the views seen at morning, noon, afternoon and evening, looking out from Edge Hill over Warwickshire.

SOAME JENYNS (1704–87). He was at St John's College, Cambridge, but took no degree. From 1742 to 1754 he was M.P. for Cambridge; from 1760 to 1780 he represented Dunwich. He was made a Commissioner of Trade. *The Art of Dancing* was published in 1729. *A Free Enquiry into the Nature and Origin of Evil*, 1757, was criticized by Dr Johnson.

SAMUEL JOHNSON (1709–84). The son of a bookseller, he went to Lichfield Grammar School and Oxford University (where he stayed fourteen months, taking no degree). His father's death left the family in poverty and Johnson worked at several jobs. He started a school at which a pupil was David Garrick. In 1750 he launched a periodical, *The Rambler*, written almost entirely by himself. He was a prolific writer and critic, and he is celebrated chiefly as the editor of Shakespeare and the author of the *Dictionary*, to which one should add *The Lives of the Poets*, *A Journey to the Western Islands of Scotland* (1775), his novel *Rasselas*, and two of his poems, *London: A Poem, In Imitation of the Third Satire of Juvenal* (1738), and *The Vanity of Human Wishes, being the Tenth Satire of Juvenal Imitated* (1749). His friends included Reynolds, Burke, Goldsmith, Garrick and his famous biographer Boswell (1740–95), who only made his acquaintance in 1763.

WILLIAM KING (1663–1712). He was educated at Westminster and Christ Church, Oxford, and became a lawyer, holding various posts in England and Ireland (where he was Judge of the Admiralty Court, 1701–7). His talent was mainly for burlesque and parody.

JOHN LANGHORNE (1735–79). He was educated at Cambridge and commenced writing for *The Monthly Review* in 1764. His poetical works were published in 1766 but he is best remembered for his translation of Plutarch's *Lives*.

ROBERT LLOYD (1733–64). He was educated at Westminster and Cambridge, became a friend of Garrick, Churchill and Wilkes, and at one point was imprisoned for debt. He edited the *St James's Magazine* 1762–3. His poem *The Actor* was published in 1760 and his collected verse in 1762.

EDWARD LOVIBOND (1724–75). He was educated at Oxford, and contributed many articles to *The World*, a weekly edited by Edward Moore. His best known piece, *The Tears of Old Mayday*, was published in 1754. His *Poems on Several Occasions* were published by his brother in 1775.

LORD GEORGE LYTTELTON (1709–73). A product of Eton and Oxford, he became a political opponent of Walpole and in 1756 was for a short time Chancellor of the Exchequer. He was a friend of Pope and Fielding and a liberal patron of literature.

James Thomson's *The Seasons* were addressed to him. His poems include *Blenheim* (1728) and *An Epistle to Mr Pope, from a young gentleman at Rome* (1750). His best known prose work is *Dialogues of the Dead* (1760).

LADY MARY WORTLEY MONTAGU (1689–1762). She was a daughter of the Duke of Kingston and wife of Edward Wortley Montagu, ambassador to Constantinople in 1716, where she wrote her *Turkish Letters*, published in 1763. From Turkey she introduced into England the practice of smallpox inoculation. She left her husband and spent the last twenty-two years of her life mainly in Italy, returning to England only to die. She wrote the lively *Town Eclogues*, piratically published in 1716, and is remembered for her quarrels with Pope, who attacked her in his verse. As her *Verses*, addressed to Pope, indicate, she could reply with equal ferocity.

EDWARD MOORE (1712–57). He was a linen draper who wrote verse and produced two comedies, *The Foundling* in 1748 and *Gil Blas* in 1751, and a drama *The Gamester* in 1753. He edited a periodical, *The World*. His patrons were Lord Lyttelton and Henry Pelham.

JOHN NEWTON (1725–1807). After a wandering life at sea, 1736–55, he came under the influence of Wesley and was ordained in the Church of England. He settled at Olney, where his friend Cowper came to live: they published the *Olney Hymns* in 1779.

THOMAS PARNELL (1679–1718). Born in Dublin, he graduated from Trinity College and in 1706 became Archdeacon of Clogher. He spent some time in London but left in 1716 to become Vicar of Finglass. He was a friend of Swift and Pope (who published his works posthumously) and his life was written by Goldsmith.

CHRISTOPHER PITT (1699–1748). Pitt's biography has a certain neat simplicity – educated at Winchester and New College, Oxford, he was made Rector of Pimperne, Dorset, immediately on graduating and remained there for the rest of his life. He wrote poems and translated Virgil's *Aeneid*; he knew Pope, and Johnson included him in his *Lives of the Poets*.

ALEXANDER POPE (1688–1744). He was born in London, the son of a Roman Catholic convert (and successful linen merchant) and a Catholic mother from a genteel Yorkshire family. In 1700 the family moved to a small farm in Windsor Forest. A serious illness at the age of twelve left Pope's health ruined: he grew to be about four foot six inches in height, crook-backed, tubercular and the victim of chronic headaches. In 1705 he first visited Will's coffee-house, one of the literary centres of London, and in 1709 appeared his *Pastorals*, followed by the *Essay on Criticism* (1711), *The Rape of the Lock* (1712), *Windsor Forest* (1713), *Eloisa to Abelard* (1717), *The Dunciad* (1728) and at various intervals the sections of *Moral Essays* and *Satires*. His translation of the *Iliad* earned him a moderate fortune and he attended the Scriblerus Club with Arbuthnot, Gay, Parnell and Swift. In 1719 Pope and his mother moved to Twickenham on the Thames, near Richmond, his residence for some twenty years. He died of asthma and dropsy, and received the last rites of the Church on his deathbed.

NICHOLAS ROWE (1674–1718). He was educated at Westminster and Middle Temple, but abandoned law for playwriting. He knew Pope and Addison, translated a good deal of French and Latin verse, and became Poet Laureate in 1715.

JOHN SCOTT (1730–83). He was a Quaker, a friend of Dr Johnson, and contributed to the *Gentleman's Magazine* from 1753. His *Poetical Works* were published in 1782.

GEORGE SEWELL (*c.* 1688–1726). Sad to say Sewell's education at Eton, Cambridge, Leyden and Edinburgh (M.D. in 1725) did not prevent his miserable existence as a bookseller's hack, writing poems, translations and political pamphlets. In 1712 he translated Claudius Quillet's *Callipædia* with Cobb, Diaper and Rowe, though the translation appeared in 1733 in Rowe's *Miscellaneous Works*.

WILLIAM SHENSTONE (1714–63). He was a contemporary of Samuel Johnson at Pembroke College, Oxford. His *School-mistress* was praised by Johnson and Goldsmith, and his elegies by Burns. He knew Graves and Jago, and wrote much miscellaneous verse.

CHRISTOPHER SMART (1722–71). Educated at Durham and Cambridge, he is chiefly remembered for his *Song to David*

(1763). He edited several magazines and was visited by Dr Johnson. He declined into debt and insanity.

TOBIAS SMOLLETT (1721–71). Educated at Glasgow, he sailed as a surgeon's mate, married in Jamaica, and then practised as a surgeon in London and wrote his celebrated novels. He was imprisoned for libel in 1759, left England in 1769 and died at Monte Nero, near Leghorn. The poem, *The Tears of Scotland* (1746), was prompted by the battle of Culloden, near Inverness, when the Duke of Cumberland defeated the forces of the Young Pretender.

WILLIAM SOMERVILLE (1675–1742). After a Winchester and Oxford education he eventually settled in the country and lived a sporting life; he published *The Chase* in 1735 and *Hobbinol* in 1740.

JONATHAN SWIFT (1667–1745). Born in Dublin, he was a school-fellow of Congreve at Kilkenny Grammar School, and then went to Trinity College. He was a cousin of Dryden. He acted as secretary to Sir William Temple, and was ordained in 1694. In the course of numerous visits to London he became acquainted with Addison, Steele, Congreve and Halifax, and later with Pope, Bolingbroke, Gay and Arbuthnot. He was a prolific writer of verse and pamphlets in addition to such celebrated works as *The Battle of the Books* (1704), and *Gulliver's Travels* (1726). He became Dean of St Patrick's in 1713 and was buried in this church by the side of 'Stella', to whom he had written the *Journal to Stella*, a series of letters mainly couched in baby-language. The poem, *A Description of the Morning*, was published in the *Tatler* in 1709.

WILLIAM THOMPSON (1712?–66?). Educated at Oxford, he became Fellow Rector of Hampton Poyle. His poems include imitations of Spenser; *Sickness* was published in 1745.

JAMES THOMSON (1700–48). Son of a Scottish minister, he attended Southdean Parish School and Edinburgh University. He went to London in 1725 and knew Pope, Gay and Arbuthnot. He had various posts as tutor, secretary etc. His celebrated poem, *The Seasons*, appeared in sections from 1726 to 1746, *Britannia* was published in 1729, and his Spenserian imitation, *The Castle of Indolence*, in 1748. Several of his plays were acted.

THOMAS TICKELL (1686–1740). He was educated at St Bees and Queen's College, Oxford, and his patron Addison made him Under-Secretary of State in Ireland in 1717. *On the Prospect of Peace* appeared in 1712, and his translation of the first book of the *Iliad* in 1715.

AUGUSTUS MONTAGUE TOPLADY (1740–78). Incumbent of Broad Hembury, 1768, he had been educated at Trinity College, Dublin. 'Rock of Ages' was published in 1775. He engaged in violent controversy with Wesley.

JOSEPH WARTON (1722–1800). He was the brother of Thomas Warton, and after an education at Winchester and Oxford he became headmaster of Winchester (1766–93). His career as headmaster is usually described as 'conspicuously unsuccessful'. He was an important literary critic and is mainly known for his essays on Pope.

THOMAS WARTON (1728–90). The younger brother of Joseph Warton, he was educated at Trinity College, Oxford, and became Professor of Poetry, Camden Professor of History, and Poet Laureate. He was an editor and critic, a friend of Johnson, and the author of many poems foreshadowing the Romantics.

ISAAC WATTS (1674–1748). Watts was educated at Edward VI Grammar School, Southampton, and Stoke Newington Dissenting Academy, and in 1700 became Pastor of the Independent Congregation in Mark Lane. He is remembered for his *Divine Songs Attempted in Easy Language for the Use of Children* (1715) – Lewis Carroll parodied *The Sluggard* and others from this volume. His hymns became popular, e.g. 'O God, our help in ages past', 'When I survey the wondrous cross', 'There is a land of pure delight', 'Jesus shall reign where-e'er the sun'.

JOHN WESLEY (1703–91) The celebrated evangelist and co-founder of Methodism was until 1735 a Fellow of Lincoln College, Oxford. He published twenty-three collections of hymns.

GILBERT WEST (1703–56). He was at Eton and Oxford, served in the army and became Clerk of the Privy Council in 1752. He published poems, a metrical version of the *Odes* of Pindar, and *Observation on Resurrection* (1747). *The Triumphs of the Gout* is translated from the Greek of Lucian (born c. A.D. 120, and author of the often satirical *Dialogues of the Dead*).

PAUL WHITEHEAD (1710–74). Whitehead experienced both sides of the law – he studied it at Middle Temple and was confined for several years in the Fleet prison. He held a minor post in the Treasury and spent his last years at Twickenham.

WILLIAM WHITEHEAD (1715–85). Educated at Winchester and Cambridge, he became Poet Laureate in 1757. He was also a playwright and *A Charge to the Poets* (1762) was a reply to unfriendly comment on his productions. *Song for Ranelagh* refers to the Earl of Ranelagh's Gardens, Chelsea, opened as a place of public amusement in 1742, with its famous Rotunda, and its orchestra, around which people promenaded. Ranelagh Gardens now form part of Chelsea Hospital Gardens.

WILLIAM WILKIE (1721–72). Known as 'the Scottish Homer', he was educated at Edinburgh University, licensed by the presbytery of Linlithgow in 1745 and became Professor of Natural Philosophy at St Andrews in 1759. In 1757 he published *Epigoniad*, based on the fourth book of the *Iliad*.

ANNE, COUNTESS OF WINCHILSEA (1661–1720). She was a daughter of Sir William Kingsmill and in 1683 became Maid of Honour to the Duchess of York. In 1684 she married Heneage Finch, later Earl of Winchilsea, who refused to swear allegiance to William and Mary. Her poems *The Spleen* (1701) and *Petition for an Absolute Retreat* (1713) are well known, and her poetry was praised by Wordsworth. Heneage Finch, who, as Lord Chancellor, appears as Amri in *Absalom and Achitophel*, was the half-brother of another Anne Finch – Viscountess Conway, friend of Henry More, philosopher, and convert to Quakerism.

THOMAS YALDEN (1670–1736). Educated at Oxford, he became Vicar of Willoughby (1700–9) and Oxford Lecturer in Moral Philosophy (1705–13). His *Hymn to Darkness*, in imitation of Cowley, was praised by Dr Johnson.

EDWARD YOUNG (1683–1765). Educated at Winchester and Oxford, his political ambitions were unrealized, and he took orders late in life (1730) and married Lady Lichfield (in 1731). He remained Rector of Welwyn to the end of his life, expecting in vain a bishopric. The death of his wife and family bereavements inspired his celebrated poem *The Complaint, or Night Thoughts on Life, Death, and Immortality* (1742–5), but his satires of 1725–8 had already been widely admired. His two tragedies of violence and passion were produced at Drury Lane in 1719 and 1721.

AUTHOR INDEX

TITLE INDEX

MORE ABOUT PENGUINS
AND PELICANS

Penguinews, which appears every month, contains details of all the new books issued by Penguins as they are published. From time to time it is supplemented by *Penguins in Print*, which is a complete list of all titles available. (There are some five thousand of these.)

A specimen copy of *Penguinews* will be sent to you free on request. For a year's issues (including the complete lists) please send 50p if you live in the British Isles, or 70p if you live elsewhere. Just write to Dept EP, Penguin Books Ltd, Harmondsworth, Middlesex, enclosing a cheque or postal order, and your name will be added to the mailing list.

In the U.S.A.: For a complete list of books available from Penguin in the United States write to Dept CS, Penguin Books Inc., 7110 Ambassador Road, Baltimore, Maryland 21207.

In Canada: For a complete list of books available from Penguin in Canada write to Penguin Books Canada Ltd, 41 Steelcase Road, Markham, Ontario.

PENGUIN MODERN POETS

Not for sale in the U.S.A.
†*Not for sale in the U.S.A. or Canada*

SOME RECENT
PENGUIN ANTHOLOGIES

Not for sale in the U.S.A.